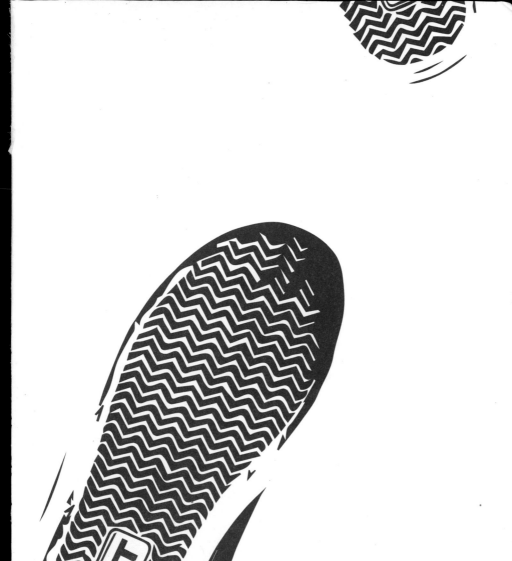

By Kevin Waltman

Cinco Puntos Press
El Paso . Texas

FIRST EDITION
10 9 8 7 6 5 4 3 2 1

Library of Congress Cataloging-in-Publication Data

Waltman, Kevin.
Next / by Kevin Waltman—First edition.
pages cm. — (D-Bow's high school hoops ; [1])
Summary: Indiana basketball prodigy Derrick Bowen—D-Bow to his friends—is impatient to start his freshman year, but his old-school coach favors a senior for a guard spot; meanwhile, pressure at home builds for D-Bow to transfer from his neighborhood school to an exclusive prep school.
   ISBN 978-1-935955-64-1 (hardback); ISBN 978-1-935955-65-8 (paperback); ISBN 9781935955665 (E-book)
   [1. Basketball—Fiction. 2. High schools—Fiction. 3. Schools—Fiction. 4. African Americans—Fiction.] I. Title.

PZ7.W1728Ne 2013
[Fic] dc—23

2013026452

Book and cover design by Anne M. Giangiulio
with b-ball advice from Bubba, as always.

Many thanks to Ben Osborne, editor of *SLAM* Magazine,
for connecting Cinco Puntos to Kevin Waltman.

For Jessica. For Calla. My dearest darlings.

PART I

1.

"Ball," I shout, but just get ignored. Instead, I watch some thirty-year-old chump with gray in his goatee and a belly hanging down over his shorts dribble and dribble and then jack one up from twenty-five feet. Barely scrapes iron.

Two possessions later my Uncle Kid backs his man down to hit the game-winner, and my five is run off. Someone's left an empty water bottle by the court and I chuck it in disgust. It clears the chain link and clatters into Fall Creek Parkway, gets squashed by traffic. I sit in the grass and watch the next five take the court, waiting my turn to get back out there. Worst of all, I have to listen to that guy run his mouth like he's some kind of baller. *Brownlee* is what they all call him, and I've seen him here before. Always the same shit. He makes one nice shot, then chucks away the rest of the game—and then has the nerve to make noise at other players about what they did wrong.

"Little man," he says. He mops his face with his t-shirt. "You, little man."

I look away, watch Uncle Kid—Sidney, really, but everyone still calls him Kid—knock in another turnaround. My uncle's pushing 40 and has seen better days, and, I mean, it's embarrassing to watch him walk up to the court with some fake limp in his stride like he thinks he's a bad-ass. But the man flirted with the NBA. Had coach after coach tell him he was *this close* to making a roster. So he can still bring it between the lines.

"Little man, you need to pay attention. I was telling you, you got to clear out some. You got in my way on that last trip."

I look at Brownlee, watch him squint at me, his sweaty black face glistening in the sun. He's got that twitchy, bossy teacher look some men get, like if he just keeps telling everyone else their business they'll think he knows what he's doing. Even his goatee is annoying, like he thinks facial hair gives him some kind of authority. And right then I hate being fifteen—because being fifteen means I have to sit here in the grass and listen to him talk nonsense even if I'm the best player on the court. It means I have to be called "little man" even if I'm pushing 6'3". It means all Brownlee's friends will pat him on the back because they've been coming to this court with him since before I was born, and they'll be damned if they admit there's not one of them can check me. And it means that come November, I'll just be a freshman trying to crack the starting five at Marion East, at least until Coach Bolden realizes I'm his best option, even if Nick Starks is already rated one of the state's top point guards.

"Little man, you still not listening?" Brownlee laughs now, like he's the funniest man in the world.

"I hear you," I finally say. "But I'm done listening to anything you got." That turns some heads. A few of them have played with me enough to know I'm no joke, but mostly everyone just wants a rise out of Brownlee. *You gonna take that?* they ask, laughing at him.

"You got a lot to learn, little man," Brownlee says. He puffs out his chest like he might swagger over and knock me around, but I know better than to flinch. He stares at me for another second, but then just repeats, "Lot to learn."

Everyone settles back for a second, waiting for the next game, and I feel the adrenaline pumping through me. My fingers feel hot and my pulse is pounding at my temples. I listen to traffic zip by, smell the exhaust from a city bus, feel the grass—dry now in the first week of October— scratch at my legs. It just makes me feel antsy, all of it, and I suddenly can't wait to get back on that court, kick game to shut Brownlee up. And more: I want my season to get here, want to see myself on the evening highlights bringing the crowd to their feet, want to see the scouts lining the bleachers to witness it all. The waiting for it makes me want to burst.

At least I don't need to wait long to get a shot at Brownlee. Kid's team wins again, but one of their players begs out of the next game. They try talking him into it, but he grabs his Gatorade and chugs, then says, "If I'm late for work today I won't have a job to go back to tomorrow." So Uncle Kid cocks his head my way, says, "D-Bow, you wanna run?"

I'm on that blacktop in a heartbeat.

One of Kid's teammates—he's good, but I've never seen him here before—mutters something about not wanting a punk on his team, but Uncle Kid says, "That's my nephew. Trust me. Young pup has some skills." Uncle Kid's word has weight on this court, even if he looks a little worse these days, growth splotchy on his ashy face, his body more wiry than ever, like he's lived all these years and nothing's stuck to him.

When the ball gets checked I'm staring straight across at Brownlee, who all of a sudden doesn't look so confident in teaching me lessons. First time down, I get my hands on the rock but slide it down to Uncle Kid—no sense in getting trigger-happy early, especially when Kid's the one who got me back on the blacktop. He knocks in a turnaround, and then, on the other end, I just hound Brownlee. He makes a couple cuts, tries to throw his weight into me to bounce free, but soon enough he starts standing, knowing he has no chance. I can smell his sweat mixed with some nasty cologne, and he keeps coughing like he's getting nervous. He was the one trash-talking, though, so he deserves what's coming.

When their shot hits iron, I rip it and am *off*. I'm past Brownlee by mid-court and only his buddy keeps me from taking it rack-to-rack. Still, I settle for a mid-range runner. As I backpedal I bark at Brownlee: "Call me *little man*, now."

"Easy, kid," he says, trying to sound wise. The wisest thing he's got, though, is an elbow in my ribs—a cheap shot to get him free. He tries floating one up from the near baseline, but I recover quick and—*Whap!*—smack that thing off the backboard.

It goes on like that for a few minutes. Between me and Uncle Kid our five pulls ahead fast. I even drop a dime to that big man who didn't want me to play, feed him right in time for him to muscle one down, and he gives me this nonchalant nod and raises a lazy index finger in my direction: subtle but serious praise from a grown-ass man.

I haven't finished with Brownlee though. We're at game point and I still haven't put my stamp on the game, on *him*. But I wait, looking for the right moment. And then it comes: on our defensive end, there's a loose ball, and it gets ricocheted back and forth in the lane for a few seconds. Everything in there is just a tangle of sweaty arms, everyone clawing for the rock, until it squirts free to me on the wing. I pluck it clean and turn. I see Brownlee hustling back, nothing but me and him and blacktop.

His eyes go wide. He knows what's coming and can't stop it. Two dribbles and I'm past mid-court. One more and I'm on top of Brownlee and in the lane. And then I rise.

The last thing Brownlee sees before I throw it down is a nice up-close look at my LeBrons, right about at the level of his silly goatee.

Game. My teammates howl and talk trash, giving me fist bumps and high fives.

"Call me *little man*, now," I say to Brownlee again. I don't yell it, just kind of throw that line at him as I saunter off the court. I'm so amped that part of me is itching for him to talk back, give me some excuse to make a ruckus.

He thinks about it, I can tell. His upper lip curls into a sneer and his eyes narrow. But then he exhales, looks away for a second. "All right, kid," he says. "Tell me your name so I remember it."

"Derrick Bowen," I say.

"D-Bow," Uncle Kid says. He's standing a few feet away, a proud smile spread across his face. The other guys are grabbing drinks, getting a breather before we run again. "I'm telling you, that's what they'll all call you someday when you're hauling in NBA hardware."

I kick at an old tattered t-shirt left near the court. It's no lie that I think about the NBA, but when I hear somebody else say it, I get embarrassed. "I'll be fine with just starting for Marion East this year."

Brownlee's gone from trash-talker to super-fan in minutes. "Oh, you'll be the best player at Marion East in years," he says. I'm not ready to have him on my side yet so I just look away, see a black Lexus with tinted windows rolling toward the court real slow. It kind of creeps. No music playing, nothing, which is in some ways a lot more intimidating than someone rolling up with beats blaring.

"He'll be the best since they had me," my uncle says. Uncle Kid's jersey still hangs in the Marion East gymnasium. He was a legend, even if he never became the superstar everyone expected. "If that coach they got doesn't mess it up. Or if you even stay at Marion East."

I look up quickly, see Brownlee checking out my uncle, too. Those last comments were loaded, like he knows more about my future than I do. I hate it when people do that—talk over my head, like just because I'm fifteen they can wall me out of the conversation.

Over on the court, guys are looking our way, impatient for us to get back out to run, but then I realize they're looking past us.

"Kid!" a voice yells.

I turn, instinctively, so used to being called "kid" or "little man" or "junior" or any variation of those names, but when I look there's only the Lexus, one tinted window down no more than an inch. And it's my uncle they want, not me.

My uncle runs his tongue across his teeth like he tastes something bad and then says, to nobody in particular, "Gotta go." He starts toward the Lexus, and the window on the car rolls back up silently. Uncle Kid turns back to me and smiles. "Catch you later, D-Bow," he says, like there's nothing strange happening at all.

2.

Once, a couple Christmases ago, I saw Roy Hibbert in Circle Centre. A train of about six or seven guys trailed him, each loaded down with about five bags worth of merchandise, and Hibbert just strolled, all 7'2" of him, right down the middle of the mall. You think he looks like a bad-ass on the court, you should see him among mere mortals. Even with his length, you could tell how ripped he is. I mean, I was already pushing 6 feet and I felt like nothing next to his mass.

The thing I remember most is how everyone—every single man and woman in that mall—stopped what they were doing and stargazed. People parted for him, like traffic making way for an ambulance, and Hibbert looked straight ahead like he was the only one in the mall, immune to all those stares. But there they were, grown men with their jaws hanging open, women frozen stock still with their Christmas gifts about to fall from their hands, cashiers stuck between ringing up sales. Even my dad, who tries not to make too big a deal out of hoops, grabbed me by the coat sleeve and pointed in Hibbert's direction. Then my dad looked over at my mom, who was staring a bit too boldly. He drummed up some mock anger and said, "Oh, come on. He's just a basketball player," and we moved on down to the next store. But I'll always remember how that whole mall just froze, astonished at the very existence of an NBA player in their presence.

That's not the reaction I get when I walk down the halls of Marion East. At least not yet. Sure, people stare. Some squint and the edge of their mouth curls up and they might whisper something to the person next to them, but for a lot of them I'm just the freshman who's six inches taller than the rest, something to be figured out, but nothing special. The most ink I ever got was last year this time, when I got my picture in *The Indianapolis Star* in their pre-season hoops section, and even then it was just a tiny picture of me squeezed into a corner for middle schoolers, about fifty words on the "kids" in a section labeled *What's Next.* So instead of Hibbert's posse following a few paces behind him, I've just got my boy Wes Oakes next to me as we make our way to Algebra, where I'm plain old Derrick Bowen, not "D-Bow."

Then, as we round the corner, I see Nick Starks, the red and green of his jacket popping against his smooth brown skin, coming the other way. And wouldn't you know it, he's getting the Marion East version of the Hibbert treatment.

"Look at him," Wes seethes. If Nick Starks is the man between me and a starting spot at the point, then he's Public Enemy #1 for Wes too. "It's like he thinks he owns the place." He puffs out his chest like he's ready to throw down, never mind that my man Wes is all of 5'5" on a good day. You gotta love Wes, though: the heart of a warrior in a miniature body.

You'd think Starks was royalty even though he hasn't been able to get the Marion East Hornets out of Sectionals—hardly anyone has since my uncle played. Still, everybody's head swivels as Starks struts along, the guys angling for fist-bumps or nods of recognition. The girls whisper to each other, eyeing first Starks and then his girlfriend Jasmine Winters. Personally, I can't figure out why someone like Jasmine Winters would hook up with Nick Starks. She's cool, but not stuck-up. Fine as hell, but not air-headed. Whenever I see her caramel face coming down the hall, always smiling like she knows some secret, I get to feeling a little wild. She's only a sophomore, but she just seems *better* than Starks. As she walks down the hall, she seems a little detached from it all. Her eyes flash here and there, and she'll smile at someone she knows, but she seems just *over* the whole scene.

Some of the other starters make a little semi-circle around Starks as if they've just broken a huddle and he's leading them out onto the floor. There's Devin Varney, the two, who depends on Starks for all those open looks he gets, and Royce Bedford, the three-man who's a senior and best friends with Starks. And then there's Moose Green, a junior. His real first name is Gavin, but nobody's called him that in years. The man is *Moose*. Six-six and a good 250. He's Marion East's best post man and—there's no two ways about it—the man is *fat*. Not "pudgy" or "bulky." *Fat*. And nobody—I mean, *nobody*—can get around him in the paint. He gets gassed after three times down the court, but Moose catches it down low and he's taking somebody for a ride.

Starks gives me the slightest of nods and says, out the side of his mouth, *'Sup*, the last curl of ink of one of his tats edging above his collar when he nods. His hair, like always, looks just the slightest bit nappy, like he's trying to show how little he cares, and he can't be bothered to really even look at me before he rolls on down the hall. Jasmine looks me up and down once, and I could swear her eyes linger, but she gets swept away with the rest of them.

Moose stops, though, lingering large in the hall like some Indianapolis version of Shaq, only seven inches shorter and with a babyface that would make him look younger than Wes if he weren't so big. "Little man!" he says and throws his arm around my neck. He's the only person who can call me that and not make me get my back up. "We gonna see you on the court tonight?" He's talking about the first practice of the season, immediately after school.

Before I can answer, Wes chimes in: "You know D-Bow's gonna be there. He's gonna be the best player you got."

Moose rears his head back and laughs. "I see you got a fan club already!" He reaches out to shake hands with Wes, and it looks like a big bear offering a paw to a cub. "I'm Moose," he says. Wes squeaks out his name in return, almost coming off the ground with the force of Moose's shake. "You all right," Moose says. "I like a guy who talks a little shit."

Wes breaks into a broad smile, which is pretty much the reaction everyone has around Moose. Even during games, I've seen the team in a huddle so tense the sweat beads on Coach Bolden's forehead. He'll shout orders to them and concentration is carved into everyone's face, but they'll break that huddle and Moose will make some crack only the other players can hear. You can see them trying to hold back their laughter even if the game's tied with 15 seconds to go.

He turns to me now. "All I can say is you got some hype to live up to." He smacks me on the shoulder and then points down the hall to Starks and his crew. "They've all been hearing about this great D-Bow who's gonna take us to the promised land. They just never gonna show it. Especially Starks."

"Fine with me," I say. And it is. Sure, I want the starting spot. I want the attention in the halls. I want my name splashed in headlines. But I know it won't happen through hype alone. I'll have to earn it.

"Good," Moose says. He leans in. "All I care about is one thing. I get open in the post, you get me the rock. You feel me?"

He's laughing, but I know he's dead serious. "I feel you," I say.

Moose pops me on the shoulder again, then gives Wes a playful bump—almost knocking him into his locker—and then he's off, bellowing for his teammates to wait the hell up, his voice deep and loud as an amped bass.

I look over at Wes. We've been friends since first grade. There's nobody as constant as he is. I always hated it when my middle-school teammates would brush him off just because he didn't ball. He's still smiling from our encounter with Moose, though.

"That guy's cool," he says, which is a pretty solid verdict on Moose Green. So we don't have to say another thing as we head on to Algebra. But I have to rein myself in—just that encounter with Moose, just the mention of practice, has me playing out the season in my head, dreaming up all the ways my hype will become reality. I've just about mapped out the whole season, right down to me hitting a game-winner to beat Lawrence North in Sectionals, plus one more to drop Hamilton Academy in Regionals and send us to State. Then we walk through the door to Algebra, where Mr. Jenks, who probably hasn't cracked a smile in a quarter century, has a stack of quizzes he's handing out as students file in. An Algebra quiz—a reality check if there ever was one.

Coach Joe Bolden keeps a somber locker room, I can tell you that. In middle school, we used to be blasting Jay-Z before practices, getting ourselves loose. In the Marion East locker room, the sound system is a beat-up old stereo stuck in the corner collecting dust. The thing's so old it's still got dual *cassette* players in front. So the only beats here are coming out of Moose's earbuds, and even Moose turns his sound down when Coach Bolden enters.

Bolden—his first year at Marion East was my Uncle Kid's last. He hasn't changed a single bit in those two decades except that once his hair started to go gray, he decided to just shave it all off. So now the locker room lights reflect on his bald, brown dome as he paces through the locker room, his almond eyes squinting so hard it forces deep wrinkles into his face as he takes stock of what he has this year. Since that first year, he's won Sectionals exactly twice, but that's not to say his teams have been bad. We've just never been good enough to beat teams when it counts. I'm sure the parents around here would like a few more Sectional banners, but it's just as important to them that Bolden's players stay out of trouble, which isn't easy at Marion East. And if anyone does step out, Bolden makes sure their next step is to the curb. The man doesn't tolerate foolishness. Just ask Uncle Kid.

I pull my new kicks from their box. I rocked Kobes, then LeBrons in middle school, but this time I've gone with the new Rose AdiZeros, black with the red trim to match the trim on our unis. It's a tough move breaking from Nikes, but I figure new school, new season, new brand. I pull them out and smell that new leather.

There's something perfect about new kicks, like you can do anything in them, like every shot's going to find bottom and you're going to win every game.

Over in the corner, I see Starks getting ready. He's got his ankles taped, his shooting elbow in a sleeve, his right knee covered by a black Ace bandage. But it's all show. He's never had an injury as far as I know of but wants to look like some soldier readying for combat. His tats creep out from under all that gear, dark against his light-brown skin. It wasn't but a few years ago that Bolden would have made a player cover all those. Seems like only since Nick came along did Bolden come to grips with the fact that young guys want to get inked up.

"Time!" Coach Bolden yells, and like that everyone is out the door. I trail out, and I see every last player lined up on the baseline. For the first time in longer than I can remember, I feel nervous. Don't get me wrong, I *know* I belong here. I know that even if I'm just a freshman all I need is a chance to unleash my skills. But there's something about everyone lined up, the coaches staring at us with their arms crossed, everyone looking grim under the gymnasium lights. I try to squeeze in next to Moose, but even he shakes me off. "Freshmen on the end, D," he says. "Don't be playin' now."

I have to take my place all the way down at the corner of the floor. When I lean forward to take a look down the row, every other player is staring straight ahead, just waiting on Coach Bolden to make his way to center court and bark orders, like we're in the damn military.

When he finally gets there and blows that whistle, I realize *military* isn't much of a stretch.

Forget about drills—he runs us. I mean *kills* us. Down-and-backs, suicides, defensive slides, and more suicides. Nobody but Coach Bolden says a word, not even Moose, who's doing all he can to hide how much of a struggle this is for him. After a while, Bolden's assistant, Lou Murphy, walks over and grabs Moose by the elbow. They walk to one of the side baskets and Murphy acts as if he's instructing Moose on post moves, but it's really just a chance for Moose to catch his breath without drawing Coach Bolden's wrath. Smart move. If Moose can't finish the runs, then Bolden would have to come down on him, but everyone in the gym knows Moose is a threat for a double-double each night out, whether or not he can finish another down-and-back.

The rest of us are still waiting for Coach Bolden's next whistle. This is nothing new. It seems like every self-respecting high school coach in Indiana has a reputation for being a hard-ass. Some places, it's all show—the coaches put on a tough face but they know their best bet to move up the ranks is to keep their players happy and position them for the scouts. But I can see early on that Coach Bolden takes a special pleasure in this. When, finally, one of my fellow freshman falls out of a sprint and bends over on the sideline like he's about to pass out, Bolden walks over. "You gonna quit?" he asks. The rest of us have finished the sprint and are gathered again on the baseline. I look over and can see Starks smiling, making some quiet crack to Bedford. It's like the seniors have come to expect this moment.

The kid just shakes his head, but doesn't look up at Bolden.

Coach shouts now: "I asked you a question! Are you going to quit?"

"No, Coach," the kid manages.

"Then get back on the baseline," Coach says.

Two more suicides and we're done.

"Free throws," Coach yells.

While we're shooting, he rides us. He points out that only the seniors had taken time to stretch before hitting the floor, that it's not up to the coaches to baby us and get us ready. He reminds us that if we can't get ourselves ready to practice, then he can't trust us to get ready for a game. He tells us that play time is over, that it's November and Arlington is ready to come at us in two weeks. And then, for the freshmen, he says that he can see fear in our eyes, but if we want to suit up for Marion East then we better grow up and get over "that coddling middle school bullshit."

Finally, the prelude is done and we jump into some drills. Bolden and Murphy spend their time on the end of the floor with the upperclassmen, but they keep sneaking peeks my way, checking to see how my jumper's developing. The J from range is the one part of my game that needs work. It's not a weakness, exactly, but if I could make myself a real threat from three, nobody could check me. While Coach Murphy is watching me, I drop in two straight from behind the arc. Just smooth as butter. I sneak a look back at Murphy, see his eyebrows rise. Then, when it's time to D up one of my fellow freshmen, I don't let any class allegiance get in my way—I pick him clean or, if he gets room for a shot, erase it fast. When the box-out drill comes around, I grab every rebound like it's the final possession of a game, and at last I see that Murphy's edged all the way down to our end of the floor. "Not bad, Bowen," he mutters after a while.

But those are just drills. I need live action to really show out, and it doesn't take much longer for me to get my chance. Coach Bolden calls the freshmen down to the other half of the floor and walks us through our basic offensive set. It's not full court, but at least we'll get to go five-on-five for a little bit. The only problem is, after he walks us through, he puts the first string in against the second—with the freshmen off to the side just watching. So I have to play spectator while Starks runs the offense.

I have to give Starks credit. He can make that offense hum. He's fast and crafty and whenever anyone gives him a sliver of daylight he darts into the lane. The difference between us, though, is that even if he's lighting quick, he's got no explosion off the floor, so when he hits the paint he either floats up a little runner or has to kick it back out to Bedford or Varney on the perimeter. Sure, those two like the open looks, but I can get the rock to the rim.

Coach Bolden's praise for Starks never stops, though. "Good look in," he'll say, or "Nice decision." Then he'll turn to the other players and explain why Starks made the right play. Meanwhile, I'm getting that itch again, like I did at the park while Brownlee was giving me shit, like if I don't get on that floor soon I'll bust.

As if he could read my thoughts, Coach says, "Bowen for Starks."

I pop up and practically bounce onto the floor. Starks, on his way off, drops the ball at my feet, refusing to even look at me. Part of me wants to tell him he better get used to watching me, but I bite my tongue. I'll let my play speak for itself.

When I get out there, though, it feels like my own teammates are conspiring against me. Devin cuts back-door when I think he's going to pop out, and when I drive and draw the defense I thread a beautiful pass to Royce only to have him mishandle it—then shake his head at me and say it was low. *Put it right in your hands*, I want to say, but again I stay quiet.

"Right play, bad pass," Coach Bolden says, and those words feel like hot little needles in my back. It's killing me. I know this is my first time on the floor with these guys and I want to put my mark on the gym immediately. I feel shackled by this offense, though. It's built for another player—*Starks*—and it's all back-cuts and cross-screens, when it'd be a hell of a lot easier to have the other guys spread out and just let me work. Worse yet, everyone else's timing is already built to Starks, and I can't tell if I'm going too fast for them or too slow. It's like the time Uncle Kid let me drive his car and he kept telling me to hit the gas every time I slowed down, but then yelled to mash the brakes every time I sped up.

I can feel the coaches watching me again, but now instead of their eyebrows raised with pleasant surprise, I can sense their expectations slowly sinking. Murphy's blank stare might as well say, *Well, this Bowen kid's okay, but he's got a long way to go.*

Then, at last, Royce zips a pass to me near the top of the key, and I catch it in perfect rhythm just in time to see the lane open up. One dribble. All it takes. *Boom!* I thunder that thing down and let out a howl. Give a short swing on the rim just to let people know I've arrived.

Once I'm back down on earth, the basket support still rocking like there's been an earthquake, I take one big stride over the kid on the floor, the poor sophomore who thought he'd try to stop me on the way to the rack. I stamp my foot and look around, get a chest bump from Moose that knocks me back a couple steps. Royce and Devin start hollering in approval, but they check that as soon as they take a glance at Starks. Murphy cracks a little smile. But Coach Bolden frowns.

"Man slid over to take away the drive," he says. He nods at Moose. "You had our best post player wide open underneath."

This time I can't contain myself: "Why dump it off when I can do that?"

The players, even Moose, look down at their shoes, and Murphy looks away as if he doesn't want to witness the crime that's about to happen. The vein on Coach Bolden's neck bulges, but he doesn't scream. Instead, he says, very evenly, "Starks for Bowen."

Nick hustles back onto the court and pops the ball out of my hand. "Thanks," he says. He hits just the right tone—not so sarcastic that his contempt is obvious, but just enough of an edge to let me know. And there's nothing I can do about it but go sit down.

That's where I stay, on the sideline, for the rest of practice. Until the suicides at the end.

3.

When you're over-matched on the court, there's no hiding. When Uncle Kid used to take me down to the park when I was only 13 I'd get in over my head trying to guard some grown man. I couldn't do it, and everyone knew I couldn't do it, but I'd get no mercy. They'd single me up every time down.

That doesn't happen to me anymore, most definitely not between the lines. But when I walk in the house and there's something I don't want to talk about with my parents, it feels about the same. Isolated with nowhere to hide. I swear, if I've got bad news—a D on a quiz, or, like now, a brutal day at practice—my mom can smell it. Marion East is only about six blocks from our door, and I bet she knows something's off before I'm halfway home.

"Derrick," she says, "what's wrong?" She's sitting at the kitchen table, where they've just finished eating, my plate still there waiting to be microwaved.

"Nothing."

She repeats the question, this time with a little more concern. My mom has skin as smooth as glass, darker than my dad, and she has these eyes that look almost Asian, so most of the time she's got a soft, young-looking face. But when she gets serious—or angry—there's nothing soft.

My dad clears his throat like he's about to say something, but he knows this is Mom's show.

"Nothing," I say again.

She pushes her chair away from the table and folds her arms. "Derrick Bowen," she says, "you either tell me what's bothering you or we are going to have one very unfriendly evening."

With that, my little brother Jayson, who was chilling on the couch watching the Pacers pre-game, snaps off the television and scoots silently to his room. My dad stands, walks across the room to take a seat in his chair, not so he can relax, but so that they're on either side of me. No escape.

"Coach Bolden," I say. When it comes out, I know I sound like a whiner. I don't want to be that player who comes home and moans about how tough coach is, who bellyaches and backstabs until he gets his way. I'm supposed to be the guy who just laces them up and gets back to work. In those summer games a few years ago if I hung my head after a bad game, Uncle Kid would come right over to me, say something like *D-Bow, if you don't like getting beat, you got two choices. Get used to it or get better.*

It's just that, right now, I'd like a little sympathy from my parents.

I explain to them what happened at practice, trying to shade the story a little bit my way. They both react, but neither with what you'd call sympathy.

My mom is all righteous anger. She's convinced Bolden should be fired. She slams her hand down on the kitchen table and shouts,

"That man has to be the most stubborn coach to ever sit on a bench." So while she's on my side, it just seems to be an excuse for her to get angry. She's lived here all her life, moving from place to place in the patch of Indianapolis bordered by 30th, 46th, Meridian and Keystone. She loves it, but she also hates it. She loves the people she grew up with and loves being able to reminisce about her old times at Marion East. She can convince herself into thinking our little three-bedroom house is a better place to live than anywhere else in the city, even better than those mansions on North Meridian. But all of that means she feels free to criticize the area like nobody else. She goes on tirades about store owners who let people loiter, about how the city lets streetlights stay burned out and neglects potholes as big as craters, or about how someone needs to "put the fear of God" into some of the teenagers in the neighborhood. But nothing draws her ire like the subject of principals, teachers and, especially, coaches at Marion East.

My dad stays silent. While my mom rages on about Coach Bolden being blind to talent, he furrows his brow and stares at the floor. He's a strong, barrel-chested man, tough enough to handle security jobs around here, but it's a sneaky strength hidden behind his wire glasses, his calm demeanor that looks more like a teacher's than anything else. Dad doesn't share my mom's love of this area, maybe because he feels like they should have better jobs and more money than they do. My dad never finished college, but he's still the most well-read security guard in the history of the city. And he always says that my mom's too good a teacher to be trapped in these schools. He's less likely to say things about the area, but he's convinced the only good thing about our neighborhood would be leaving it behind. When *The Star* runs stories on crime or exposés on failing high schools, they'll sometimes snap some pics of our streets, of Marion East, to accompany their stories. To me, that's easy enough to ignore. I know there are places in this city a lot worse than the blocks I rep, and it's like *The Star* thinks every black guy in Roca Wear is some banger. But my dad gets grim when stuff like that comes up. Cranks out numbers on income levels. Starts rattling off graduation rates at Marion East and shakes his head. Now, when my mom finishes her tirade on Bolden, my dad says simply, "Well, maybe he shouldn't play for that coach, if he's as bad as you think."

Mom stops, puts her hands on her hips and fixes my dad with an icy glare. "And just what exactly does that mean, Thomas?" I've seen that stare before, heard that tone. Pops better tread lightly.

Instead of answering my mom, though, he turns to me. "What do you think about Coach Bolden?" he asks. "You want to play four years for him?"

That tone is even worse than my mom's. It's the one people get when they ask a question that means something other than what they're saying. Teachers, coaches, parents—they all do it, like they're holding something back. I grab an apple from the counter and take a bite, trying to act nonchalant. I shrug my shoulders as I chew and then say, "Sure."

"Thomas," my mom says, "let's not get into this now." She clears their plates from the table and puts mine in the microwave.

"I'm just asking a question, Kaylene," he says. "You were the one running down Bolden."

"Well, I don't like Coach Bolden, but I'm not going to let whatever happened with him and Kid way back when give you an excuse to mess things up now."

The mention of Uncle Kid tears it for my dad. He's slow to

anger—unlike my mom, whose temper goes zero to sixty in two seconds—but she's hit a sore spot with him. He stands, and though he doesn't yell—he never really yells—he raises his voice just enough. "The only thing that bothers me about my brother is that he's damn near forty years old and people still call him Kid instead of Sidney," he says.

There's silence in the room now, and I can tell that even though this conversation is about me, there's a lot more to it than what they'll say when I'm around, like they've had these little coaches meetings but can't decide what they want to tell the players yet. The microwave gives three long beeps to break the silence, and I pop it open, grab my dinner and beat it to Jayson's room. I've had enough conflict for one day.

I plop down next to my little brother. "What's banging, D?" he asks, but doesn't look up. He's deep into a game of NBA 2K13, taking the sticks with the Thunder against the Heat. I cling to beliefs that the Pacers will break through some day, but Jay's a front-runner, and as I finish my dinner he throws an alley-oop from Westbrook to Durant.

I pick up the other controller. "Start it over," I say.

"Naw, D," he says. "Lemme finish this."

I nudge him with my elbow. "Start it over. I'm gonna run you off the floor."

He laughs, cocky. "Bring it," he says. There's nothing better than spending time with my little brother. As soon as the season starts, though, we don't get to hang as often so he's excited to get a little attention. "I got the Thunder!" he calls.

"Take 'em," I say. "I'll run with whoever you want and I'll still take you."

He laughs again, then locks me in with New Orleans.

"Fine with me," I say. "I can drop fifty with Gordon." That draws more laughter from Jayson, but it's not far from the truth. Being a young point guard from Indianapolis, I heard that name—Eric Gordon— whispered more than a few times last year. As in: *That kid's the next Eric Gordon.* Sure, I know the line—I'm supposed to be the first Derrick Bowen, not the next anyone else—but I've followed Gordon's rise in the league. Even slicing through his defense with Gordon, though, it's not long before Jayson opens up a lead on me and starts talking trash.

"You too slow on the sticks," he says.

"You got no skills," he says.

"Oooh, I'm goin' by you again," he says.

I have no problem with my little brother running smack. He sure runs enough from the stands when he's watching me play. Last year I swear he almost made the kid guarding me cry.

Finally, at the end of the first quarter, he looks up at me. "How'd your first practice go, D?" he asks.

For a second, I think about telling him about Coach Bolden getting on me, but then I realize I shouldn't worry him. It made enough of a mess between my parents so no reason to drag Jayson into it.

"Let's just say this," I say. "All those things you do in the game with Westbrook? I'm gonna do that in real life."

"Cool," he says. As he looks up at me, I can see his imagination spinning out, envisioning all the buzzer-beaters and championships in my future. His excitement is so infectious it kind of puts things right for me again.

We turn back to the game. For a while, the only sounds are our thumbs on the sticks and the play-by-play on the television. At timeouts, though, I can hear my parents droning in the other room. They're not yelling at each other, but I can tell they're hashing out some serious stuff.

I ignore them and turn back to the game, but even as I do it, I know that those conversations won't wait forever. As much as I resent not being treated like an adult—by my parents, by guys like Brownlee down at the park—I know that when I enter that world, it won't be just games anymore.

4.

Wes and I walk down 34th toward school. My parents both have to be at work early, and my mom takes Jayson to the same school where she teaches, so Wes and I hoof it. In some ways, I like it. Wes lives two doors down from me on Patton, and when it's just us walking these streets—these blocks we've known our entire lives—it feels like we own the city. That creepy old house on Patton with the two cement lions spray-painted black and gold manes, guarding the porch: ours. The old apartment complex on 34th where Wes and I used to explore abandoned units before the city boarded it up: ours. All that traffic flying down Central—the buses wheezing along, the businessmen hustling through what they think is a shady part of town—that's ours. And, amid all that, these old houses here and there that have been kept up nice—no peeling paint, no rusting scooters or overturned wheelbarrows or piles of bricks in the yards— they belong to us too.

"So why'd Bolden get so pissed?" Wes asks. He shivers inside his big coat when the wind whips around the corner. The sky is watery gray and there's just a drop of rain now and then. It feels like it could sleet, lay down a sheet of black ice.

"Who knows why coaches do what they do?" I say.

He elbows me in the side. "C'mon Derrick," he says. "You don't have to put up some front. Why'd Bolden jump you?"

"Honestly, Wes. All I did was show off my hops. But, you know, coaches have to prove their points."

Wes laughs but tells me I better not mess around, that he doesn't want to hear noise for four years about *Coach this* and *Coach that*.

We go another block and then he says, "We got time." He's got that tone he used to get when we'd search through those old apartments when we were kids. I'd think we were going to get caught, but he'd always egg me on: *Nobody's coming*, he'd say, *let's hit one more unit. Bet we find a TV left behind!*

"Naw," I say now. "No time. Place isn't even open."

"Hell, yes, we got plenty of time," Wes says. And with that he's off, down 34th. Instead of stopping at the Marion East campus, he goes on to Central and up the street. I know where he's going. 38th. Window shopping. There between the Domino's and a payday loan place is Ty's Tower. Not much of a tower, really, just two stories, but it's the nicest place on 38th, and in that front window Ty's got all the fresh new kicks on display. Wes might not ball, but he's a sneakerhead extraordinaire, and when I catch up to him he's got his hands wrapped on the metal gate, his nose between the bars, checking out the displays.

"Those," he says, "are butter." Wes is always looking for something new. He comes down here weekly to stare at the same pair of Lunar Hyperdunks, even though he can't even dribble with his head up.

"You don't even play." I give him a little punch in the arm.

"Doesn't mean I don't need new flavor for Christmas," he says. He points up to some sharp Timberlands. "Those are what I need." If he had his way, his closet would be waist-high in kicks, a fresh pair for every day of the year, but we both know he'll be getting just one new pair for Christmas when his dad makes it in from St. Louis and swings up here with Wes—best day of the year for both of them.

I don't really care about window shopping in near-freezing weather, but it's just cool hanging with Wes, killing 10 minutes before first bell.

Yes, this is our part of Indianapolis. Like my mom, I love it. It doesn't matter that those old apartments are boarded up—that's where Wes and I played when we were kids. And it doesn't matter that for every house on Patton that's kept up there's another that's beat to hell—that's my street.

But, like my dad, I know what's beyond Fall Creek, beyond 38th. How can you not? I mean, you get across Fall Creek on Central now and the first thing you see is a fancy coffee shop and a yoga center. Not that I want to ever set foot in a yoga center, but there are times when I can see my dad's point: somebody high up decided to care about those blocks. The world doesn't end at our neighborhood, and what's outside of it has plenty of promise.

For now, though, even Wes knows it's time to get back down to school. We run. I lengthen my stride to pull ahead of Wes, who's hilariously slow with his choppy little steps, so I slow back down so we're step for step up the stairs to Marion East.

The grip on my shoulder is tight, and I flinch under it, thinking maybe it's some junior or senior wanting to start some shit. When I turn, though, it's Coach Bolden, his brow furrowed so deep that grooves form halfway up his bald head.

"This way," he says, nodding toward the gym.

"I'll be late to History," I say.

"I told Mrs. Henderson already," he says. "She won't mind."

I nod to Wes and he gives me this wide-eyed look like I might be in real trouble.

I walk a few paces behind Coach Bolden, trying not to look too much like I care, but inside I'm hoping like hell that nobody sees me, especially not Starks.

We exit the main building and walk across the grounds toward the gym. When we get to Bolden's office, he just points to a chair across from his desk. His office is pretty bare—a desk with a single lamp and a blank notepad on it, his cushioned chair behind it, and my uncomfortable folding chair on the other side. Behind him there's a huge equipment locker that seems to hold every sporting good known to man: racks of basketballs, boxes of knee pads, deflated volleyballs, baseball helmets, rackets of varying sizes.

"Look at me, Derrick," Bolden says. The man is all business. There's part of me that wants to resist him, to rebel against his strictness. But Wes had a point. I don't want to be the guy who sulks his way out of a starting spot.

Bolden starts right in: "You've got a chance to be the best player I've ever had here. The best. Do you know that?" I start to say something, but it's not a question he wants answered. "I've had a dozen players that have gone Division I, but none of them have had the promise you do. I saw some of your games last year. I see how far you are beyond other players your age. I might be a mean old pain in the ass, but I know basketball." He smiles then, just briefly. "But there are things you can work on. You need to be better at the stripe." This one stings, as I know I should be better than a coin toss at the free throw line. "And you need to clean up your jumper. Your motion takes too long. It'll cause you problems down the road. And you need to see the whole floor better, especially as the game gets faster. And it gets a lot faster, believe me. First when we start playing against schools like Lawrence North, then at college, and so on."

He gives a little pause now, but I know I'm still not supposed to speak. He just wants that *so on* to linger because it can only mean one thing: the NBA. He knows that's a real possibility in my life, and he wants me to know he knows. "So here's the thing, Derrick. You can work on those things and become a really special player. Or you can just keep doing what you do well. You can explode to the hole and dunk on somebody every chance you get. Just like you did yesterday. And that would be nice. We'd win a bunch of games and you'd score a bunch of points and every girl in school will be all over you. Everyone will know D-Bow.

"But we'll never go to State. And you'll never become as good as you can be. And you'll get a scholarship somewhere but never really do all that much. Because Derrick—I hope you can believe me here, because it's the most important thing I can tell you right now—you can do what you did yesterday against a lot of people, but soon you're going to step on a court and the opposing team will have a big man who will knock that junk into the fifth row. I swear it. Yesterday that was Tyler Stanford, who can barely crack our starting five. Dunking on him means nothing. So you've got to make a decision right now. Do you want to just be D-Bow? Or do you want to be Derrick Bowen, the player nobody can stop?"

He finishes his lecture. Normally, you'd hear noises coming from the gym, which is right down the hall. You'd hear people shouting and shoes on the hardwood and the thump of dribbles. But right now the only noise is the whoosh of heat coming out of the dirty vent in the ceiling. Just me sitting there across from Coach Bolden, who's staring at me so intently you'd think I just stole something from his house.

"Now," he says. "Get your ass back to History class before Mrs. Henderson fails you on principle."

5.

I still bring it when I get the chance. Still get a rip on the perimeter and hammer one down on a breakaway. One-hand throwdowns. Tomahawks. Once, when Bolden had to go into the locker room to get his clipboard, I popped it off the backboard to myself before throwing it down. My teammates hollered loud enough to wake the dead over in Crown Hill Cemetery. All but Starks, who just took a long sip off his water bottle and then spit into a garbage can.

I know why Starks acts that way. It's because, between dunks, I'm making the plays that Bolden wants. Our offense isn't that complex, and it never takes me long to get impatient. I'll see that baseline open up and it kills me to not just attack the rim, but instead I reverse it back up top and let the offense clip along. All that matters is earning Coach's trust so when the games get here in a few more days, I'll have plenty of chances to punish people who want to try and check me. I'm also finding a rhythm with Moose, who's a legit beast on the blocks. I get him the ball where he wants it and there's nothing the guy guarding him can do. If little guards bite down on him they bounce off like pinballs. No doubt, Moose has enjoyed my arrival.

Royce and Devin aren't so quick to warm to my presence. I know it's not because they worry I'll take their minutes, but because they're tight with Starks. They've been balling together since they were in middle school, and those bonds don't break, I guess. Even when I drop a dime to one of those two for a wide-open shot I get nothing, but if Starks hits them for a shot they act like he's the second coming of Chris Paul: *Great look, Nick*, they'll say, *Beautiful pass, man*.

Now we're running fives, prepping for the first game against Arlington tomorrow night. I'm splitting time with Starks with the 1s. Right now I've got the O's engine humming. First time down Moose seals his man. I hit him with a perfectly timed lob for a deuce. Then Royce deflects a pass on the defensive end and I push it ahead for an easy two-on-one break, Devin finishing at the end. Next time I rip the board and can't help myself—I just motor past everyone and finish strong in the lane, getting the hoop and harm. One more time down and the 2s finally get a bucket—Devin falling asleep on a backdoor, and getting an earful from Coach Bolden—so they're set again when we come down. I drive right, then kick to Royce in the corner. I cut on through to clear the lane for Moose, but when nobody can get him the ball down low, it gets reversed to me on the left side. Shot fake. Drive to the elbow. Shot fake again. And before the defense knows what hit him, I've slipped a little left-handed pass into Moose's mitts. Bucket again.

After that, Coach subs me back out for Starks and I get a round of fives from my teammates, even Devin and Royce. I catch my breath while Starks runs the point for a few possessions. I stifle a grin when he bounces a pass at Moose's ankles. Don't get me wrong—I don't want the team to fail. But if I raise the bar and Starks can't jump over it, fine by me.

They go up and down a few times, with nothing special happening except Tyler Stanford getting flipped from first to second team at the four spot for Chris Jones. They're both sophomores, and neither one does much more than take up space at that power forward position. There are times you can almost see Bolden's patience stretching thin with them. Some days he'll alternate them back and forth possession after possession, the vein in his neck bulging. Finally, Coach Murphy walks over and whispers something to Bolden. I know what's coming.

"Bowen, in with the twos," Bolden says. I flip my practice jersey inside-out, going from red to green, and jump back on the hardwood. Every day, they do this at least once—match me up against Starks. I always have to run with the 2s, but I don't mind. It just makes it that much more impressive when I turn him inside out as quick as I do my jersey. Any day now, it'll be Starks with the 2s. I can feel it.

I take a look at my squad—bump fists with a few of them. "Let's run these guys off," I say. The rest of the back-ups love it when I'm in their five, because all of a sudden things even up and they've got a fighting chance.

"Quit yappin'." This is Starks, who's waiting between mid-court and the top of the key, basketball nestled in the crook of his elbow. He won't even make eye contact with me, but says, "Less talk, more play, Bowen. This ain't middle school."

That draws a little laugh from Devin, but when I give him a look he shuts up quick. I go out to check Starks. Up until now we've gone at each other pretty good, but he's ignored me as much as he can. The fact that he had to say that to me lets me know I'm in his head.

He checks it and I get into him. I know where he wants to go, so every cut he makes is met with a little bump from me. Nothing that catches the coaches' attention, but enough to bounce him off course. After a few passes, Devin gets impatient and flings up a weak fadeaway that skips off the iron and into Tyler Stanford's hands. He outlets to me up at the hash and I push it into the front-court. Starks is back quickly, and if there's one thing I've learned against him it's that you shouldn't underestimate how crafty he is on the defensive end. He'll make it seem like you've got a good look at the rim, only to cut you off or poke the ball away. So I ease up on the throttle and settle us into our offense. It's clear pretty fast, though, that nobody else with the 2s has a prayer of making something happen, so when I swing back to the top of the key I catch a pass on the move and lower my shoulder, get myself to the elbow and rise up over Nick's outstretched hand. Bucket.

When they inbound it, I jump right on Starks. It's hard to turn him over, but the more I get into him the more frustrated he'll get. Sure enough, as he crosses mid-court, I flick at the ball and get a fingernail on it—not enough to steal it, but it slows him down again. Starks flashes a look at Coach Murphy, all but begging for a foul, but when Murphy just stares back, Starks gives the ball up and barks at me: "Don't reach, man. That's a foul."

"Less talk, more play," I say. That comment receives a subtle elbow from Starks as he tries to free himself on the wing. Sure enough, Royce feeds him the ball and Starks darts back baseline, but when he floats up his little runner, I get part of it. "Piece!" I yell, and Stanford yanks down another board and we're off.

At the other end I drive and kick to the wing. No shot. I pop back out to the perimeter for the rock and feed Stanford low, but he just gets off balance, so I swing baseline and get it again. Reverse it back to the top. Wait a beat and then cut across the lane. Starks is trailing me, so I stop in the paint and just open up. It takes the three-man a second to realize it—he's not used to a point guard who can post up near the basket—but he finally gets me the ball and Starks is still buried behind me. He tries to reach, but I keep the ball high and rise for an easy turnaround, only to see Moose flashing over. I know I can still score, even with Moose running at me. But I drop to it to Stanford who's all alone for a layup.

"Good look, Derrick!" Coach Bolden shouts. Then he jumps on the first team. "You guys are getting it taken to you by the second team! How are you gonna handle Arlington? How you gonna handle Cathedral? How you gonna handle Lawrence North?"

"Come on!" Starks yells at his teammates, trying to rally them.

I don't let up. As soon as he gets the in-bounds pass I'm on him again. I flick my hand in again near mid-court, and he seethes at me: "Don't reach!"

So next chance I get, I reach again. This time I pick him clean. And here's the thing: Nobody picks Nick Starks. So as I scoop the rock and push down the floor, I can hear a few people behind me—*Ooooh.*

Two dribbles. I'm in the paint. I rise. Then, just as I'm about to finish, my feet go out from under me. For a second I'm weightless in mid-air, my back parallel with the floor. Then down. Hard.

My shoulder gets the brunt of the fall, but my body twists, pushing weight up through my back and into my neck. Multiple whistles blow. As I lie on the floor I can hear the rumble of everyone's feet as they sprint down to my spot.

I leap to my feet and step to Starks: "What the hell was that?" I yell. "You trying to get someone killed?"

"It's a clean play! I was going for the ball." Even as he protests, though, he's backing up, looking out of the corner of his eyes for his boys Royce and Devin, who hustle over to get between us.

"It was a dirty play and you know it," I yell, but as I step forward, two things happen. First, Coach Bolden's hand grabs my jersey. You wouldn't think to look at the old man, but when he gets a hold of you, you're going nowhere. Second, I get dizzy. My legs wobble and I just have to stand there for a second trying to gather myself.

I worry that maybe something's really wrong, but my hesitation gives Starks confidence. He steps my way. "You want to accuse me of playing dirty? You wanna go, we can go!"

"That's enough!" Bolden screams. The gym goes quiet, except I still feel a little buzzing in my neck and head. "You're supposed to be getting ready for Arlington. For the goddamn basketball season. Instead you're trying to fight each other like a bunch of ten-year-olds."

With that, the buzzing and numbness in my neck turns to heat. I can't believe Bolden's jumping my case too, when it was Starks who undercut me. I know to bite my tongue, but all it does is make me want even more to put Starks on his ass.

"I ought to put both of you on the damn bench," Bolden yells.

I see Coach Murphy's eyes widen a little when he hears that. I guess Bolden's enough of a hard-ass to actually do something that crazy, so Murphy pipes up. "Okay, okay," he says, "we got that out of our system. Now let's put that energy in the right direction and have a good rest of practice."

Coach Bolden looks at Murphy. He doesn't like getting interrupted, even by another coach. But I guess Bolden decides not to make a bad day worse, so he sends us all off to shoot free throws and calm down.

For the remainder of practice, I kept my cool. The coaches don't match me back up against Starks all day, and there are no more fireworks.

In the locker room, with Bolden and Murphy keeping an eye on us, Starks came over and gave me a little fist bump.

"We cool?" he asked.

"Sure," I said. But we're not cool. Both of us know it.

During practice, it didn't take long for my numbness to fade. I most definitely didn't want to let the coaches think I was hurt the day before our first game, but now that practice is over I play it up. I keep stretching my neck and rubbing it, even ask our trainer—some pint-sized but solid guy named Darius—to get me a bag of ice.

So out of the gym I stroll, ice pack held to my neck even in 30 degree weather. The gym doors open up onto Fairfield, right where it meets Central, and the traffic is creeping in the early evening, a few flurries sparkling in the lights. I know my Mom's got dinner waiting for me, but I like nights like this. Cold and crisp, all the city lights coming on as the sky gets dark, so I zip my coat up, pull off that ice pack, and decide to head up to 38th and College for a couple cheeseburgers before heading home.

I text Wes and tell him to meet me there when I see Jasmine Winters. She's leaning against a car in the corner of the gym lot, waiting on Nick, I guess. As always, she looks fine. She's got on this big red coat that kind of stands out, this one flash of lively color in the black and gray of the city. She's got her hands shoved in her pockets and she's shivering, but she must sense me looking at her because she looks up and smiles, gives a quick wave.

I head on up Central, trying to be cool, but I wave back and call *Hey* to her.

"What happened?" she asks. I don't know what she means, and she points to the doors. "I saw you had ice on when you came out."

"Nothing," I say. "I got undercut and landed on my neck, but I'm straight."

She takes a couple strides toward me. "Let me see," she says, sounding seriously concerned.

I should know better. I really should. But here's Jasmine taking an interest in me, so I walk into the parking lot, and when I get close I have to bend down a little and tilt my head so she can take a look. Her fingers are cold as little icicles against my skin, but I can feel her breath warm against my neck. I peek over at her, see the smooth caramel of her skin, see her simple silver necklace glimmering in the night. "I don't see any swelling," she says.

I smile at her. "See," I say. "No big deal."

She folds her arms across her chest, almost like she's embarrassed for having tried to nurse me a bit. Then she pulls out her phone and looks at it, but she's just checking the time, growing impatient for Nick to make his exit. "Who undercut you?"

I consider lying, but then I figure why lie to protect Nick? "Your boy," I say.

"Nick did that to you?" She sounds alarmed again, almost angry.

"It happens," I say. Out of the corner of my eye, I see a couple of the other players leaving and I don't want to be caught talking to her.

"Gotta bolt," I say. "Peace."

"Take care," she says. "Don't go getting yourself hurt."

I swear she's flirting as she says it. As I walk away, I think I see her wink, but the flurries are turning a little heavier now so I can't be sure.

I head up Central and I'm just about to 36th when I hear someone call out my name. I turn and see Moose, so I wait for him at the intersection.

"Good practice," he tells me when he arrives. "We gonna beat the hell out of Arlington."

"We better," I say. "I'm so amped I can barely stand it."

We cut over toward College, our heads bent into the wind.

"One thing, though," Moose says.

"What?"

"You're already about to take Nick's starting spot. Don't screw it up by trying to take his girl."

I play ignorant. "I'm not doing anything like that."

"I saw you," Moose says. "Running game with her in the damn parking lot. I mean, come on, man."

I try to laugh it off. "Shit. I wish I had game to run. I was just talking."

Moose stops then, right there in the middle of the lane on 38th. "I know game when I see it," he says. "Just stay clear of Jasmine." We head on across the street. I tell him I'm meeting Wes for some eats so he decides to join us. Then, even though he was dead serious for me to stay away from Nick's girlfriend, he pushes me on the back, messing around. "A freshman trying to get down with Jasmine Winters in the parking lot," he says. "You a dawg, D-Bow." We laugh then, and duck into the warmth of the burger joint, leaving Indy's bluster outside.

6.

Game Day. Is there anything that gets the blood flowing more than those two words? Wes gives me a fist bump and wishes me luck as we bust out of final period and head down the hall. He's off to practice with the band so I won't see him until we hit the hardwood tonight. I stroll down the hall, give a quick smile to Jasmine as she waits on Starks, bounce down the Marion East stairs, put Kanye on headphone blast and start focusing on the game tonight.

I only get about four steps before I see Uncle Kid waiting on me. He's leaning against his dinged-up Nova, skinny as a lamp-post and a little disheveled. He's got no coat on, just a dingy Nike sweatshirt that looks about as old as he is. He shivers in the wind. Still, when he sees me, he gives a big smile. "D-Bow!" he shouts, so loud I can hear it over my music. "You gotta be ready, son! Game day!"

I wanted to retreat into my own world for an hour or two before reporting back to the gym, but Kid's energy is infectious. It's almost like it's his game tonight. I slide my headphones down around my neck and walk over. I offer a handshake, but he pulls me in and gives me a half-hug. "You're my man, D-Bow. It all starts tonight," he says. We stand there in the chill for a few seconds. I can sense the other students looking at us as they file out of school. I love my uncle, but he does look out of place so when he asks me if I want to take a ride, I jump on in.

That Nova of his is a sorry old bucket. Even as we climb in, I can hear the shocks squeak under our weight, and when the heater kicks on it sounds like somebody's shuffling cards behind the dash. It smells like glue and stale food too.

Instead of taking me back home, Kid goes down Central, hangs a right on 32nd, then another right on Fall Creek Parkway. I figure he just wants to cruise around a bit, but when we pass under the red bridge of the Monon Trail, he points up at it, and I realize he's got some lesson in store for me.

"See that?" Kid asks. "They connected that trail all the way from the North side to downtown, but they hit our neighborhood and they put it right over us, so all those people out biking and jogging with their dogs can pretend like we don't even exist."

"Yeah," I say. I've heard this story before from my dad, as if I'm supposed to be offended by that trail. But like my mom points out, they just followed along the old railroad line, so if we're supposed to get pissed off, then she says we might as well look up who the hell originally designed the city and then go shout at their graves. It's just as productive as bitching about people from Noblesville riding their bikes, she says.

But there's an edge to my uncle's voice as he talks, and he grips the wheel a bit tighter with every block. His old sweatshirt hangs off his arm, and underneath it he looks thinner than usual. For as long as I can remember, Uncle Kid—Sidney, as my dad would stress—has been kind of a problem. I don't mean he's a bad guy. But there's always been some kind of bad news swirling around him. He can never keep a job for long, he doesn't get arrested, but he's got friends in and out of jail, and he's always got some scheme that's going to turn things around that just makes my dad shake his head in disgust. And sure enough those schemes always lose money for Uncle Kid and he's got to pound pavement to try to find someone who will hire him again.

He guns it to beat the light at Keystone. The whole car rattles and squeaks as he bounces through the intersection. He slows down then and goes quiet, but he frowns as he stares ahead. All this frustration started for Uncle Kid before I was born, back when he came out of Marion East only to see his basketball career go nowhere—or at least not as far as people thought it would. So he shuffled around, a disappointment to everyone. And that's the thing. Even now, I feel like he'd be okay except that the weight of everyone else's disappointment presses on him until he lives down to what they think of him. The only time I don't see all of it weighing on him is when he's on that Fall Creek court, schooling guys.

We roll north until Fall Creek becomes Binford. The houses on either side of us start to rise from more and more impressive lots. We go past a few commercial intersections—gas stations and fast food joints like anywhere else—but soon the lights get brighter and suddenly my uncle's Nova appears out of place next to the luxury cars and new model SUVs.

"This is where you want to be," Kid says, almost to himself. "Up here with the beautiful people." In his voice, though, I hear both my mom's resentment and my dad's desire.

Then he hangs a right on some residential street and we wind back and forth through neighborhoods, some houses rising three stories up.

"I could have lived in places like this," he says. "Just needed a break here and there."

I don't say anything. The truth? Hell yes, he could have lived in a mansion if things would have played out. But it seems rude to agree with someone who says something like that, like you're calling attention to all the ways they screwed up. I'm not sure exactly where we are once we go under the interstate, but at some point I see us pass a sign that says we've crossed from Marion County into Hamilton County.

Uncle Kid just stares straight ahead. "Not that I'd want to live like all these people, but, D-Bow, up here they look after each other. It's impossible for people up here to fail." Then he looks over at me. "But, my man, down where we are, you have to look out for yourself. I learned that the hard way."

He's leading to something, and it doesn't take me long to see what. We come down a hill past a country club, then hit a bigger intersection, and he turns onto 126th. Then there it is: Hamilton Academy, its lights up since their first game is tonight too.

"If I'd have played ball at a place like this," Kid says, "instead of wasting my time with Joe Bolden, things would have been a lot different, I can tell you that."

I slouch down in my seat and fold my arms. Hamilton's a power in the state, cranking out Big Ten talent every year. Champs of our Regional five years running, with a state title to boot. Right now, there's a junior there—Vasco Lorbner, 6'8" with range and skills—that has every college in the country beating a path to his door.

"I'm not stupid, you know," I tell my uncle. "I hear what Mom and Dad say. I know what you're getting at."

"Well?" he says.

"Well, if you want to tell me something, tell it." I look out the window now at Hamilton Academy. Ten years ago, that school was a little 2A hole-in-the-wall, but every year the people pour North. And they bring their cash. Now that place is a cathedral—brand new facilities and trees lining the drive—compared to the old decaying brick of Marion East.

Uncle Kid just laughs, that kind of aggravating sound people make when they think they know better than you. He wheels into Hamilton Academy and then hangs a U-turn, starting our journey back home. "All I'm saying is you have options I never had. Think about it."

We don't say a word to each other for a while then, and soon enough he's got us back out to Binford, puttering south into a cold drizzle.

"Can we get a move on?" I say. "I got to get my head ready for Arlington tonight."

Uncle Kid pauses and shakes his head, but then he hits the accelerator. The Nova jumps forward, the whole car rattling with the effort.

5 – GREEN
4 – STANFORD
3 – BEDFORD
2 – VARNEY
1 – STARKS

That's what's written on the chalkboard in big white caps when I come through the locker room door. I'm one of the last ones there, thanks to Uncle Kid burning up my time, and nobody even looks up at me.

Everyone's getting taped up or already pulling on their gear. Coach Murphy, standing at the front of the locker room, is the only one who nods at me when I come in, but then he tilts his head in the direction of my locker as if to say, *Hurry up and get ready before Coach comes in.*

I get dressed quickly. It's for the best that I have to hurry. That way I don't have time to burn on Bolden's starting five. Moose at center, and Devin and Royce at guard and small-forward? That makes sense. But everyone who's been at our practices knows I've outplayed Starks. I guess Bolden is too stubborn to budge this early in the season. But by the time I've got on my #25—Derrick Rose's high school number—it doesn't matter. Not really. What matters is that, starter or not, this is my Marion East debut, rocking the white with the red and green trim, and I plan to make it memorable.

Soon enough I've got my AdiZeros laced tight, and we're sprinting out onto the floor for warm-ups. The gym's hot as a sauna, and I can smell popcorn and polished hardwood. We hit that floor and the band starts up, the crowd rises, the opposing team stares us down, and my adrenaline jumps through the roof. Warm-ups, Coach's pre-game talk, the huddle before we break—all of it's a blur, until we break huddle and, for the first time I can ever remember, instead of readying for the tip, I slump back to my spot on the bench. I stand and clap with my teammates, but soon my eyes wander. I see my parents and Jayson, with Uncle Kid sitting beside them. Kid's got his arms crossed, angry, and Jayson seems to be asking my mom something—probably about why I'm not in the game, because Mom answers quickly and then squints at the court. She's got that same look she gives you if she thinks you're lying about something. I'm suddenly afraid she's about to storm down out of those stands and jump Coach Bolden. Only my dad seems content to watch the game.

On the wall above the South basket, the jerseys of former standouts hang. There's my uncle's #31 among the others, but none of the numbers up there represent guys who made it to the league. Even the best—a guy who was a surefire All-American in college—got in a car wreck after his sophomore year and was never the same afterward. Sometimes it does feel like all the best things that come up here are doomed.

I look over toward our basket where the band's stationed and make eye contact with Wes, who gives me the thumbs-up from behind his saxophone. Then he offers a little fist-pump of encouragement. I figure at least he's got the right attitude. I try to re-focus, remember that all I can control is how well I play once I get my shot, but then there's a roar from the crowd and I look back to the court, where Starks has just blistered his man with a cross-over and a jumper that finds bottom. I figure somewhere Jasmine is standing and cheering for him, looking good as she does it.

The first few minutes of the game are uneventful. We trade a few buckets with Arlington, but then Stanford makes a stupid reach on a driver, sending him to the line for a three-point play. That sends Coach Bolden into a fit. You never want to be on the receiving end of his anger, but when he goes ballistic you can't help but enjoy the scene. It's as if seeing bad basketball causes him physical pain. When Stanford reaches on that kid, Bolden rocks back in his chair and then grabs his head, pressing his fingers into his temples. It knocks his collar up on one side, but he doesn't even seem to notice. He's too busy cursing under his breath and calling for Chris Jones to get in there for Stanford, and when Stanford trots off the floor—he looks surprised when Jones calls his name, like he expects Bolden to be subbing for somebody else—Coach meets him two strides onto the court, already lecturing him about "playing D with your head, not your damn hands."

The end result, though, is that we fall behind Arlington, one of the few teams in our Sectional we usually beat. Then our offense goes cold. They sag way back in on Moose and cut off Nick's driving lanes, so all that's left is Devin and Royce chucking up threes. They're usually solid, so maybe it's first-game jitters, but they offer miss after miss—first getting bad rolls and then throwing up uglier shots each time. Soon enough, there are only a few minutes left in the first quarter, and we're down 15-8 to Arlington—a team that has only one senior getting DI offers, just places like Eastern Illinois and Ball State.

Coach finally turns my way. "Bowen for Starks," he says. As soon as I rise, I hear it—those murmurs rippling through the crowd. Those who know hoops have heard of me, and there's a little buzz in the gym now. I also hear my family cheering, and I think I can hear Uncle Kid heckling Bolden for waiting so long.

A few more subs come in with me, so the only starter on the floor is Devin. Doesn't matter. I walk to him, look him in the eye. "Let's take hold of this game," I say.

"I can't get anything to drop," he says.

"It'll drop," I say. "Keep firing."

Then the ball's in and we're on D. The kid I'm checking is pretty good, the junior who's getting that DI interest, and I know they want to run through him. So as soon as he gives it up, I'm chest-to-chest, killing his chances of getting the rock back, and Arlington isn't exactly patient in working it to him—they squeeze off a bad shot after about ten seconds and I get the outlet. And you know I know what to do with it: *Push.*

I get on top of Arlington's guards right away. As quick as Nick is, his size didn't bother them. Mine does. At the elbow, I give a little hesitation, then power into the lane and rise for a 10-footer. Their off-guard swipes at my elbow with no call, but it doesn't matter. I bury it. Just like that the crowd's back into it, and I can feel the energy on the court turn. Everyone in the gym knows Arlington's got no answer if we just attack.

As I backpedal I can hear my teammates calling out to me—"Shot, D-Bow. Good shot."

The run we put on Arlington is quick and merciless. Devin for three from the corner. Stanford, who looked lost as a lamb his first go-round, banks one home from the shallow wing. I overpower their guard and hit a fifteen-foot turnaround, prompting Arlington's first time-out. Moose, back in after his breather, scores a garbage bucket on an offensive board. I drive and dish to Devin for three again. And then, when I feel like I control the whole rhythm of the game, I bait them. I sit back in the lane and wait for them to reverse the ball to my man—then I'm in that passing lane like a fired bullet. I pop it loose and track it down, push on down into the frontcourt. No less than three Arlington guys sprint back to close on my drive, so I just drop a dime behind my back to Moose trailing the play. And, damn, Moose brings heat. Brings his weight down on that rim, and the whole bucket is still swaying with the force of the blow even when we're back at our bench after Arlington's second time-out.

By mid-second quarter I'm subbed back out for Nick. My point's been made, though. A ton of them, really—we're up on Arlington

28-18, a 17-point swing during my minutes. After that, there's no looking back. Nick helps push the lead out to 15 by half, and we give Arlington a thorough thumping. A 72-46 final. My line: 12 points, 4 assists, 3 steals, 4 boards. That's better than Starks in every category but assists, and I did it in fewer minutes. When I talk to people afterwards, everyone's sure that tomorrow night when Lawrence North rolls in, Bolden has no choice but to start me.

7.

5 – GREEN
4 – STANFORD
3 – BEDFORD
2 – VARNEY
1 – STARKS

This hits me when I walk back in the locker room like a slap in the face. For a second I think maybe it was just left up there from last night. But, no, it's fresh chalk. Same damn starting five.

After last night's game, my parents and Jayson were thrilled with the win and with the plays I made when I got my chances. Wes and Uncle Kid came over afterward and we all crowded into the living room. My dad ran out for some pizzas and everyone felt celebratory, talking about how Arlington couldn't check me, laughing about how late in the game when it was wrapped up Chris Jones went up for a dunk and popped it right off the front rim, Jones nearly falling down in the process. The play sent Coach Bolden into a fury on the sideline, stomping up and down the coach's box in a ridiculous tirade, but now it was just material for our amusement: our back-up four-man playing the fool in the waning minutes. Wes scooped a slice of pepperoni from the box and said, "Yeah, Jones got blocked by Joe Rim on that one." I've heard Wes crack that joke about a dozen times, but we all laughed like it was the funniest, most original thing we'd ever heard. We all stayed up late, even Jayson since it wasn't a school night, and watched the West Coast game—Spurs-Blazers—and nobody even breathed a word about me not starting. Until the 4th quarter of that late game. Wes had gone home and Jayson was in bed and my mom was asleep on the couch. Uncle Kid leaned forward in his chair to get my attention. "I see Bolden's out to mess with you, just like he did me," he said.

"Sidney," my dad said. He was over on the couch, Mom's feet propped on his lap, so he said it softly so not to wake her, but there was a real warning in that one word.

"Tom, you know Derrick shouldn't be sitting on that bench."

"Let's just watch the game," I said, nodding toward the TV.

"We've talked about this," my dad said.

That was it for a while. We watched Duncan own players half his age. Then, like an afterthought, Kid muttered: "Well, we're gonna talk about it again sometime."

And now, lacing up my kicks and staring at that starting five, I feel like talking about it. Last night, I just wanted Uncle Kid to let things be, but I almost feel like I deserve some kind of explanation for why my name's not on that board, especially after the way I outplayed Starks last night. Maybe Coach Murphy senses it, because he comes over and gives my shoulder a quick squeeze. "Different ballgame tonight," he says. "Lawrence North makes Arlington look like a bunch of grade schoolers, so we're gonna need you to be ready."

"I'm always ready," I say, though I want to tell him that if they need me so much then Bolden best get my name up there on the board.

Murphy was right about one thing: Lawrence North's no joke. There's a reason they're the favorite to win our Sectional, and why they're a real threat to bounce Hamilton Academy in Regionals. Squad is loaded. Every single one of their starters is scholarship material, but the primary weapon is Marcus Tagg, a rangy 6'5" swing-man. All-City, All-State, Kentucky-bound blue chipper.

Bolden stuck Royce Bedford on Tagg, and even before the tip you could tell Royce was in too deep. You could see it in the way he dried his hands on his shorts a bit too nervously, cocked his head back and forth and rolled his shoulders like he was trying to act tough: he was scared. Royce is a good shooter, a decent athlete. On his best days he's usually a good match-up for us out there—but nobody can play scared. First time down, Tagg catches it shallow corner and just rises for a 17-footer. Filthy good. Next time he cuts to the wing and Royce, wary of Tagg's burst to the hole, doesn't challenge hard. Bucket for three. And next time it's just ugly: Royce tries to anticipate the pass to the wing and gets back cut. By the time he realizes he's lost him, Marcus Tagg is up in the clouds, soaring for an alley-oop that has the Lawrence North fans jumping in our bleachers. Timeout. A 7-0 hole and their other stars haven't even gotten warm.

"Shit, he can play," Royce says in the huddle.

"Well, damn, Bedford," Bolden says. "At least you've figured that much out. Took you long enough."

"You all right," Starks says, and gives Royce a quick pop on the shoulder to try and shake him out of it.

"No, he's not!" Bolden shouts. He looks at me for a second, his eyes bulging and angry, but then he turns back to the starting five. "We can't expect Bedford to just check Tagg on his own. We all have to know where he is. Help on drives! Hedge on screens! Now let's dig our heels in and protect our home court."

That rallies guys for a little while. Nick makes a few nice plays and Moose knocks in a mid-range shot off the glass. But it doesn't last. Tagg and Lawrence North are just too much, and soon enough Tagg gets loose for another thunderous dunk. Coach Bolden hangs his head momentarily, hands clasped behind his back, looking more like a man lost in deep thought rather than one in the thick of battle. It lasts for a few seconds and then he pops his head up like he's heard someone suddenly call his name. "Bowen, next whistle," he says. I jump from the bench. In the background I can hear a few cheers, but as I start for the scorer's table Coach grabs me by the sleeve of my warmup. "Not for Starks," he says into my ear, "for Bedford. You get into Tagg and see what you can do." I take another step and he pulls on my sleeve again. "You know what you're doing out there? You know the three spot in our offense?"

"I'm straight, Coach," I say, but that's not entirely true. I've never played anything other than point guard, not even in practice, so though I know what the three does I've never actually done it.

By the next whistle, we're down 9, and when Starks looks up to see me checking in, a pained expression flashes across his face. The thing is, when I point to Royce instead, Starks looks even more pissed. I watch as Starks walks toward the sideline with Royce, like he's some police escort—in his ear the whole time. This is their third year as starters together. Whatever Starks is saying to his best friend it's certainly not complimentary of the freshman coming in to replace him.

When I body up next to Tagg, he just gives me this long staredown, like *Who you think you are?* He's bulkier up close, and his dark scowl makes him look like he's about 25. On the offensive end, I get out of rhythm. Any time I'm a step slow on my cut, Starks shouts at me, once giving a frustrated look toward the bench—as if I'm the one that dug us a nine-point first quarter deficit. Moose has my back, though, and guides me a bit more subtly: "Flare now, D," he'll say. Then, during a dead ball, "You all right, D, just stay at it. Next time you catch it on the wing, I'm clearing for you." And, sure enough, he does, so I dip my shoulder and get past Tagg, exploding so quickly that he has to relent so he doesn't foul, and I get us a quick deuce off the window.

At the other end of the floor, it's an even greater challenge sticking with Tagg. The guy is in constant motion—posting up down low, then spinning for that lob, faking to one baseline and dashing to the other, setting a cross-screen and slipping it to cut into the lane. Their point guard, a shifty kid named Patterson who's a ringer for a younger Jason Terry, is always on the lookout for him too. I stay glued to Tagg, and the one time he gets me pinned on his back in the paint, Moose slides over to scare away the entry.

We dig. We claw. We fight. Bolden shouts maniacally from the sideline. But we can't make a dent in their lead except to shave it to 8 with the ball for the last shot of the first quarter. With just under ten seconds, we get it to Starks at the top of the key so he can work. He idles for a moment and we all catch our breath. There's just a hint of a buzz in the crowd. I look up in the stands and see Uncle Kid on his feet, urging us to get a bucket. I realize that if we could knock one down here, we'd actually be in the best shape we could have hoped for after that disastrous start. I'm on the wing to Nick's right. He jukes a couple times up top, then crosses hard to his right and knifes into the lane, so when Tagg helps I drift deep into the corner. I know Nick wants that last shot, but he's drawn a crowd in the paint, so when he leaves his feet he has no choice but to kick it out—and I'm his best option, standing all alone in the corner for a beautiful look at a three. The pass comes crisp but low and I have to re-gather. In just that hesitation, Tagg is rushing at me, hand outstretched. I've still got time to rise up for a look, but his presence bothers me. The release just feels off, a little flat and short. Sure enough, as the buzzer sounds, my shot scrapes front iron and drops straight down like a stone. Our crowd is dead again.

In the huddle, Nick doesn't waste time putting a knife square in my back. "We need another shooter out there," he yells. Coach Bolden frowns but doesn't say a word about it, so Murphy steps in and rattles off about five straight clichés to try to raise our spirits. When Bolden finally does get in the middle of the huddle, he just re-iterates all the things he's already told us: everyone help on Tagg, push the ball whenever we get a chance, be patient in the half-court. Like saying it all again will make any of it work better for us. Just before we break, he rattles off substitutions, putting Moose and Devin on the bench too. So Starks and I break huddle to face Lawrence North, down eight, with nothing but sophomore back-ups surrounding us.

It goes about as well as you might expect. I stick with Tagg, but with Moose out of the paint, he's content to just feed their bigs. Even when we force a miss, they pound the glass, getting second, third, fourth shots until something drops. On the other end, it's like I'm invisible. With this five on the floor, Nick decides he's got to play savior, so he drives and drives and drives, penetrating into the teeth of the D but never kicking it out for shots. He never once looks my way, even when I pop open in the paint. "Ball!" I shout, but he just drives right at me, bringing more defenders with him.

"Get out of the lane!" he yells at me. He dribbles back to the top of the key and shouts at me again: "The three isn't supposed to be in there. Learn the offense, man!"

Soon enough, Bolden gives up on his little experiment and sends Moose and Stanford back in along with Royce, so now I slide into the two spot that Devin usually occupies. But Royce arrives with instructions that I'm still supposed to check Tagg on the defensive end. The return of our starters gives us a little jolt and we slice away at the lead, getting it back to single digits. Our little run is fool's gold, though, because Lawrence North cranks the intensity back up. They don't explode like they did in the first few minutes, but they methodically stretch their lead, and our crowd goes kind of numb as if they're watching a funeral procession edge along to the graveyard.

As the half nears an end, I'm spent. I've given everything I have keeping Tagg reined in. On the offensive end I haven't had a single touch except to inbound the ball. It just wears me out. I'd as soon strangle Nick as look at him. Even Moose isn't offering any words of encouragement. The silence of the crowd has been replaced by grumbles here and there. It's not that they all expected us to beat Lawrence North, but they're not exactly thrilled with our effort.

That's when it happens: for the briefest of moments, I think about how Uncle Kid drove me up to Hamilton Academy and told me how I should consider taking my talents there. Tagg's gone faster than a finger-snap, spinning away from me and throwing one down on a lob: the same move that froze Royce in the opening minutes. He backpedals to the defensive end and smirks at me. "Gotta stay awake, kid," he says.

Next time down the clock's dwindling, so they iso Tagg. He jabs at me once, twice—toying with me—then dips his shoulder and starts baseline only to pop back and bury one from three. I hang my head and hear the Lawrence North crowd go nuts. The buzzer sounds and I shuffle toward the locker room, not looking up. I don't want to make eye contact with Wes, my family, anyone. I just stare at my AdiZeros as they make one step after another toward the locker room, until I almost bump into Coach Bolden.

"What the hell was that?" he yells.

"Tagg's too good," I say.

Bolden's back stiffens and he puts his hands on his hips. "Don't you ever say that again," he says. "You make him good because you lose focus." He started off in a controlled tone, but as he goes on his voice gets louder and louder. I realize we're near the bleachers where Wes sits. "Then you're out on the perimeter with Marcus freakin' Tagg," Bolden continues, "and you've got your hands down below your waist. You let your hands sink like that and you're just waiting around to die."

Waiting around to die. That's about what halftime feels like. And much of the second half. By mid-fourth quarter most of the crowd has cleared, which is fine by me, because it's fewer people to see me pile up garbage minutes with the other back-ups.

I listen to Coach Bolden's post-game talk. After Bolden exits, I listen to Starks slam his fist into his locker and scream that we should be ashamed of ourselves. I listen to Moose talk shit about how it doesn't matter if we win or lose, he's still going to have himself a Saturday night, rattling off names of all the girls he claims want to share that Saturday night with him. I listen to a few guys laugh, unable to stay down around Moose even after a 19-point thumping. I listen to the shower hiss. I listen to the door to the locker room slam again and again. I listen to the sound of my footsteps echo in a dark, empty gym. Then I listen to someone call my name.

It's Wes. He's been waiting for me this whole time.

"You're unbelievable," I say.

"Derrick, if I'm gonna hang with you after wins, I'm gonna still be around after you get your ass beat."

I laugh. "We did get our asses beat, didn't we?"

"Like a drum."

We go out the doors and get whipped by the cold November wind.

"You coming over to hang out?" I ask Wes.

"Hell, naw," he says. "Your place will be depressing. Let's go get some eats. We'll pretend like basketball was never invented."

8.

Sundays mark moratoriums on basketball, at least as long as my dad has his way. He'll usually relent by late afternoon and let me watch a game, but in the mornings the very topic is banned. Been that way since I started playing.

First thing is the early service at Church of God. Neither one of my parents is super religious, so I'm pretty sure they think church is just a great excuse to get me and Jayson up and moving early on a Sunday morning. Uncle Kid usually attends too, but he never goes with us, always opting instead to slink in a little late and lounge in the last pew.

Anymore, though, while Pastor Baxter is up in the pulpit warning the faithful about the wages of sin, I'm running play-by-play in my head, dreaming up acrobatic dunks and buzzer beaters, plays that send the Marion East crowd into a frenzy. Honestly, when I do pay attention, Baxter isn't bad. He's a young, energetic guy, who can build up a cadence and get more than a few Amens from the congregation. He even does his best to tie his sermon into what's going on now, so it's not just some musty old history lesson. Every time he sees me after church he asks me about my game before he asks about my faith. But the more he builds up a rhythm on Sunday, the more I build up a rhythm in my head, and I can almost feel the leather leave my hands as I drain a shot over Tagg to win a rematch against Lawrence North in the Sectional Finals. And then I snap back only to hear Pastor Baxter tell us that our intentions mean nothing if we fail to act upon them.

I don't worry about Hell any more than any other freshman, but when I'm sitting in that dusty pew by a stained glass window, I can't help but think that it must be some kind of special sin to be imagining whole basketball games as the preacher's giving his sermon. So, really, the only time I ever think I'm doing something bad enough to send me to Hell is during church itself.

I check Jayson and can tell he's paying even less attention than I am. He fidgets in the pew and rocks his feet back and forth, like it's all he can do not to leap up, kick those uncomfortable shoes off, and run for freedom. All it takes is our mom giving him a sidelong glance, though, and he straightens right up. We know from experience we don't want to earn Mom's wrath on a Sunday—she's not above marching us down the aisle and out the doors while giving us a sermon of her own.

At last, Baxter gives us one final, rousing Amen. The congregation echoes it, and we rise for the final hymn. When the singing's over, I look at Jayson and he gives me a triumphant wink back. We both made it through another service without incident. Our parents linger in the pews and chat with a few neighbors and friends, but Dad gives us the nod to go ahead. So we walk swiftly down the threadbare red carpet and break into a half-run down the stairs and to the daylight of the lobby.

Today brings a break in the cold. Though it's still morning the sunshine feels good, hinting that it might even get up into the 50s, so Jay and I snag our coats and linger on the top steps. We watch people stream out, mostly old people, all of them frowning like they've just been convinced again that the world is a wicked place. There are also some younger families like ours. They all look more hopeful, smiling in that rare November sun. There are several with daughters near my age who are looking fresh in their Sunday best.

"She's fine," Jayson whispers to me about one in particular. "You should go talk her up."

"She's standing next to her grandma, Jay. That's not the best time."

"You're just scared," he teases. "Man, when I'm your age I'll have all the girls. I won't even have to be a baller. Just walk up and start talking game."

I laugh and tell him he thinks way too much of himself, but the truth is he's probably right. He sure didn't inherit it from our dad, who can go days without saying a word, but Jayson can talk—especially to women. He's too young to have anything come from it, but he knows how to make a girl of any age smile. It makes me think of Jasmine and how she smiles at me in the hall sometimes when Nick's not around. I know I shouldn't be thinking of that, but I can't help it. Truth is, I might not be a talker like Jay, but none of these girls—fine as they may be—are the one I want to be talking to.

I text Wes to see if he can meet up with me later, but he hits me right back saying his mom has him tied up with chores for the next few centuries, so instead I busy myself by asking Jay if he's so smooth then how come he doesn't have himself a girlfriend yet.

He pauses and thinks about this, then looks at me, all cocky. "Why limit myself to one woman? I've got to be free, D."

We both laugh, but we stop short when we see Uncle Kid leave church. Our uncle looks agitated, more than usual. Every once in a while he gets this way. It's never long before we learn about some stupid thing he's got himself twisted up in. Today, he doesn't even look at us, just bolts down the stairs and starts looking up the street like he's waiting on someone. I didn't see him after the game last night, but I know he'll have plenty to say—both about how we got drilled by Lawrence North and about how long it took Bolden to get me on the floor.

"Uncle Kid," Jayson yells. "Uncle Sidney!"

He looks our way and nods, but he still seems distracted and annoyed, as if we caught him shoplifting. "Hey fellas," he calls. Then he sees what he's after: a car idling by the curb—that same black Lexus that picked him up at the park last month. He waves at us quickly and disappears inside the car.

The Donut Shop is the best part of any Sunday. From the outside it looks like a place you'd want to avoid. A fading orange sign that says, simply, Donut. Windows that look like they haven't been washed in decades. A parking lot pocked with potholes. But the truth is it's one of the best breakfast places in the city, and it's our favorite destination after church. We walk in that door and Jayson suddenly looks like a five-year-old again, his eyes wide with the dilemma of choosing from all those donuts. Mom keeps a pretty good watch on what we eat, but here she cuts us loose to have our fill—éclairs, jelly-filled, fritters, anything. My parents opt for coffee, eggs, hash browns, but Jay and I eat ourselves into sugar highs.

The rule is still no basketball talk. My dad quizzes us on what we're learning in school. My mom, maybe out of a sense of obligation, quizzes on the sermon we've just heard, and—every single week—acts dismayed at first and then gives up, laughs and asks, "What in the world are you two thinking about during church?"

Jayson answers honestly: "I think about what I want for Christmas." This makes both my parents laugh, and it's good times all around. My mom tells us stories about how strict her mother was when she grew up. "One time," she says, "she took my brother out behind the church and whipped him for breathing too loudly." She laughs at her own story and then says she's glad she doesn't act that way with us. "But start paying attention during the sermons!" she warns.

We finish up then and my dad marvels at the bill and says the same thing he says every week: "Four breakfasts for fourteen dollars. My God, you can't beat that."

But when he goes up to pay and Jayson hits the bathroom, my mom tells me to hang in the booth for a second. She waits until my dad's out of earshot and then gives me a serious look.

"Derrick, I'm going to tell you something, but you can't tell your brother."

"Okay," I say. She has me worried, because the expression on her face is usually reserved for when she's about to lace into me or Jayson. She must sense it, because she relaxes and tells me it's not that bad.

"It's just that a couple places are cutting back on your dad's hours," she says. "That means we might have a little smaller Christmas than usual."

"Is Dad fired?" I ask. He works security part time at two different businesses, and then a couple nights a week for a big apartment complex up on Binford. He used to work full-time security at a college, but they stripped down two years ago and he's been scrambling to make up for that lost income.

Mom shakes her head patiently. "No," she says. "It's just a few less hours here and there. You're just so sensitive when we keep things from you that I didn't want you to get upset."

I check my reaction. First off, I hate to be called sensitive, especially with the tone my mom had. Ballers aren't sensitive. And I also know my parents aren't telling me everything from their conversations about Hamilton Academy that they have with Uncle Kid. But if I react badly, it basically proves my mom right, so I just sit there and nod. Try to be a man about it. "Your job still good?" I ask.

"Mine's fine," she says. "If that school ever lost me they'd be overtaken by fourth-graders in revolt."

When Dad and Jayson get back to the table, my dad—still in a good mood over how cheap breakfast was—suggests we head downtown to the bookstore. This, too, is sometimes part of our Sunday non-hoops regimen, mostly because both my parents are convinced that reading books is more important to our well-being than everything else—exercise, discipline, studies—put together. Now, though, I shoot my mom a nervous look. Books aren't exactly games for the X-Box, but they still cost money. She just smiles, letting me know it's all right.

I don't find much that interests me in the stacks. Between them, though, is the prize: Jasmine Winters, sipping hot chocolate and wearing her scarf indoors, even on a warm day. There's something about her pose—so quiet, so wrapped up in her book—that makes her look impossibly older than me, like she's a student at one of the local colleges, unapproachable. Crazy, I know. I can take the court on Fall Creek against grown-ass men who have sixty pounds on me, and I never flinch. But the sight of Jasmine Winters with a cup of hot chocolate steaming up beside her freezes me.

The first thing I do, once I regain power, is look around for Nick Starks. Then, when I don't see him, I keep casing the place for people who might want to run down the hallways of Marion East with a few rumors. It's all clear, though. People keep passing by, but it feels almost like there's only me and Jasmine, alone in the bookstore. She still hasn't noticed me so I scramble to find a decent book on the shelves—something that will impress her, that will make me look more mature and intelligent. When I look, though, I realize I've wandered into the travel section. I try to think what kind of travel book would seem cool to her. But maybe I'll need some kind of explanation for why I'm looking at a travel book, and Jasmine knows no freshman at Marion East is planning an overseas vacation.

"Derrick? Derrick Bowen?"

I turn, still no book in hand, and look at Jasmine Winters looking back at me. She gives me a big smile, and just like that I feel calmed.

I nod, trying to act nonchalant. "'Sup, Jasmine?" I say.

She smirks. "'Sup? Really? That's how you greet people?" I start to stammer an apology, but she just laughs. "Take it easy," she says, "I'm just teasing."

I relax again, and when she motions toward the chair next to her I go sit down. "Where's Nick today?" I ask.

She frowns. "Still in a foul mood because of last night's game. I swear, you guys get so worked up over that stuff. Drives me crazy. Besides, Nick Starks wouldn't be caught dead in a bookstore."

I try to think of something intelligent to say, but all I can think of is how she seems kind of down on her boy Nick, so I just muster a worthless, "Yeah."

She smiles again. "I'm surprised to see you here," she says. "I didn't think bookstores were your thing, being a basketball star and all."

"My parents make it pretty clear. No books, no ball."

I must have sounded too defensive because again she says, "Teasing. I'm just teasing." This time she gives me a playful pat on my wrist.

Behind her I see my little brother eyeing us from afar. He purses his lips in the pose of a kiss, trying to mess with me. I give him a glare that tells him I won't hesitate to come over there and smack that look off his face, but all it does is just make him laugh.

My time with Jasmine is short-lived though. "I've got to go meet my mom," she says. "But it was good to see you. And it's nice to know at least a few guys have some interests outside of hoops." She smiles again. She wraps her scarf tighter. She takes her cup back up to the counter and waves goodbye to me. And for the first time ever I thank heaven that my dad insists on non-basketball Sundays that include trips to the bookstore.

Jayson, however, doesn't fare so well. My dad catches him at checkout with a *SLAM*. There's nothing wrong with that, but it breaks my dad's primary Sunday rule.

"You didn't even make it out of the sports section, did you?" he asks.

Jayson shrugs his shoulders and says, "No. So?"

This is not the kind of response my parents want and so the

SLAM quickly gets replaced with a book of my father's choosing. "You are going to learn about things besides sports," he says. "Even if you only learn that it matters to me that there are things besides sports."

It's all entertainment for Mom and me. We watch Jay protest, watch my dad spin him around and march him to the counter. She rubs my shoulder real quick. She has to reach up awkwardly to do it, but her hands are strong. Whenever she does that I still feel like I'm back on our living room floor as a little kid, sitting in front of my mom's chair and trying to stay awake while she massages my shoulders and talks with dad and my Uncle Kid, the three of them laughing and telling stories from back in the day. "Don't you worry about what I said earlier," she says. "I just told you because you're becoming a man. But you're also still my little boy. I won't let anything happen."

She lets her hand linger on my shoulder for a second, then notices my bag. "What did you get?" she says. I show her, and she gives me a puzzled look, wondering why on earth I'd be buying *Their Eyes Were Watching God*.

"Just looked interesting," I say. I don't feel the need to tell a soul that it's the book Jasmine was reading.

9.

We keep alternating wins and losses. Knock off Manual by 8, lose the first round of a weekend tourney to Lawrence Central, then bounce back the next night to take down Carmel by four. None of it is outstanding in any way, but after that Carmel win I realize we're already a week into December, and—snap, just like that—a quarter of the season is over.

I still haven't cracked the starting lineup. Suddenly I see that it's a very real possibility that I won't do that this year. I'm doing fine off the bench. Jayson has the stats to prove it. He keeps track of my +/- minutes, and says we're always better when I'm on the floor, never fail. And that doesn't even tell the whole story. Bolden's decided to play me with Starks more and more, which means half the time I'm boosting Starks' minutes with my play.

I get it. I do. Bolden just wants to get his two best perimeter players on the floor at the same time. But it means I've got to slide over to the two, which isn't a natural fit for me. Every time I rattle out a three, Nick just shakes his head and looks over at Devin on the bench.

Only one thing to do, though: work. If there's one thing I've learned from my folks, it's that you can't sit back and wait for things to come to you. Work. So after practice on Monday I hang back near the court while the other guys hit the showers. I help Darius round up the loose balls, but tell him to leave one rack out for me. Then I wheel the rack back onto the hardwood. I start in one corner, work my way through the rack, then reload it and go again. I tell myself I have to make 80% off a rack before I move to the next spot. It takes me a while to find the touch, but then I get it rolling—bucket, bucket, bucket, bucket. Each time the rock finds bottom, I picture Nick's expression on the court when I shoot our way to a win.

From the other end of the floor, I hear a shout. "Bowen! Come to this end." I turn and see Coach Bolden, hands on his hips. I grab one more from the rack, turn and fire—bottom—and then jog down to see what Coach wants. He puts his hand on my shoulder and looks me in the eye. "That's what I like to see. Put in a little extra sweat."

Out of the corner of my eye, I see a few of my teammates filing out, hear them laughing and messing around. Then one of the figures stops and stares—without turning my head, I know it's Nick. I can't acknowledge Nick's stare in front of Bolden, so I tell Coach what he wants to hear: "I know I've got to be a better shooter to help the team, Coach."

He smiles and nods. "Well then, let's make sure you get better. Let's have you practice the right way." He moves me aside for a second and shouts all the way down to the other end of the gym, where Coach Murphy is just about to make his exit. "Murphy! Our freshman wants to work on his shot." Murphy's got one hand on the door already, but he stops and turns back toward us. He's in the shadows far away, but I can see him give a glance at his watch.

"He needs someone to feed him, instead of him pulling balls from a rack," Bolden says. "Thing is, I have a wife and family to get home to. But you're a young bachelor still. Right, Murphy? You probably have some time on your hands."

In the distance, I see Murphy's head lower for a second. But he calls back, "Sure thing, Coach."

Murphy heads our way, walking quickly now that he's resigned to having to stay late. When he gets there, Bolden shakes his hand. "Good man, Murphy. I really do have to go tonight." Then he turns to me. "Bowen, I've been coaching for decades. I know when a kid stays late, it's as much about his scoring average as it is about the team. But you want to get better? That's what we're here for. Next time you want to stay late, I'll work with you too."

I work up a good lather with Murphy feeding me, going baseline to wing to top of the key, then down the other side. There's something kind of pure about working out in an empty gym. No whistles, no chatter, no noise but kicks on hardwood and the leather finding bottom. Murphy chimes in now and then: "Atta way to stroke it" when I make a string, or "Straighten it up now" when a shot bangs off.

I can feel my knees starting to tire. On one trip around, I miss my last four, the last one a brick so ugly I groan in dismay and grab my shorts, bent over in fatigue.

"Can't end that way," Murphy says.

"I hear you," I say. "Let me catch my breath." There's part of me that wants to stay there tightening my game all night. Just pretend like all that noise outside doesn't even exist—Uncle Kid isn't running some bullshit about Hamilton Academy, Jasmine Winters isn't all wrapped up with Nick Starks, and my parents aren't having any hushed discussions about me. Just this. Just ball.

Murphy walks to the free throw line and sets the ball on the stripe. "Shoot free throws when you're tired," he says. "Then some game when you're spent but need to knock two home, you can do it."

I stride to the line, scoop up the rock. I toe the dot with my AdiZero, take a deep breath. Two dribbles, spin the rock once in my hand, let it fly: spins off.

"Tough roll," Murphy says. He grabs the ball and starts to feed it back, but he stops mid-motion. "I want you to work on something," he says. "The stroke you've got on your pull-up is perfect. You get your feet under you and pull up straight as an arrow. But at the line or when you shoot off the pass, you get all this junk in your motion." I've heard this before, to varying degrees. Even my coaches in middle school wanted to fool with my shot, but the changes never stuck. Finally they figured to leave well enough alone rather than mess up their best player. Murphy must notice me make a face, though, because he tells me just to hear him out. "Your last two shots that last time around—how'd they miss?"

"First one was right, second one was left," I answer.

"See. That's motion, Derrick, not your legs getting tired. Good shooters miss short and long, either they don't get their legs into it or they fire too strong. But they're always on line. When you miss left and right that means something else is wrong." He sends me a bounce pass. "Shoot your free throw."

I go through my ritual and let fly: right again, even worse this time.

"Now try it just as a pull-up. Dribble to the stripe and rise," Murphy says.

He zips the rock to me and I do as told. Of course, I find bottom on this one.

"You're in a straight line from knee to elbow to wrist on that, D. But other times you get all twisted up." Murphy grabs the ball to demonstrate, spinning it to himself and bending his knees like he's about to shoot. He cocks his head to one side like a fighter dodging a punch, and his right arm comes overhead all crooked.

"I'm not that bad," I say.

Murphy laughs. "Okay, maybe not. But you get your head off center and it throws the shot off. That's also what slows down your release."

He feeds me a few for jumpers at the free throw line with instructions just to focus on keeping my head still. I knock a few down and Murphy gives his approval. It didn't take long to figure out that Murphy's the good cop partner to Bolden, the young guy who's always got to clap his hands and rally the troops when the old man is down on us, so I take his praise with that in mind. Still, it's good to finally hear something positive about my J.

"Now back it up a few steps but keep the motion the same," he says.

I do, but at the top of the key that motion feels awkward, the way it felt when I was first starting to play and Uncle Kid made me drive only with my left. The first two shots come up way short, and the second one hits glass first before ricocheting off so far that Murphy has to sprint to the corner to track it down.

"Shit," I say. I'd never cuss if Bolden were in the gym—that's a set of stairs for sure, even if Bolden can cuss himself blind in the heat of a game. But instead of getting on me, Murphy just walks back to the lane, tells me to stick with it. He feeds me another bounce pass and I catch it in rhythm, rise up with my usual form, and knock one down.

"No, man," he says. "I know you made it, but that form isn't going to make you better." He sends me another pass, and shouts: "Head still!"

I miss.

He does it again. "Head still!"

Front iron.

Again, again, again. Still can't get one to drop.

"Damnit!" I scream. What had started as a nice after-practice workout has disintegrated, made me more doubtful than ever that I can play the two spot. And that's one thing I know about hoops: If you doubt you can do something, then you can't do it.

"Easy," Murphy says. "Take it easy. If it were simple to stroke it like Stephen Curry then every damn body would do it. Just give it some time."

"That isn't gonna help me Friday against Gary Roosevelt," I say.

Murphy looks down at his shoes and shakes his head. He's not going to rip me like Bolden would, but he just gives me this look of disappointment. "Derrick, I want to beat Roosevelt too, but you've got to aim a little higher than that, man."

I want to tell him it doesn't matter where I aim if I can't shoot, but I check myself. Instead, I tell him I'll work on it—only half-believing myself—and hit the showers after a long day. I let the hot water soak me and try to forget about it all, but when I hop out my cell is flooded with texts—two from my mom wondering why I'm so late, one from Moose telling me to meet him up later to catch a flick, one from Uncle Kid asking why the hell Bolden isn't starting me yet, and two from Wes asking where I am, reminding me that we were supposed to get together to study for our Algebra test tomorrow.

"Stop crowding, people," I say. Then I get dressed and pack up my things, hoof it across the gym to the exit where Murphy's waiting to lock up and kill the lights.

Wes and I are hanging at The Castle, this place on 36th that's been there since my mom was my age. Part record store, part arcade, part junk food stand. My mom's always a little leery of The Castle now, positive that it's gone downhill since her day, just another place for trouble. But there's nobody causing any drama on this Tuesday night, just me and Wes and a few others flipping through the racks looking for some good beats. Too cold to make much noise tonight even if you wanted to, with all of Marion County in a deep freeze, weathermen crazy about record lows.

We went up to Gary and ran Roosevelt off their own floor, then came back to Indy on Saturday night and knocked off Washington, both solid wins over decent teams that have beaten Marion East in the past. I should be pumped over our little streak, but the truth is I haven't done that much to help the cause. I still jump off the bench and energize our five on the floor, but no matter how many extra hours I put in with Murphy, that jumper doesn't translate to live action. There are times when I'm running at the two spot that make me feel like I'm a liability on offense, and it's not until Nick gets a breather that I can make a little magic on the floor—drive and dish, get out and lead the break. In those moments I feel free, like I've been playing with a weight chained to my ankle and now I'm loose, playing at the tempo I want. But it's never long before Nick's back at the scorer's table, popping his gum and adjusting the wrap on his knee in anticipation.

"You here, D?" Wes asks. He's got a stack of cds in his hand, none of them by people I've ever heard of. Like with kicks, Wes fashions himself a music aficionado, but I know from experience that even if he's got a diamond in that stack the others will be weak amateurs. Either that or some old school jazz he'll use to impress his dad when he comes for Christmas next week.

"I'm right here," I say.

"You haven't said a word in half an hour, man," he says.

I realize he's right. I've been all wrapped up thinking about the game. "Sorry, man. I just get obsessed during the season. You know that."

"Yeah, I do know," he says. "Some days it's like my man D's gone and there's just this robot in his place going from practice to game to practice to game."

"I feel like that myself sometimes. But I gotta put in the hours if I want to get to where I'm going."

"I know, D," he says. "It's cool." Up front, a few older guys come in. They look a little ragged and they're arguing as they enter. You can tell they're both running nonsense, just disagreeing with the other for the sport of it. Then they both shut up and stare when a woman in a fur coat walks in and starts flirting shamelessly with the man at the counter. She's up to no good, but I can't tell exactly what. I nod at Wes and he sneaks a quick peek at her, but shakes his head at me like she's not his style.

I hear a text hit up my phone, but I don't check it now. I feel out of rhythm with my boy Wes—same way I get out of the flow when Nick's running point and I'm in at the two—and I need to just relax with him some. Problem is, I'm so locked in on hoops I don't know what else to talk about. My only lifeline to the non-basketball world lately is that book I bought that Jasmine was reading, and half the time I don't see why anyone would bother with that stuff. I guess this is why my dad always wants me to think about other things, too—*cultivate other interests*, he'll say—but none of those things compare with ball. Even as sixth man for a high school team, I know there's nothing that can compare. That quick inhale of the crowd as I rise up on somebody, and then that eruption after I throw one down. It's like having lightning at your fingertips. You just set things on fire any time you do something. Then there's the bond of a team—nothing like that in Algebra or Geography. Sure, I feel that twinge, that little jealous burn, when Nick hits a big shot down the stretch, but when we seal a win, when a shot finds bottom and everyone knows it's all wrapped up, that feeling is like we're given a gift from the heavens. Nothing else like that.

Problem is, Wes is outside that. It's the one thing we can't share, and it defines my life during the season. But Wes saves the moment—always does. "One thing about high school," he says, "every day you see some fly girl you haven't seen before. Fine girls too, not like…" He trails off, but nods at that woman at the counter again.

Now I may be out of step with Wes lately, but I know my boy. When he says "some fly girl," he means one girl in particular that he's got his eye on.

"What's her name?"

"I didn't mean anybody, D. Just there are a lot of fine honeys."

"Wes, please. You don't have to play. Is it Natalie from Algebra?"

"Nah, man. Nobody."

"Arielle? She's pretty fine."

"Stop man. You're way off base."

"Iesha? In History class?"

"Just drop it, D," Wes says, but he looks down at the music racks real fast, thumbing through like he's concentrating on something.

"Ah, Wes, you got it for Iesha? That's cool, man. She seems alright."

"I just said drop it. I don't even know who you're talking about." But even as he says it he gets this grin like he's got some secret he just can't wait to tell.

"You talk to her yet?" I ask. "I know she's good friends with Moose. I'll hit him up and get that number for you." I pull out my phone like I'm about to call.

"Naw, dog." He's through pretending and takes a step my way like he's afraid someone will overhear. "Alright, man. I got it bad for Iesha, but I don't know what to say to her. I think she's all about those big guys on the football team. And me?" He points to his own pint-size torso and gives a discouraged shake of his head.

"Don't sweat that, man," I tell him. "You got more game than any of those guys. You're funny. You're cool. You just get a chance to talk to her and she'll be down in no time."

He shakes his head again. "Nawww."

"Seriously. Talk to her. See if she wants to come out with a bunch of us after the Hamilton game on Saturday night. You can make it all casual so it's not some big date, but you'll have a chance to hang with her."

Wes pauses, thinking it over, and then agrees, suddenly amped about the idea. "I figure by that time you'll have Jasmine all up on you too," he says, trying to get after me the way I got after him.

"Man, that's Nick's girl. I got to accept that."

He looks around for a second, again like he's about to share some secret he doesn't want anyone to overhear. But there's just those old guys hanging out by the door, and the man behind the counter focused on that woman. Still, Wes leans in again. "You haven't heard? Man, yesterday she and Nick went at it in Senior wing. Like at each other's throats. She's about to tell him to walk, D."

I get a weird feeling in my stomach, this kind of mix between excitement and dread. It would be sweet if Jasmine dumped Nick, but it almost makes me worry about what I'd do if she did. As long as she's off limits, I can't screw things up. But if she were free? I might have to take my chance with her, and there's always the chance she'll shoot me down.

"Look, man," Wes says. "I gotta jet before my mom gets mad, but you mean that about after the Hamilton game?"

"Most definitely," I say.

He gives me a quick fist bump and then goes to check out. Once he's out the door, I stand in the middle of The Castle feeling lightheaded with possibility.

That's when I remember to check my phone. It's a text: *Derrick. Something I need to talk to you about. Give me a call when you get a chance.*

Jasmine.

Damn.

"Head straight!

Head straight!

Keep your head straight, D!"

It's Bolden working with me this time, trying to get my J tightened up. I'm about to pop if I hear *Head straight* one more time, but it's good to get some hours one-on-one with Coach. I catch a crisp bounce pass in the deep corner and pull. Bottom.

"Good, Derrick. Real nice."

I have to admit that as much as I've resisted them changing my shot, now and then I snap off one so true it feels like it's in the bucket as soon as it leaves my hands.

Bolden zips the next pass to me and has Murphy run at me with his hand up. Shot fake and go. One dribble to the rim and I throw one down.

"Good again, Derrick." Bolden has Murphy do that every so often to keep me honest, and then once in a while Murphy will give fake pressure—just a quick show of his hand so I don't just bury my head and drive every time I see him move.

I roll from baseline to shallow wing to top of the key and down the other side. Jumper, jumper, drive, jumper, drive, and so on, getting nothing but praise from Bolden the whole way around and back. I finish on another real solid J, just rising up over Murphy when he comes at me half-heartedly, so pure it pops through the net with authority.

"There it is," Murphy says. "Bring that tomorrow night when

Hamilton Academy waltzes in here, they won't know what hit them, but that new jumper's gonna swing down like a sledgehammer."

I have a good sweat worked up. When I bend down to catch my breath, a few drops run down my nose to the floor, a sign I've put in some work. I think, just for a second, about hitting up Jasmine's digits, but I know that would seem like I was trying too hard. Too obvious. All she wanted the other night was to ask me if Nick was okay, if I'd seen him upset at practices. She said she thought she could trust me to tell the truth about Nick, but I know she just wanted an excuse to chat me up a little. Jayson was convinced that was it. *Talking about her boyfriend? Shut up, D. That's what her girls are for. Honey wanted to talk to you and just needed an excuse.*

I lift my head back up and push all that away. *Focus.* It's Hamilton Academy tomorrow night. I'll be damned if I let them come in and push us around. We knock them off and people will start talking about Marion East in a whole different way—and Uncle Kid and my parents won't be whispering back and forth about me transferring up there anymore, that's for sure.

"Twice more back and forth," I tell Coach. "Or just keep working til I drop."

"That's what I like to hear," he says. He rifles me a chest pass—the old man can still make that leather pop—and then scolds Murphy. "Don't just stand there. Get a hand in his face. Instead of telling the boy how good he is, help make him better!"

I get after it for another fifteen minutes, getting more comfortable with my form all the time, until even Bolden has to praise me. "It's looking better, Derrick. Just keep working on it." Of course, he's always got to push me too, so just as I peel off my jersey and head to the locker room, he calls after me. "Once we get that spot-up perfected, we'll teach you to come flying off screens ready to shoot."

I just nod at Coach and disappear into the locker room. Alone in the gym after a good workout, you just feel right. Even back in the locker room, you can kind of feel the dark and cold of December pressing in. It's so quiet that if you listen hard you can hear a wicked gust rip down the street. I know there are a ton of other good players in the state. If I'm honest I have to admit that some are still better than me. There's Tagg at Lawrence North for one, not to mention a couple juniors down in Bloomington who have all the scouts salivating. And there might not be a more celebrated player in all of Indiana than Hamilton's Vasco Lorbner, who's about to visit along with three other players destined for big-time programs. But at times like these—the dead of December in a darkened gym, or a stifling hot summer day out on the Fall Creek blacktop—I like to think about those players already done for the day, resting up at home and taking it easy, while I'm still on the court, gaining on them.

10.

It's two hours before the Hamilton tip and our house is packed. Wes is over, as is Uncle Kid along with, of all people, Brownlee, the guy I had to stomp at the park before the season started. He's shaved his goatee and looks even sillier without it, like his chin is too small for his face. Uncle Kid keeps acting like he and Brownlee are old friends, and I can tell it's got my dad wound up. Dad's usually a pretty steady guy, but Uncle Kid can always set him on edge.

To add to all this, Jayson is blasting some old school Biggie from his room so everyone has to shout over the beats. Every once in a while, he'll pop out of his room, rapping along. He gets as juiced as anyone before games, but he's also doing this just to get under people's skin. He always likes to stir things up.

"Could you please turn that down?" Dad finally yells, but Jay just scoots back into his room, pretending like he doesn't hear.

Brownlee has Wes cornered over by the TV, lecturing him about how music was back in his day. I'm sure Wes could school Brownlee on the subject, but he can't even get a word in. My mom and Uncle Kid are over at the kitchen table, arguing.

"Turn it down, Jayson," my dad hollers again, and the music cuts off for an instant. But it's just Jay changing tracks, and "Mo Money" kicks in full blast, breaking the momentary silence. "Jayson," my dad yells, but there's no response this time.

In the middle of it all, I'm sitting on the couch, picking at some of the frayed brown threads and trying to focus. Last time we went up against one of the best teams in the state, Lawrence North smoked us. Everyone knows the mighty Hamilton Academy Giants are even better. Vasco Lorbner is like a 17-year-old Nowitzki. The plan is for all of us to know where he is at all times. We've got to dig down if he catches it in the post, but the bigger problem is when he's on the perimeter. Out there, Moose has to get into him to deny the three, but we all know he's got no prayer of staying in front of Lorbner on the drive. So we've all got to be ready to help. Then the problem is that Hamilton surrounds Lorbner with shooters. The best of the bunch is their point, Deon Charles, a junior who played his freshman year at Arlington before Hamilton lured him away. Now he's a key piece of their championship team, and the word is he's heading for Illinois in a couple years.

"Enough of that talk, Sidney!" my mom yells. She slams her hand on the kitchen table and everyone stops and looks, the rickety old table shaking in aftershock. Even Jayson must have heard, because Biggie gets in one more rhyme before the sound gets turned down fast. Brownlee shoves his hands in his pockets and edges toward the door, looking like a man who just got caught trying to lift from a store.

"Babe," my dad says, taking a light step toward the kitchen table.

"Oh, don't give me that *Babe* stuff!" she yells. "Why don't you talk some damn sense into your brother instead of trying to talk me down like I'm a little girl."

I look up at Wes and give a slight nod toward the door. He picks up his bag from the floor as delicately as a doctor performing surgery.

Brownlee sees his chance and coughs quietly and mutters that maybe he should be going.

"Don't duck out now," my mom shouts. "I know you're in this nonsense with Sidney so don't act like you're all innocent. Come into my house and try to tell me what's best for my son."

"Can we not talk about this now?" my dad says. He's trying to keep his composure, but when Uncle Kid tries to interrupt he snaps. "Damnit, Sidney, shut up! I told you this wasn't the time to talk about it."

Uncle Kid tries to interject again, but this time it's my mom drowning him out. "Well, let me tell you all something. It's never gonna be the time to talk about it. My son plays for Marion East High School. The same high school we all went to, in case you're all getting too damn big-headed to remember. And that's where he's going to play. Nothing wrong with that place! Something might be wrong with you all, but there's nothing wrong with going to Marion East!"

By this time, Wes and I have edged to the door. Dad's right about one thing: the timing couldn't be worse. Right now, I need to be thinking about how to stick Lorbner and Charles, not what side to take in some family war.

Wes shakes his head like it's nothing and whispers, "Don't sweat that, Derrick. Just do your thing tonight."

"Thanks, Wes."

"And we're still on for afterward, right? You gonna set it up to get some people together so Iesha and I can meet up?"

"I got you, Wes," I say.

We kick it out the door then, but before we make it all the way to our street, I hear Jayson's stereo again. He blasts it, probably thinking everyone's calmed down, but it only takes a second before I hear all the grown-ups shout together: *Turn it down!*

Pre-tip, I look up into the crowd and see Jayson. He's pumped. Got his headphones on and is practically bouncing from bleacher to bleacher, this little pinball of energy ricocheting between my parents and Uncle Kid and Brownlee, all of them sitting there with their hands in their laps, obviously still tense from the argument back at the house. The rest of the crowd is more in line with Jay, though—maybe not jumping around, but there's an edge tonight. Not only because Hamilton Academy is in town, but because people actually think we've got a chance to take them down now that we've reeled off three Ws in a row. I do see one other difference in the crowd: an SEC assistant, easy to spot in his school colors. He's probably soft-recruiting one of Hamilton's seniors as an excuse to get a better look at Lorbner. Maybe I can give him a little extra show for his trouble.

Bolden tries to calm us down in the huddle, going over our game plan again, but when I look around I can see it in everyone's eyes: the adrenaline is loose. Of course, once we break I've got to take my usual spot on the bench, right next to Murphy. I hate to say it, but at this point I've got my routine on the bench, checking all my people before the ref tosses the ball in the air. I eye my family again, and see that my mom's on her feet now, as is Uncle Kid, though Dad and Brownlee are still seated. Then I look over at the band, check Wes. Every time, he's looking at me, like he's on to my pre-game ritual, and gives me a fist pump of encouragement. Next, I look for Jasmine in her spot—always on the far end with Nick's parents. Only this time she's not there. I file that one away for later, because before I can make too much of Jasmine's absence, Murphy gives my shoulder a squeeze. "Don't get comfortable here," he says. "We're gonna get you on that floor real soon. We need your A game tonight, D."

Then why not start me? I want to say. But this is no time for that kind of negativity. Not with Hamilton Academy swaggering in here undefeated.

The ball goes up and Lorbner controls it easily. He's listed as 6'8", but no way he's a millimeter under 6'9". Guy's gonna be a handful all night.

Sure enough, on one ball reversal he catches it on the shallow wing and pulls—a soft little kiss for two.

Nick comes tearing up against their man-to-man press and pops it Devin's way on the perimeter, setting the offense in motion. Right away, there's a different feel to this game. Everything's crisp, and you can hear the cuts even over the buzz of the crowd. That doesn't mean Hamilton isn't guarding the hell out of us. They slip through every screen, cut off every drive, challenge everything we want to do. But no cheap fouls, no grabbing or elbowing. Coach Bolden had us so focused on how to defend them, we never really talked about how hard they guard.

Finally Nick gets frustrated and floats up a runner in the paint. It scrapes iron and Lorbner grabs it. When that man squeezes the orange, nobody's gonna rip it from him.

We get back against their break, so Hamilton eases into their offense. Despite a slow start, our crowd is still into it, louder when we're on the defensive end, but Hamilton's unfazed. They get this treatment everywhere, so they're not going to get shook just because the Marion East faithful make some noise. They pass up decent looks, waiting and waiting for a better one. Then Lorbner catches it on the perimeter and gets Moose off his feet with a shot fake. He drives, then kicks to Charles, who's in the corner wide open. Bang.

Our crowd sits. Just like that it's 5-0, but it feels like we're down a dozen. Nick comes racing back up, and zooms right by Bolden who's signaling him to call timeout. Nick drives all the way to the baseline and gets cut off, almost traveling before he kicks back out to Devin.

"Time out!" Bolden yells. Even before the ref blows his whistle, Bolden is headed for Nick. I can hear him from the bench: "When I tell you to call a timeout, you do it."

Nick glares back at him, that same look he had on his face the day we squared off in practice. "I saw a crease. Chance for a bucket!"

Bolden just points at the bench. "Sit." Then he looks at me and motions for the scorer's table. "Bowen for Starks."

I get back to the huddle just in time to hear Bolden still riding Starks, who apparently didn't take that substitution very well. "Now listen to me! I'll get you back in there, but you got to calm down. All of you need to calm down. We can't be taking bad shots against these guys, or leaving Charles to go chase a driver. Even if it's Lorbner. God, you'd think we hadn't talked about Charles. Now focus. We can play with these guys, but we've got to be smart. Make each possession count."

Then, before we hit the floor again, Bolden grabs me by the arm.

He doesn't yell, but he speaks in a way that lets me know I damn well better listen. "We don't need a savior out there. Run the offense and stick Charles. That's all."

Sticking Deon Charles isn't as hard as checking Tagg, but a few possessions in, I learn that you can't have a lapse. Just for a second I look ball-side, and he disappears on me—poof, like a magic trick, he's all the way baseline and I'm caught on a Lorbner screen. He buries it again, but had a toe on the stripe. On the way up, I tap my chest and look at Coach. *My bad*, I mouth to him.

"I know it was your bad!" he screams. "Don't let it happen anymore."

I don't. I'm chest-to-chest from that point on.

Getting buckets against Hamilton is even tougher. Lorbner isn't their only talented big, so there's not much to be had in the paint. And they have speed to burn out on the perimeter. Royce and Devin each shake free for jumpers, but Moose is swallowed up inside, so the only point in the paint we get early is when I find Stanford—can't blame them for losing sight of him—a no-look laser for a quick deuce. I see seams here and there, but I'm trying to follow Coach's instructions. I don't force anything, hoping to avoid Nick's fate.

As the first quarter winds down, though, Hamilton's got the ball up 15-7, cruising. That's when Moose gets lazy, gassed without his usual breather. Even though there's still 10 ticks left, Lorbner lets fly from a good twenty-five feet—the ball's still in the air when I hear him shout *Good!* as he backpedals. When it hits bottom, our crowd just deflates, and the Hamilton fans are so loud it feels like we're on the road.

Disgusted, Moose slings me the in-bounds one-handed, and Charles almost picks it, but when I get the handle and look upcourt, I see that the other Hamilton players are still in celebration mode, too busy high-fiving Lorbner to pay attention to the backcourt. Out of the corner of my eye, I see Murphy on our sideline, windmilling his right arm. *Go!*

By the time they realize what hit them, it's too late. Even Lorbner is slow to turn his head. When I hit the lane I can feel our crowd rising again, exploding when I throw one down on their three-man who's foolish enough to swat at me at the last moment.

"That's what I'm talking about!" Moose yells from mid-court, and Royce and Devin practically knock me into the bleachers with their chest bumps.

I sink the freebie, and we're still down 8, but at least I pumped some life back into the gym. Even Bolden seems energized. "Hey, we took their best shot and we're still standing," he says in the huddle. "Let's dig in a little bit now! It's just a bunch of teenagers from Hamilton County over there. Not the Miami Heat!"

I've got the taste for the game now, and I can feel my pulse in my throat when we hit the hardwood for the second quarter. Bolden has me slide to the two so Nick can run point again. He gives Moose a breather since Lorbner's catching a break too. But it doesn't matter who else is out there on the floor. That one dunk and I feel it, like right now I can do anything I want with the rock.

First touch I rip past my man so fast he gets whiplash, then finish off glass. Next time Nick finds me in the lane for a little ten-foot pull-up. True.

I backpedal, woofing at my boys the whole time. "We on them now. Let's show them how we ball at Marion East!" I see Hamilton's coach—Henry Treat, a young, tanned guy in suit and tie who acts like God himself put him on the sidelines of Hamilton Academy—pop up like someone lit a firecracker under his seat and motion for Lorbner to check back in.

They stop the bleeding with a cheap put-back. Next time down they're set, so there aren't any quick looks to be had. Their whole team knows where I am now. When I try to drive baseline all five jump, so I zip a crisp pass to Devin on the wing. Soon as it leaves his hands, though, I can see it's off. I spin on my man to get to the other side of the rim and go up among the trees to rip the board. Pull it down with authority too, and I can hear the fans under the basket react. A shot fake doesn't free me, so I back it out to the perimeter, and that's when I see my man give me space. He's so worried about my first step now that he's got his heels on the free throw line. It's like I can hear Bolden and Murphy: *Head still.* Jab once for show, then cross back between my legs to make even more room. And when it leaves my hands it's so pure I don't even have to look.

"*Money!*" I holler, my head cocked toward Lorbner who's crouched at the scorer's table, keeping my follow through held high for everyone to check the new form. Keep it up as I backpedal, as the crowd goes insane, as Coach Treat tells the ref *Timeout.* Only on my way back to the huddle do I lower it, giving a quick point to my family up in the stands. We're still down three, but looking at Jayson you'd think I'd hit a buzzer-beater in Game 7. He's practically climbing on my uncle's shoulders. Even my dad is pumping his fist and high-fiving some stranger in the next row. Marion East hasn't seen hoops like this in too damn long.

I can't help but sneak a peek at that SEC assistant, and when I look up he's busy writing something down in his notebook—probably, *Forget these Hamilton players, let's offer to Derrick Bowen!*

Put-backs, pull-ups, flavorful finishes at the rim. It all comes out in the second quarter and early third. I don't keep track of my own points during the game, but I know I passed my season high long ago. Bolden is even starting to draw things up for me in huddles. He may have told me he didn't need a hero, but that's what he's getting. Every now and then Devin or Royce will knock down a J, but it's mostly me on the attack—doesn't matter if I'm running at the two or back at point with Nick on the bench, Hamilton has no answer.

Problem is, we can't find defensive stops either. For every J I bury, Lorbner knocks one down, and their shooters keep sniping away from the outside. Our crowd has stayed at a fever pitch, but as we hit mid-third, I realize that none of this bothers Hamilton. It's like they know they can keep it up longer than we can. Lorbner has the look of a guy who's just shooting a quick game of Horse with a younger brother.

Down 6, I pop free on the baseline again, but this time I can feel my form let me down and the shot sails right, just scraping. Lorbner rips it and I swear for a second I see him smile, like this is the moment he's been waiting for. He waves Charles off and brings it up himself, that smile replaced by a look of stony concentration. He crosses mid-court and takes a rhythm dribble, same spot he hit that bomb in the first, but this time he's just baiting Moose. He's past our big man in a flash, then takes one last power dribble in the paint. Boooom. With Tyler Stanford hanging off him, he throws it down two-handed, hangs onto the rim for just a beat, then drops himself straight down in the lane with his hands still over his head. That's some authority.

While Lorbner toes the line, Charles edges my way and whispers, "You didn't think the white boy could do that, did you?"

I just ignore him, but the truth is, no, I didn't. Not because Lorbner's white, but because he drops Js so consistently that you forget about the man's power. Even Tagg's game isn't that complete.

It's not like I'm intimidated, not like any of us are, but the play changes the energy in the gym, and next time down we get a little hesitant in our offense. Devin passes on a look. Then Moose forces one that gets swatted out of bounds. Lorbner again. I know it's up to me, so when I get it back on top I wave everyone down so I can solo up with Charles. In the back of my head, I know that forcing it is the same thing that got Nick sent to the bench in the first, but we've got no other options at this point. I can hear some fans urging me on, a voice I'm pretty sure belongs to Wes shouting *It's all you, D-Bow*.

This time when I step back on the crossover, Charles jumps my shooting hand, so I spin back left and zip into the lane. Their off-guard reaches, but I'm already past him, so I take one last dribble and gather. *Rise.*

Lorbner comes up so fast. There's some contact with the body, but up top he swats me clean, so I know there's no sense in crying to the ref. They scoop up the rock, outlet, find Charles on the wing for a three and just like that the rout is on. And before I even make it to the bench at the timeout Bolden says, "Starks for Bowen."

Nick doesn't fare any better out there, but as the lead goes to 14, then 16, then 18, Bolden just hovers next to me, arms folded.

"Bowen," he says at last, and I start to stand, thinking he wants me back in for one last frantic charge. "No. Sit. Game's gone. Soon as you blink against a team this good, it's gone. But, damnit, Derrick, I told you. Remember when I called you into my office and said some day you'd face someone who'd knock your shot into the second row?"

I nod. I want to just stare down at the floor, but I force myself to look up and meet Bolden's eyes. Thing is, he doesn't look angry. His brows are pinched down and he's shaking his head slightly, almost like he feels sorry for me.

Then he motions out to the floor, where Lorbner is busy knocking down a 12-foot turnaround. "Who the hell do you think I was talking about?"

11.

I just walk. Forget about curfew, about the dangers of the city night. After that game, it's all I can think of to do. I shut off my cell so I can't see people texting consolation messages or hear my mom call to ask when I'll be home. Just hit the showers, slump out of the locker room and try to put some distance between myself and the 27-point beatdown Hamilton put on us. Worse even than the pasting from Lawrence North.

The thing is, this time we were right there. And I was leading the way. When I finally checked the stat sheet at the end of the game, I realized I poured in 24, and that's with Coach sitting me for the rest of the third and part of the fourth. But I know it doesn't matter. I could have scored 50 and it wouldn't have mattered. It's like we were in a race with those guys and they were just toying with us, then once the finish line was in sight they mashed the gas and left us for dead. Or, as Coach Bolden put it to me afterward, "You were so damn busy talking trash over shots you made in the second quarter, you forgot there's four quarters in a game!"

I head on Meridian toward downtown, put the school and my neighborhood behind me. Far ahead, I see the Chase Tower and the

OneAmerica Tower rising next to each other, lighting up downtown Indy. I go ahead and cross Fall Creek. The water gives off a slight stench in the night. I'm so frustrated I just want to give up. I stare down at that water, see the moonlight reflecting off its cold surface, think about how none of this is turning out how I planned. I think about that day back on the court, when I showed out against Brownlee. Just a few months ago, and just up the water from where I'm walking now, but back then everything felt certain: my starting spot, a great season, the first few steps toward basketball stardom. Just playground dreams, I guess. Because right now it's only bitter cold, with bad losses piling up.

I keep hoofing toward downtown. Past the Taco Bell, past the Wendy's. I don't have anywhere I'm headed. I keep thinking I'll stop somewhere to get warm and grab a bite, but it's like I can't, like the only way to keep from going crazy is to keep walking.

Past 16th and the late night traffic cruising from the bars to White Castle. Down the lonely stretch to 14th and soon enough, under the interstate where I hear the whoosh of the traffic above me. I know I've got a couple miles back to my house, not all of them the best blocks to be on at night, but I keep on. I think about all those cars racing up and down 65, burning up to Chicago or down to Louisville. I look around me at the swirl of the city. A couple office lights still glowing high in the office building at 10th, cars going in and out of the lot of the news station, horns honking from far off, shouts from distant doorways. Here's the good news: Nobody cares about what happened in the Marion East gym tonight. I know that's not entirely true, but in the scheme of this city it's nothing. They care about the Pacer game tonight or the morning deadline or how they're going to afford Christmas presents. Or they care about one more drink or making it further up the highway. So Hamilton Academy drubbing Marion East doesn't even register. I'm not Roy Hibbert strutting through Circle Centre. Since I don't get that kind of glory, at least nobody notices when I fail on the court.

Problem is, I know. Damn. I might be just a freshman, but I already know this much about winning and losing: The way people look at you after a win, all the laughter back home when people are celebrating, or the way they avoid your gaze after a loss or give your shoulder a squeeze and tell you *Good game*—that stuff counts, but it doesn't matter. What matters is how that win makes you feel inside, the way it fills you up with a kind of light, something all yours that nobody can touch. And what matters is how a loss sits in your stomach like you ate something rotten, how there's no getting rid of it, like a loss is its own being alive inside of you, gnawing on your insides.

So the fact that this city doesn't really care if we won or lost doesn't help one bit.

Finally I get to where I'm going. I didn't even know it when I set out, but when I see the Soldiers and Sailors Monument, standing proudly right in the heart of the circle downtown, I realize this has been where I've been going all along. I remember being a kid, younger than Jayson is now, and my parents bringing me down here at Christmastime. The city would string lights from the top of the monument, making it into a Christmas tree for everyone. They still do it, though I haven't been down for the lighting in years. But when I was little I thought it was the coolest thing in the world, all those lights coming on at once. It's lit now, but there's nobody else looking at it, just some late night cars making arcs around the circle before shooting east on Market Street.

My mom used to say this is where they'd have the title celebration if the Pacers ever won one, and as a kid I couldn't help but imagine myself on the steps of that monument, just above the heads of all those sculptures of soldiers, throngs of fans below chanting my name for bringing a banner home to Indianapolis. Those fantasies feels pretty far away too. The Pacers are always a step behind the Heat, and I'm a long, long way from being any help to an NBA team.

A cruising car honks at me, and the driver shouts something I can't understand. Probably something obscene, but it doesn't matter. It snaps me out of my little daydream. I shiver in the cold. I turn around, see the Statehouse lit by spotlights behind me, flags rippling overhead. This really is a beautiful city at night. As I turn back home, I try to hold onto the best of it, the best of me, try to remember all those fantasies I had and remember that no matter how far away they feel, they can all still be realities.

Mid-afternoon and Wes still hasn't returned any of my texts. It's a Sunday, church and stops at the Donut Shop and bookstore behind me, in front of me just homework and—if I can convince Dad I'm prepared for school tomorrow—the Colts on primetime. I'm looking forward to that, me on the couch with my folks, and Jayson sitting on the floor, all of us watching on that old TV, the plastic Christmas tree lit in the corner with a few boxes stacked beneath it. I can't quite settle into the evening though. I want to do something before night closes in, even if it's just browsing through Ty's Tower for the millionth time, so I hit Wes up again.

No answer.

I knock on Jay's door. Little brother's cranking out a little homework of his own, but as soon as he sees my face he throws his books on the floor. "'Sup, D?"

"Not a thing, little man. What they got you working on?"

"Some nonsense," he says. "Just English vocabulary." Jayson tries to act too cool to study, but he's still our parents' son. He'll get that work done whether he admits it or not.

"You want to take a break and hit the sticks?" I nod toward his console.

"Nah, man. You don't really give me much competition anymore."

I laugh, but I can tell he's serious.

We decide to raid the kitchen instead. Mom's at the store and Dad's taking a nap, so there's nobody to get on us about ruining our dinner. We load up with chips and Cokes and snag a couple candy bars from my mom's stash in the freezer, then head to my room, Jayson sitting on the floor and me on my bed, back against the wall. Jayson stares up at my posters and pics, nearly every inch of my walls covered with my heroes: Rose, CP, Durant, LeBron.

"You think any of those guys would struggle against Hamilton Academy?" I ask.

"You didn't struggle. You lit those kids up."

"Yeah, but we lost."

Jayson laughs then. "You didn't just lose, bro. You got flat run out." I know there's nobody who roots harder for us than Jay, but he can't pass up any chance to talk a little smack.

I finally get a ring, but when I look down it's just a blunt text from Wes: *busy.* I wonder what's got him so tied up he can't give me more of a message than that.

Jayson shoots a candy bar wrapper across the room, but comes up a foot short of the can, so he scrambles across the floor like it's a rebound and slams it in.

"What's wrong with our team, Jay?"

He stands up, taking the question seriously, and puts his hand on his chin as he deliberates. Thing is, I asked him seriously too. He might be a runt, but he knows hoops. "You really want to know?"

"I asked, didn't I?"

He starts to answer, but then stops, as if he heard some strange noise in the other room. He picks up a basketball from the corner of the room and stares down at it. "Ah," he says, "only problem I see is they don't get you the rock enough." He was going to say something else, I can tell, but before I can pin him down he changes the subject. "What about that honey who's been all about you? Jasmine?"

"She's disappeared, man. I haven't even seen her in the hallways."

Jayson shakes his head, disappointed in me. "You can't just wait to bump into her, D. The girl wants you. All you gotta do is hit up her number and it's butter from there." He pump-fakes a pass at me for emphasis.

"Like you know a thing about it. Butter? Please, son."

"I know more than you do!"

I spring off the bed and pop the ball out of his hands, act like I'm dunking over him. "You don't know, Jay! You don't know a thing!"

Jayson takes a pratfall to the floor, playing the part of a posterized big man, but he's laughing the whole time. This kind of foolishness, a little messing around with Jay, is just what I needed after last night. Then we hear Mom come through the front door, and he pops up to help me erase the evidence of our binge.

12.

Last practice before Christmas, and everyone's itchy to be done for a few days. Moose is joking around in the locker room, messing with a couple sophomores. He'll steal their jerseys while they're not looking. When they go to put their jerseys on, he swipes their shoes. "You want your shoes back? Then you got to get the juniors Christmas presents," he says. When they protest, he insists it's a Marion East tradition. When they appeal to Nick he doesn't miss a beat. "Moose ain't lying. He bought me a signed Chris Paul jersey last year, I swear."

Everyone laughs, but the door to Bolden's office pops open and as soon as the old man enters all that Christmas cheer is squashed.

"You fools," he seethes. "It's like we didn't just get our asses handed to us two nights ago. On our *own floor!* And you're all just kidding around acting like you don't have a care in the world." He runs his tongue over his teeth and then squinches up his mouth like he ate something sour. "When I was your age, if we lost a game, we *felt* it. Sure didn't joke around about Christmas. *Shit.* You guys don't even *deserve* Christmas the way you played."

We file out to the floor then, nobody making a sound.

Bolden does have a Christmas gift for us: a set of suicides. The man runs us like he's intent on killing someone, blistering us as we go by—*You should at least care that we got blown out*, or *I swear I've never had a bunch of kids this damn soft*, or simply, *Run harder!*

He doesn't let up. This time, when Murphy pulls Moose aside to work on free throws, Bolden calls him out, saying this is not time to be giving a breather to the player who needs conditioning the most.

Finally Bolden blows his whistle and breaks us into fives, but has Murphy put a bubble on top of the rim—a killer drill where we go full speed, but nobody can make a shot because of the bubble, so we work like crazy on boxing out and crashing the offensive glass. Everyone's getting a little weak-kneed, so Nick shifts the offense down a gear so people can catch their breath. A bad move on this day.

"Bowen and Starks flip jerseys. Bowen with the ones," Coach says.

I don't hesitate, but I sure don't act like it's a big victory because I can see any little thing is going to draw Bolden's wrath today. Nick doesn't take it in stride though. He doesn't say it loud, but it's above a whisper: *Bullshit.*

To everyone's surprise, Bolden doesn't explode. Instead, he calmly tilts his head toward the bleachers. "Stairs," he says.

Nick knows better than to argue further so he trots off the court obediently. I can hear his kicks on their ascent—*slap, slap, slap* on the cement stairs—as I set the offense in motion. With the bubble still on the rim, I work the boards relentlessly, using my size to keep possession. It leaves the twos on defense forever, and they start to quit a little. After a few minutes, Moose and I are just grabbing board after board at the rim, the back-ups swatting at us in vain attempts to get possession.

"That's right!" Bolden shouts. "Stay after it!" Then he blows his whistle and looks at us. "That's the kind of tenacity we need."

I sneak a peek at Nick, who's finished his set and is on one knee on the sideline. He bites his lip and looks away. I realize this is the moment I've been waiting for since pre-season practice, the time when even Bolden can't rationalize keeping Nick in front of me. The thing is, there's something kind of bittersweet about it. I can't place it exactly, but I know this isn't how I wanted it to happen. *Forget it,* I tell myself. *Not your fault Nick dug his own grave.*

"Here's the thing though," Bolden says. "You guys are awfully courageous when you're beating up on our second stringers. But where's that kind of fire when teams like Lawrence North and Hamilton Academy are putting it to you?"

Damn. The man just can't be happy. Not ever. He just can't praise us for playing hard without cracking on us in the very next breath. But as he starts us into the next drill, I have to admit that the question he asked is a good one.

Christmas Eve. I get out of the night service to see a text from Jasmine wishing me a Merry Christmas. Just like that, a freezing Indianapolis night feels awfully warm. On the way to the car I elbow Jayson, show him the text.

"Girl's all about you, D," he says. This time, I believe him, and I figure it only makes sense. Come next game, I'll most likely be taking Nick's spot in the starting five, so why not take his spot with Jasmine too?

Our parents walk a few strides in front of us, arm in arm, my mom's head leaning against Dad's shoulder. They're all business most of the time, but the holidays bring this out in them. They'll curl up under a blanket on the couch, my mom stretching her legs across my dad's lap, and listen to music while the snow falls. Or they'll laugh and tell each other stories about the old days, tease each other about past girlfriends and boyfriends—*You're lucky I came along and saved you*, my mom might say. *You'd be a mess with those trashy girls you were chasing.* And my dad will laugh and laugh. Before they do that, the tradition is to have Wes over with his dad, who will be in town for a few days, to hang out and open a present—just one present on Christmas Eve, my dad's rule. My dad will mix up drinks, something he only does on Christmas Eve and New Year's Eve. I don't know what he makes, but my parents and Wes's dad will have about two of those honey-colored things and start acting like fools.

Problem is I still can't get Wes. Haven't heard from him in days, and that's just not the way we roll. I'm starting to think something's wrong with him. In the back seat, I check my cell again, but the message from Jasmine is all there is. I look out the window at the houses strung with lights, some with wreaths hung on the front door. I get a pang of longing for when I was younger and Christmas was more magical. I still look forward to it. I love the mood it puts my parents in, but now some of those decorations look cheap and sloppily hung. The dusting of snow on the ground looks meager and dirty. When I was little, it all seemed so perfect I'd stare out in wonder at every house. Now it just is what it is.

When we get to the house, my dad leaps out of the driver's side and runs around the front of the car to open the door for my mom, offering her his hand like some gallant gentleman. She loops her arm through his elbow and he helps her along the walk even though there's not even a trace of ice. All of this makes Jayson groan. I think about doing that for Jasmine, how incredible it would feel to have her hugged up on me like that.

Inside, Jayson sprints to his room to shed his church clothes, my dad hums in the kitchen as he starts dropping ice in glasses to mix drinks, and my mom goes over to the tree to decide what gifts to select for tonight. I check the home phone, figuring Wes must have called there, but there are no messages, no missed calls. I go to my room to call him, since he must be blind to texts. After only about five hundred rings, he picks up.

"Wes, what's the word, man?"

"Nothing," he says, his voice cold as a wind down Central.

"You coming over tonight?"

"Oh, was I supposed to meet you tonight?"

Now he's just being rude, playing me off. I kick my dress shoes from my feet and send them thudding into the corner. "What's your deal, Wes?"

"Oh, is it a *deal*, Derrick? Is it not cool to just stand you up without even bothering to call?"

"What?"

"That's the *deal*, man," he says. His voice is rising almost to a shout. I haven't heard Wes this angry since someone swiped his iPod from his locker in 7th grade. "You don't even know why I haven't called you!"

"Wes, you're starting to sound like—." I'm about to call him a little bitch, something I'd regret saying to Wes almost as much as I'd regret my mom hearing me say it, but he cuts me off before I can get it out. My man is *boiling*.

"You ditched me, Derrick! You've got your head so wrapped up in your game—in whether you can get ahead of Nick freakin' Starks—that you ditched out your best friend!"

"What are you talking about?" I ask.

"I'm talking about me and Iesha after the *Hamilton game!* You were supposed to call me to meet up and you just *bailed!*"

I feel exposed. It's like getting caught flatfooted in the lane with a driver coming fast as a freight train, nothing you can do about it but take the punch. "Ah, Wes. Man. I am so sorry. I just spaced on it. I was so juiced for that game and then afterwards I was so down that I just walked around the city to forget about everything."

"I know," he says, "including me."

Then he hangs up.

My dad comes in the room, smiling, about halfway through one of those drinks, and he leans leisurely against the doorjamb. "So," he says, "when's Wes and his old man coming over?"

13.

"Derrick, come into the kitchen and sit down."

My dad says this, but my mom's also sitting at the kitchen table. She motions to the open chair beside them. All they need is a hot light to shine in my eyes and a lieutenant listening in behind glass and this would be a perfect interrogation set-up.

I do as I'm told. I can feel the table tremble from my mom's leg bouncing up and down in agitation. She's not pleased about something, and I figure I'm about to find out what. I rack my brain to think about some way I've messed up over the past week, some secret they must have discovered, but there's nothing. I screwed up with Wes most definitely, but they already know about that. The only sketchy thing I've done is send a few texts to Jasmine to see if she wants to get together over break, but there's no crime in that.

It's the day after Christmas, and there are still some shreds of wrapping paper here and there on the floor. From my brother's room, the play-by-play from his new NBA 2K14 fills up the house, pretty much the way it's been since he opened it. Everything seems normal and untroubled, so I don't know why I'm called to the kitchen with my mom's leg bouncing a mile a minute and my dad taking long, pensive breaths as he stares into his coffee cup.

"You start, Thomas," my mom says. "You're the one who wanted to talk to him."

My dad looks at her for a second, but her eyes are like two loaded pistols right now, so he turns to me. "Derrick, how much do you like Marion East?"

So this is it. "It's okay," I say.

"What do you mean by *okay?* Do you mean it's just average, or is everything good there?"

"Everything's good, I guess." I know my answers are non-committal. I'm not sure what they want me to say here so my words come out all hesitant, the way some players get when Bolden quizzes them on the upcoming opponent and they're scared to give the wrong answer.

Mom can't take it anymore. She stops bobbing her leg, stands up and puts her hands on her hips. "For God's sake, Thomas, quit dancing around the issue." She turns to me. "What we're asking is if you want to keep playing at Marion East because there's some interest from other schools about having you come there."

"What schools?" I ask.

"Hamilton Academy," she says. She spits the words out like she's saying the name of the Devil himself.

"I thought you hated them," I say.

Now my mom softens. It's her turn to struggle with what precisely she wants to say. "Well, I do. Kind of. But there are some things that we need to consider. Extenuating circumstances."

The only circumstances I care about are the ones on the court. The truth is, with Deon Charles up there, I'd have a lot tougher time cracking that starting five than the one for Marion East. But what a five we'd be. I'd be playing point for a powerhouse. Packed gyms every night. Scouts at every game. A sure path to state finals at Bankers Life Fieldhouse. Better competition and exposure during AAU in the summer. It's not like it didn't cross my mind before, even when I was telling Uncle Kid I didn't have any interest, but now that my parents have brought it up, I realize what kind of an offer this is—especially after the way they ripped us the other night. The leap in the level of hoops is large. "What do you mean?" I finally ask.

"They've offered me a job there," my dad says. "But only if you come along too."

"No joke?" I ask.

"Not at all. Full time security. Decent money."

I remember my mom talking to me about my dad's hours getting cut back. Then I think about the price tag on those gifts we unwrapped yesterday. They didn't lose their minds shopping, but they still gave me and Jayson a solid Christmas. In his room, Jayson reacts to a three-pointer on his new game. How can I say no now?

"Listen, Derrick," my dad continues. "Your mom and I are making it work as is. We're not about to go up to Hamilton with our hands out begging. If you don't want to go there, then there's nothing in the world they can offer us to make you go."

He kind of trails off, holding something back. "But?" I say.

"But it's worth you taking a visit up there next month," my dad says. "Just hang with some of the players, see what you think."

"Drive around and look at the pretty people," my mom says sarcastically. Even now, she can't hide how much she detests the place.

"Kaylene," my dad says, "we've talked about this. You know as well as I do that Hamilton Academy sends ninety percent of their students on to college."

She exhales sharply and shakes her head, but then she looks up at me, all her anger evaporated just like that. "He's right, Derrick. It is a good school."

Then I remember the blow-up before that game with Hamilton, how my mom went off on Uncle Kid and Brownlee. "What about Uncle Kid? What's he get?" I ask.

My dad answers, very evenly but sternly, his words like a door being shut and locked, "What my brother does is my brother's business. It has no bearing on your decision."

"Okay," I say. We all look at each other for a few seconds, and then I say, "That it?"

"For now, sure," my dad says.

"No rash decisions," my mom says.

"Just think about it," my dad says.

"But for now keep giving everything you've got to Marion East," my mom says.

I get up and leave the table, walk past Jayson's room, his face lit in X-Box glow, then go and lay on my bed.

Some Christmas. My best friend blows up at me and now this. For a second there at the table, I got excited about the notion of playing somewhere else. With the offer they've given my dad, I don't see how I can refuse. But then I think about having to tell Coach Bolden, about having to tell Moose. I think about what it would be like as a sophomore playing against them. It wouldn't be so bad to light up the coach who refused to start me, but when I try to picture myself in that Hamilton Academy blue and red, it just seems wrong.

This isn't the way things were supposed to happen. Not at all. I look around my room at all those All-Stars hanging on my walls. That's who I'm supposed to be someday. In the end does it matter if I come out of Marion East or Hamilton Academy or anywhere else so long as I get to where I want to be? I don't know. Over on one wall is D-Rose. Simeon High School, Chicago's South side. But he'd still be every bit Derrick Rose if he went to some private school in the northern suburbs, right?

Then I look over at LeBron, an old poster of him still in his Cavs uniform. He took his talents to the place that was best for him, and everyone hated and hated on him. But what did he do that was so wrong? Making the hometown folks like you isn't as important as winning championships. At the end of the day, the ring is the thing.

PART II

14.

Times like these, the court makes a good getaway. No worries about Wes being angry with me. No sweating Hamilton's offer when there's live action—drivers to stop, cutters to hit, Js to bury. It's always been this way for me, like I can sweat out whatever troubles I have. And on Christmas break, ball is all there is. No homework, no tests, nothing. Just practice during the day and ESPN at night. And now, tonight, we're in Brebeuf's gym, ready to take on another North side squad, one who won their sectional last year.

Up here, they pack the gym out, the whole place flooded with their maroon colors. I know what all those private school kids are thinking—just more city scrubs coming up to get a beatdown before the new year. They better think again. I've run with the 1s all week, and tonight's my first start. I know I'll remember this one, and I'm about to make it a night the Brebeuf fans want to forget.

In the lay-up line, I keep bouncing, trying to get a little sweat worked up to push the nerves out, and each time through I run all the way to the mid-court stripe so I can look around to take it all in: Coach

Bolden rolling and unrolling a program in his hands, the Brebeuf photographer crouching at the baseline to snap pre-game pics, their cheerleaders flirting with boys in the stands, the splash of Marion East red clashing with the Brebeuf colors in the far corner. I saunter back into line and grab Royce's shoulders. "You ready, my man? I'm gonna drive and dish on these fools all night, so you best knock some down."

Royce stiffens his back and glances over his shoulder. "Just be ready to help out on Henderson." He's talking about Lex Henderson, Brebeuf's three man and Royce's responsibility. He's no Marcus Tagg, and I tell Royce that, but he just cuts me off. "The guy lit us up for 24 last year," he says, then snatches a bounce pass and darts toward the rim.

Doesn't matter. Let Royce worry about that. I got this. A week removed from that Hamilton game and the loss still stings, but what I keep reminding myself is that I torched those guys, so I'm not about to sweat Brebeuf. Moose zips the rock my way and I take a dribble like I'm sticking with the lay-ups, but then zag back out to the perimeter for a deep fade—pure. I'm telling you, Brebeuf better pray for a blackout in the gym—that's the only thing gonna save them.

I don't waste any time. First time down, I create some space and knock down a 12-footer. A minute later, I turn my man around with a cross-over then drop a dime on Moose for the hoop and harm. Next possession I get the outlet from Royce and rip it right down their throats, kicking back to Devin at the last second for an open three. With each play, I can hear our little corner making more and more noise. Pretty soon they're drowning out the Brebeuf crowd.

Then Nick checks in. And just like that, the rhythm's thrown. I slide over to the two-spot, but I might as well be invisible. Only time I get a touch is when I rise up over their guard and pluck an offensive board for a put-back. After that, I run back on D and shout at Nick to get me the damn orange.

He shoots me a look like I just spit on his mother's grave, says, "Other people need touches too!"

For the rest of the half it's like we're running in sand, getting nowhere for all our efforts, and we go into the locker room down a half dozen. I know better than to bellyache to Bolden, so I grab at Coach Murphy's sleeve as we leave the floor. We're standing right at the corner of the bleachers, still visible to the crowd. Some of the Brebeuf kids heckle us—weak stuff like *Take that game back where it came from* and *Five years running we've beat you guys*. I glance up, just to let them know I heard. The guys yelling at us are scrawny and riddled with acne, two punks feeling brave since they've got 20 rows between me and them. I just smile, give them a head nod, and they slap each other five thinking they've rattled me. "You gotta talk to Starks," I tell Murphy.

He frowns and motions to the locker room. Darius holds the door, waiting on the two of us and looking pretty nervous that there's a player who's in no particular hurry to hear what Coach Bolden has to say.

"No, for real," I holler. That makes Murphy turn back around, and those hecklers up above me start in again. Now I can feel more of the crowd staring. It makes my neck feel hot. If I can just get Murphy to talk some sense into Nick, I can really give these people a show worth watching.

"Derrick," Murphy says, "don't do this. Not the time or the place."

"He's freezing me out," I say. "I could drop 30 on these guys if he'd get me the ball!"

That's too much even for Murphy. His good cop routine drops, and all of a sudden I see him for what he is: a 6'5" grown-ass man who is 100 percent out of patience. "Locker room! Now!"

I follow along, but as I do I hear a familiar voice piercing the hecklers'. "You don't have to take that, D!" it says. I get to the locker room door and hear Darius saying *Hurry, hurry* under his breath, but I take one last second to look back. It's Uncle Kid, who's made it all the way from the opposite corner to get that message to me.

The second half is more of the same. I get loose early for a quick half dozen, but as soon as Nick checks back in we hit that sand again. Brebeuf feeds off Henderson, and the later the game gets the more Moose starts to drag, so their big man starts to get rolling too.

With three minutes left, we're down two with the ball. Royce has a pass deflected away. It rolls out of bounds and past the corner bleachers. As the ref hustles to retrieve it, there's a pause in the crowd noise. "Get D-Bow the ball!" someone screams. I know it's Uncle Kid, but as soon as he yells it other Marion East fans join in: *Yeah, get it to Bowen*, they yell, and *Iso for Derrick!*

Nick shakes his head and sneers. "Classy," he says. "Should have Devin back out here so we have another shooter."

I walk over to him, get right up beside him, tight as if I were guarding him, but I don't act hostile or puff out my chest or make it look like I'm showing him up, a move that would just get me banished to Bolden's dog house. "I know we've had some static, Nick," I say. "But, man, give me a touch. Trust me."

"Trust me," he mocks. "That what you been telling Jasmine?"

So that's it. Not even about minutes. It's about his girl. Ex-girl, but I guess that doesn't matter to him. I want to tell him to ease off, that he's got no claim to her anymore. Even if he did, there's no law against me texting her. No time, though. The ref hands the ball to Royce to throw in and it's back on. I V-cut and pop out to the wing for the in-bounds, sweep through on the catch and drive toward the free throw line. They're ready, though, and I pull back and pop it to Nick, who catches and pauses, just for a second, to look at me like he's sizing me up, then waves me down to the baseline so he can solo with his man.

It makes me want to scream. Here's a senior about to sabotage a game over some nonsense. As I float to the baseline though, Nick keeps watching me as he dribbles up top, giving little hesitations to keep his man occupied, and then—almost imperceptibly—Nick motions at me, just a little tilt of his chin toward the rim. It takes a second for me to realize what he wants, but he drops a filthy crossover on his man and darts diagonally into the lane, coming my way. I step behind the stripe and show my hands, and my man bites, taking a lunge for a pass that isn't coming. I cut baseline as Nick pulls up, but instead of floating up his little runner he loops a lob my way, a pass that seems to hang in the air forever as I gather and go get it for a perfect alley-oop. I take it with two hands and rip it through, quickly and efficiently before Brebeuf knows what's happening. Tie game.

As I backpedal, hearing our crowd go insane, I point to Nick. "Good look, Nick! Way to be, baby."

He just gives me another quick nod, almost like he's angry for having done it, and says, "Let's just get a stop, D."

We dig into Brebeuf, get their guards back on their heels. Royce jumps a baseline pass and almost swipes it clean, but it ticks off his hands out of bounds. He pleads with the ref, saying it's a double-tip off his man, but no way we're getting that call up on 86th Street.

When Brebeuf inbounds, their coach reminds them they're in no rush, so they work it around to Henderson, who's trying to get free in his favorite spot on that right baseline. Royce is ready though, and cuts him off every time he tries to duck in. But they stay patient, reversing the ball again and again until one of their bigs slips free on a diagonal cut. Moose meets him at the rim, but the ref sees him get body and his whistle puts Brebeuf at the line for two with just under two to go. Worst of all, that's the fifth on Moose and he lumbers back to the bench as the Brebeuf fans jeer him with every step. Bolden's left with no option to go with both Stanford and Jones at the big spots. More than ever, it's up to me and Nick.

As their big toes the line, I look up in the stands and see Jayson, who's shouting to try and rattle him. I look for Wes over with the band, but he hasn't made eye contact with me all night.

Big man drains the first, ugly form and all. Sure enough, on the second he catches front rim and it pops up, glances the window, and drops through to re-establish their two point lead.

Their crowd rises in unison, begging for a defensive stop, and their guards slap the court and clap their hands in determination. Nick just gives me another nod—*They can't check us*, it seems to say—and when we cross half court he motions me back toward the same corner. This time my man doesn't lunge, but Nick's just baiting him again. He shakes his man, gives a sick hesitation like he's kicking it to me again, then ducks into the paint and kisses it high off the glass. Tied again.

Our whole bench leaps to their feet as the shot drops, except for Bolden who bends down on one knee and urges us for another stop, almost like he's praying. They go right at Stanford and Jones, just spreading out on the perimeter so their big men have room to work in the post, so Royce, Nick and I have to dig back in on every feed to make their bigs kick it back out. If they were stronger, they'd just drop step on Stanford or Jones no matter how much help comes, but I can see that with the game this tight they don't really have the onions for it, so they keep passing it back to Henderson, hoping he'll save them. Royce sees it too. The longer the game has gone on, the more he's locked into Henderson's timing. With just over a minute left, Royce jumps back in on a post entry. But it's false pressure, and when they try to kick it back out he tips the pass, then outhustles Henderson for the loose ball in the corner.

The outlet goes to Nick and he pushes. I'm out ahead, staying wide as the hash so he can kick it to me, but he keeps ripping it up the center of the floor. I just stay wide, floating toward the baseline and when he finally kicks it out—after he's driven all the way into paint— I'm so open I can take my time. I catch. Set. Stroke.

Front rim, back rim, out.

Brebeuf corrals it and eases into the frontcourt, holding for one last shot. Nick and I keep trying to jump the passing lanes, but their guards are too steady for that. That clock just ticks, ticks, ticks. Agonizing. Finally, with ten seconds to go, they set a pick to get Henderson a little separation from Royce and kick it to him on the perimeter. Then everyone flattens out and it's just Royce and Henderson. Royce has done about as well as you can on the guy all night, but this is a brutal spot, on an island with him as the time dwindles.

Henderson starts right then crosses hard to his left, lowering his shoulder as he nears the elbow of the lane. Royce jumps the move, cutting him off, but Henderson spins back on his right foot and arches up a turnaround with two to go. Nick runs at him, but he's too small to bother the look, which is true, just as the horn sounds. Ballgame.

"Damnit, damnit, damnit!" Nick yells, stomping the bottom of his locker with each word.

"Take it easy, before coach hears," Darius tells him.

"Shut your mouth, Darius. We lost a goddamned game we should have won," Nick yells.

The rest of us just slump in our lockers, heads still hung in disbelief at the most brutal loss of the season. Lawrence North and Hamilton hurt, but we had these guys.

"Come on, Nick," I say. "No need to jump Darius."

Starks spins from his locker and takes two quick strides across the room to mine. "You can just keep your fucking mouth shut too."

I stand and get my back up. I'm exhausted from the game—exhausted, really, of constantly battling Nick, but there's no way I'm letting him talk to me that way. "I'll say what needs to be said," I tell him. "Ain't no need to come down on Darius. And if you run up on me like that, I'll make sure you're shut up for good."

The other guys are up now. The last thing they want is for Bolden and Murphy to come in on the two of us going at it. Nick must sense it too because he relaxes his pose and smiles. He cocks his head in a kind of reflective pose. When he speaks his voice is calm, like someone answering a question in class. "You're right. No need to yell at Darius. He didn't choke away our last possession."

I've had about enough. I rip off my jersey and throw it in a ball in my locker. It almost feels like I'm taking that thing off for good. At least at Hamilton I won't have to deal with this kind of bullshit, I think. "You're blaming me? Why? I carried your ass out there. If you wouldn't have frozen me out for half the game, we'd have won the damn thing."

"Riiiight," Nick says. "The savior D-Bow can do no wrong. Except when you launch a three when we should be holding for the last goddamn shot."

I get as close as I can without touching him, so close I can smell his sweat. "If you'd have kicked it ahead to me earlier, I'd have thrown it down no problem. Instead, you got to dribble to nowhere."

"I know if my man Devin was the one open in the corner, that thing would have been buried," he says.

"I thought just a second ago you said it was a bad shot to take!"

"It was a bad shot because *you* took it!"

Before I can respond, the locker room door thunders shut. There stand Bolden and Murphy. Who knows how long they've been listening. The room is completely silent. Then Bolden speaks. "I want everyone to get showered. I want everyone to get on the bus. I don't want anyone to say a goddamn word."

We do as we're told. Not even a word from Moose. When we do get situated on the bus, Bolden and Murphy stand outside for a few minutes to talk. The engine rumbles and I can smell that sickening mixture of gas fumes and the old plastic seats. If Nick just would have kicked it ahead to me. If Bolden and Murphy wouldn't have messed with my shot. But no, it's no use thinking that way. We lost. I had a shot to bury them and it rattled out. Those are the facts, and there's no use wishing otherwise.

The doors whoosh open and a blast of cold air rushes in with Murphy, who walks with his head down all the way to the last seat of the bus, where he can keep an eye on everyone. Then Bolden comes in. He stands at the front, his hand on the first seat, and in the darkness he's just a silhouette. "I wasn't going to get mad," he says, "because the truth is you guys played well and battled hard. So I'll just say this. We don't practice again until the new year. That gives you three days to think about what it takes to be a member of a team. If you show up to that practice on New Year's Day, I'll expect that you've thought about that quite a bit."

He sits down and faces forward, then leans slightly toward the driver. "Let's go home," he says.

15.

"I don't think you can understand what kind of pressure he's under as a senior," Jasmine says. "Things are ending for him here and he wants a scholarship to Ball State, but they keep waiting to offer."

We're eating in the Artsgarden, a glass dome that connects the mall to other downtown buildings. We can look out on the traffic going up Illinois, everyone rushing around to get ready for New Year's Eve. There are a few businessmen in coats and ties, putting in one last grind of the year, but mostly people seem festive on one of those cold but clear winter days.

"Anyway," she says, "Can we please not talk about Nick? My ex-boyfriend isn't exactly my favorite topic, Derrick."

"Cool here." Not only do I regret bringing up the subject of Nick, I regret bringing up hoops at all. For the first time I can remember, the very idea of basketball makes me anxious. There's nothing better in the world than playing the game, but all of a sudden it seems like one big task, as much of a job as the ones that have those businessmen running around with their phones glued to their faces. I know, too, that it will only grow worse. Some drama over Hamilton Academy is nothing compared to what will happen when my parents start letting recruiters in the front door.

I exhale. Remind myself all that stuff is still on the horizon somewhere. Right now, it's just me and Jasmine in downtown Indianapolis. Eating in the Artsgarden like two grown folk being civilized on the last day of the year.

She smiles and shakes her head. "That means you're supposed to change the subject, Derrick."

"Oh. Well, how do you like Marion East? Whose classes are toughest for sophomores?"

She smiles again, but it's different this time, more genuine instead of this puzzled little grin. "I love our high school," she says. "I mean, I know there are better schools if you want a shot at college, but our teachers are good. And I swear, Derrick, they're so beaten down from years of people slacking off that if you show the slightest bit of interest they'll think you're the best student ever." She continues, talks about some colleges she'd love to go to, about how she's had good luck with all the Marion East teachers so far, but I might try to avoid Mr. Marshall since he's notoriously brutal on athletes. I try to pay attention, I really do, but as she talks I start to focus on those brown eyes of hers, how full of life they are, and how her lips pout out just slightly when she's trying to think of the right word. She's wearing this brown top that perfectly matches her eyes, and comes down just a thread shy of her jeans, so you can just see this glimpse of smooth skin. It makes me nervous. And it's not just that she looks so fine, but that she seems so put together. So many people my age look like they're a series of parts that don't quite make up a whole. But Jasmine looks as put together as anyone in downtown Indy.

"Derrick?" I re-focus, and see that her eyes are wide, expecting an answer. "What about you? How's your first year?"

"It's cool so far," I say.

She pauses, leans back from the table with that puzzled grin again. "That's it? It's cool so far?"

"What?" Really, I know I could say more, but it's not like I can throw the whole thing down on her, especially about how Hamilton's recruiting me.

She leans her head back and looks up at the glass ceiling, exasperated but amused. "What is it? Is there some blood oath you guys sign in the locker room that says you can't ever give more than a three-word answer to things?"

"Be fair," I say. I hold up my hand, counting off with my fingers. "It's—cool—so—far. That's four words!"

She nods, her mouth slightly ajar like she wants to laugh but won't let herself. "Okay. Very cute."

"Fine. You want the real deal? You want to know about everything?"

She teases back now, piling her trash up on her tray and looking away like she has no idea who this fool is across from her. "I'm not interested anymore," she says. "You missed your chance."

She even flirts like someone older, and when she walks across the Artsgarden to the window overlooking Illinois my heart leaps a little bit. So even though I want to play it cool, I walk over to her. She's staring at one of the art exhibits, something that to me looks like a random swirl of colors on a canvas with no discernible shapes. Most people just walk right by on their way to the mall, or, like me, eat lunch right beside these exhibits without even noticing they exist. But here's Jasmine, checking one out.

"Jasmine, you want to come out with me after the Ben Davis game next weekend?" I try to sound confident as I say it, but she looks at me as if I'm speaking in a foreign language and it makes me more nervous than one of Bolden's staredowns.

She folds her arms and cocks her head a little, considering. "You do realize I just broke up with Nick, like, a week ago, right?"

"I thought we weren't talking about Nick," I say.

She bats her eyes at me, cute. "I'm just saying that I don't know about going on a date right away."

"Okay," I say, "it's not a date. Just hanging out." As soon as I say the words I want them back, like a pass that leaves your hand just as you see a defender jumping it. Backing down from a date to hanging out is a chump move. I can almost hear Jayson in the back of my head telling me as much.

She considers some more then says, "Fine. We'll hang out." She goes quiet again and stares at that painting. Then after she's soaked it in all she wants, she turns to me. "Hanging out after a Marion East basketball game. Derrick, you ever think about how big the world is? About all the things there are to do? I mean, here's this city all around us, and it's just a tiny little spot on the globe. The world doesn't end at Marion East, not by a long shot." She pauses again and frowns a little, like whatever she meant to say came out wrong. Then she smiles and tries to sound enthusiastic when she says, "But, yeah, let's hang out after the game."

She turns and walks into the mall then. I follow close on her heels, but even after we've killed some time in Circle Centre and gone our separate ways to meet our parents, I can't tell how much what she said was teasing and how much was serious.

Nick's right. Not about how this team should play and not about whose fault it was we lost the Brebeuf game, but about us needing another shooter on the floor. There are about a hundred things I can do on the floor that Devin can't, but even though I've improved that J a bit, defenses don't have to run at me the way they do at Devin.

"There it is, D," Murphy says. "Doesn't matter that it came up short. Form's looking better all the time."

But it does matter that it came up short. That's what I want to shout at him every time he tries to say it's okay that I've missed one in our little post-practice workouts. The more frustrated I get, the more I want to forget about everything the coaches say and just rip it to the rim every time I get a touch. Forget the offense, forget ball reversal, forget working on a form that hasn't paid off except for a couple times against Hamilton: Just drive! Maybe if I did that every time, we'd be sitting a little better than 5-4.

Here I am, though, staying late after the first practice of the new year, listening to Bolden tell me to keep my head straight while Murphy trots out his little encouragements. I catch one on the shallow wing and this time as soon as I let it go, I can tell it's long, so much that I'm lucky to scrape back rim. "Don't worry about that, D! Just keep it lined up."

I grit my teeth and ignore him. Hell with this. I catch Bolden's next pass in the corner and blast down the baseline, cock the pill back and throw it down.

"What was that?" Bolden asks.

I'm standing right next to him under the bucket, my chest heaving, and the question makes me want to scream to the dark rafters: *A dunk, old man! The easiest deuce there is!* Instead, I just put my hands on my hips and stare down at the red baseline. "I just had to get that out of my system, Coach."

"I understand, Derrick, but you don't need to practice that. It's your jumpers and free throws that need work." I wonder if he'll think as much next year if I'm throwing down in a Hamilton jersey. I don't say a word, but he must read something in my expression because he raises his eyebrows and steps back. "There's no rule that says you have to stay after practice," he says.

Five days until we take on Ben Davis. In the past, every time I've gotten frustrated at practices I've put all that anger on the next opponent, so by the time they take the floor I've got a strong hatred working, their very colors an offense to my pride. Right now, though, I can't trick myself. It's not the players at Ben Davis riding my ass over every little thing.

"Let's go around again," I say. I jog back to the baseline and wait for Bolden's pass, only this time he gives me a little dig every time he zips me the rock.

"You could be so good, Derrick!" I catch on the baseline and fire. Long.

"But you want it to be easy!" I catch on the shallow wing and fire. Long.

"Even staying after practice isn't enough!" I catch on the wing and fire. Good, but it feels as wrong as a miss, just kind of spinning in from the side.

"Extra time doesn't help unless you make it work!" Top of the key. Left and short. Awful.

"Not just for you but for the team!" Other wing. Short.

"Get better for the team!" Shallow wing. Short.

"Get better!" Opposite baseline. Long. Way long, another scraper.

"Goddamnit," I say. I don't care if Bolden hears. He tries to make me run, I'll walk instead. "I'm getting worse!"

I put my hands on my knees, trying to catch my breath. When I lower my head the blood rushes into it and I can feel my pulse pounding at my temples. Then I feel a hand on my shoulder. Like an angry dog, I pull back from it but Bolden squeezes.

"You're not getting worse, Derrick," he says. "You're up to seventy percent at the stripe and you're about to break through on this shot. When it finally clicks, it'll stick. And you need to stop playing like you're angry all the time."

"I'm not angry," I say, but in my heart, I'm so mad I want to boot the ball into the bleachers, kick the scorer's table into a million pieces.

Bolden sighs and releases my shoulder. When I look at him, I don't see any of his temper flaring back. Instead, he looks kind of tired. I suddenly see every loss of every season worn into the wrinkles around his eyes. "Let's call it a night," he says. "Save your legs for the game." He nods at Murphy and tells him to lock up, then walks away with his hands in his pockets and his head bent in contemplation.

16.

Ben Davis is a disaster. The noise starts even before tip, because as I'm lacing up in the locker room, Coach Bolden walks in and puts the starting five on the board:

5 – GREEN

4 – STANFORD

3 – BEDFORD

2 – VARNEY

1 – STARKS

Unbelievable. I'm the one busting ass every day after practice, and this is how I get rewarded? Meanwhile Nick has sulked ever since the Brebeuf game, but he's right back in the point guard spot while I'm riding pine. I keep my mouth shut, but I'm so mad I can barely look at Bolden. I watch Ben Davis jump out to a six-point lead and I don't even care—might as well be watching a movie in History class. Ain't a thing to me. In my heart, there's a part of me that's already elsewhere, like I'm closing the door on this season and just biding my time to opening night up at Hamilton next November, where we sure as hell won't get run by Ben Davis.

By the time I check in it's a nine-point deficit, and I just don't have it in me to try to pump up my boys.

"Come on, D. Let's jump back in this," Moose says.

I just give him a tilt of my chin to say *Yeah, sure*, and he stares at me for a second, then turns his back in disgust. Soon, instead of making a dent in the lead, it's grown to double digits. Every time down, Ben Davis works it inside to Stanford's man, who just deals like a fiend. When Bolden sends in Jones, it just gets worse. And on our end, we play like five strangers who just happened to show up at the gym on the same night. Nick passes it to the wing just as Royce back cuts. Next time down Royce chucks a 22-footer on the first touch he gets and leaves it a foot shy. Then it's my turn, so frustrated at not getting looks that when I touch leather I drive baseline—square into a double-team—then get an off-balance pass swiped. Nobody's immune: Moose swings an elbow to get free and gets called for a flagrant; Devin checks in and flat-out drops a nice pass in the lane; Nick just dribbles and dribbles and dribbles, getting nothing to show for it.

By the end of the first we're down 13.

By half it's 20.

By mid-third we're down 26 and when Bolden calls a timeout he simply looks at us. Just stares, those old almond eyes burning holes in every one of us. He doesn't say a word. Coach Murphy clears his throat like he's about to bust up the silent treatment, but Bolden swivels his head Murphy's way real quick—like a man tracking motion with a gun—and Murphy edges back behind the scrubs in the huddle. The staredown keeps on for thirty seconds, Bolden shifting that gaze slowly from one player to another.

At last, Nick offers a meek, "Coach?"

"What?!" Bolden snaps. "What, Nick?"

Nick stares down at the floor, and the rest of us join him, withered by that cruel Bolden stare. I can promise you there's never been a timeout like this one at Hamilton Academy. Then again, what is there to say? We're way past the time for a rousing speech. Whatever competitive fire any of us had was extinguished before half.

The buzzer sounds to call us back to the court. We rise, wobbly as beat-up boxers, to head back out for more punches.

"Where the hell are you going?" Bolden yells.

We stop, puzzled. If he had a message for us, he missed his chance. He just points at the bench. Then I get it: that silent timeout was the message.

"Twos in for the ones!" Bolden shouts, and the back-ups rip off their warm-ups, not so much eager for the minutes as to be the hell away from that bench.

For one last insult, Bolden exiles all the starters—and me, lumped in with them in punishment if not for the opening tip—to the end of the bench, putting Murphy and every last scrub in between us, as if he can't bear to even breathe the same air as we do.

Showing some mercy, Ben Davis responds in a few minutes by sending in their second team too, but it doesn't stop the onslaught. We have to endure those embarrassing cheers of their crowd responding to a scrub getting a jam on the break, and then some pasty kid who can't be more than five-three—looking like even less of a baller than our manager Darius—draining back-to-back treys in the last minutes.

The final damage: 75-40. But it's more than the score. Hamilton was brutal, but they're stocked with D-I skills, so they're bound to put the beatdown on squads now and then. Ben Davis? They got nothin'. A couple guys sniffing mid-major scholarships, a couple bigs who might go D-II. No way—*no way*—we should get thumped by them. When I looked down our schedule before the season, this one was a sure W, even on the road. Everyone else must have felt the same way too, because the locker room might as well be a funeral home. Everyone looks listless. Even Nick, who you can usually count on to throw his gear around after a loss, just quietly drops his uni to the floor and heads to the shower.

Bolden doesn't say a word the whole ride back. Then, when we reach the school, he just stands and leaves the bus. That leaves Coach Murphy to tell us when to be at the gym tomorrow night for the game against Indianapolis Northwest. Then he turns and leaves too. It's just the players sitting in a darkened bus, smelling the smoke from the driver's cigarette as he puffs away against the bus out in the brutal cold.

Finally Moose stands and hulks down the bus toward the door.

"Ain't nobody gonna say anything?" Stanford finally says.

Moose spins around, a quicker move than any he used on the floor tonight. "Fuck you want me to say, Stanford? You want a pep talk? Man, we're dead. Dead in the water. And we got two months of this shit left."

So that's the verdict on the Marion East bus after the first week of January, handed down by the most relentlessly optimistic player we've got: Dead in the water.

Later, I'm kicking it with Jasmine at Free, this under-21 club she knows about. I'd never even heard about the place, but maybe that's because I'm bound by where my feet can take me, while she's got a car. I figured we'd just hang downtown killing time like everyone else in Indy, but she laughed that idea off. We cruised through downtown and onto Southeastern, then across the tracks into some desolate area before she told me where we were going. "There's a lot more to do than sit around downtown until some fast food place kicks you out," she said. "My cousin's on stage tonight." All I know about clubs like this is that they opened one on Central back when I was still too young to enjoy it. That place lasted about two months before some noise started between a few guys. Soon as you can snap your fingers, they shoot at each other and end up spraying the crowd. Two teenagers wound up killed. That was the death of that club, too.

But here we are, Jasmine's cousin up on stage throwing rhymes into the mic. He's all geared up like some old-school hip-hop kid—got the oversized Bulls jersey and his hat on backwards and cocked down over his left ear, off to the side enough so you can see he's rocking a little bit of a fade. I don't know if I dig the look, but after a while I have to admit he's got some skills. The dj behind him has the bodies moving after a while.

"All right," her cousin shouts between cuts. "This one's for all those fine brown-skinned honeys out there." And everyone—especially the white guys in the crowd—shouts when his dj drops the first few beats, so this must be some kind of signature song for him. Even the security guards, huge black mountains of muscle stationed in each corner, start to bob their heads.

Jasmine tugs on my coat sleeve, like a little kid pleading. "Come on, Derrick," she says. "Dance!" I feel good being out with her, but truth is I can't put enough distance between me and that game to feel any bounce. But when she starts dancing around me, shaking and swerving her hips, I give it a try just to see her smile.

I didn't even go in my house after the game, just sat on the stoop and waited for Jasmine. She pulled up in her dad's dented Subaru, the exhaust puffing hot clouds into the cold night air. I was sitting shotgun in the blink of an eye. She looked good, her hair done in little brown and amber ringlets framing her smooth, caramel-colored face, her smart brown eyes peering at me from across the car. It made me stammer out a hello and feel a bit shaky inside. When I took a deep breath and smelled her perfume, I damn near passed out. Good thing for me she shifted into gear and I could collect myself while I texted my parents to let them know why I wasn't back yet. They understood, I'm sure, because nobody wanted to see anybody in the aftermath of that game.

God, that game. I've lost basketball games before, but there's never been anything like that. They treated us like we were a JV squad. It happens, I know. I mean, even the NBA champs came out on the wrong end almost twenty times last year—but, no, never like that. Good teams just don't get curb-stomped like that.

"Derrick!" Jasmine yells again. "Where's your head, boy? Have some fun."

I realize I've stopped dancing with her and have been staring blankly at the stage, letting images of the game play out in my head—a missed pull-up in the lane, Stanford losing his man for a nasty jam, Bolden staring at us in silence, and Moose leaving the bus like a sulking, hulking bear.

"All right," I say. "It's all good. I was just thinking for a second, but it's cool." The music's loud enough that I have to bend down to her ear so she can hear me. I get a deep breath of her perfume and a brush of those ringlets against my cheek. Ben Davis who? This girl can make bad things disappear in a hurry.

For the next few minutes, I just lose myself in the sound, in watching Jasmine bounce around me, her shirt riding up just so I can see that razor-thin slice of skin above her jeans again. But I feel a cold blast on my neck every time the club door opens and a mean Indianapolis January intrudes on us. This time when it opens, the cold air keeps on. I turn to see a couple guys standing there as leisurely as if they were basking in the June sun. People start shouting for them to close the door, but they don't seem to care. Instead they survey the scene like they're kings, these smug sneers across their faces, one of them a sandy brown and the other dark chocolate. The darker-skinned one, long enough to fill up the door frame, is Marcus Tagg. The lighter one is his point guard, Patterson, from Lawrence North.

Just seeing them undercuts everything good I'd been feeling. I try to ignore them, but that lasts about 30 seconds because after they finally come in from the cold it's as if they're drawn to me like a magnet. Soon they're head-bobbing to the music not ten feet away.

I know Tagg recognizes me, but he doesn't acknowledge me. Patterson pipes up first.

"Hey, it's the great D-Bow," he shouts. "The second coming at point guard, if you believe all the hype."

Tagg looks my way for a second, just kind of snorts like I smell bad, then turns back to the stage. Patterson stays at it though. "Yeah, new kid in that uni, same old sorry-ass team." He laughs. I get my back up. But before I can do a thing Jasmine grabs my wrist—her fingers are like little electric coils on my skin—and tries pulling me away.

We don't get far enough. Tagg decides to run smack too. He's just as deadly efficient as he is on the court: "How'd you do against Ben Davis tonight?" he asks, his voice booming across the room so other people hear, all of them swiveling their heads back and forth between us. He just stands there with a smug look on his face. Of course he knows how we did against Ben Davis tonight. He just wants to make sure everyone else in the room knows it too.

That rips it for me. "You two a long way from 75th Street!" I shout. I shake free from Jasmine's grip and step at him. "You come all this way just to start shit, you might not like how it ends!"

As I walk to them, people start parting for us, the crowd quickly turning their attention from the stage to see what's going down in their midst. Tagg laughs like he's above all this noise, but Patterson steps to me, his chest out. "Who the fuck you think you're talking to?" he says. "You think you gonna do something, little man?"

He shoves me on that *little man*. It's like a curtain falls behind my eyes. All I see is a violent, bloody red for a second. I snap—push Patterson right back and cock my fist. And then the both of us are on the ground, our heads pinned to the floor. I'm so locked in on Patterson I'm still looking at him, still trying to get at him, before I realize that security has us. They don't waste time. We get hoisted up and dragged to the door, getting lectured the whole way that there's no room for nonsense at Free, that we best not show our faces until we know how to act like grownups. I try to wrest my arm free and fight back, but the guard who has me wrenches it so tight behind my back I think it's about to come out of the socket. After that I just let it happen—I may be big for a point, but this guy's a whole other kind of big, like Colts D-line big, a big you don't test. Finally, when I let myself surrender, I think about Jasmine again, about whether or not she's still standing on the other side of the club where I left her. That thought makes me ache somewhere deep inside.

"Do you know why I broke up with Nick?"

We're idling outside my house now, Jasmine talking to me but looking straight ahead into the cold Indianapolis night, as if she were asking this question to the stop sign at the end of our block.

I don't answer. I shrug, and my coat makes an awkward scrunching sound against the seat. I feel like I'm a little boy whose mom just caught him in a lie. The wind kicks up and makes the Subaru shudder, a little of that biting cold sneaking in through the windows.

"Do you think it was because Nick was stupid? Because he was ugly? Because he cheated on me?" I just shrug again. Something about the way she's talking about Nick makes me uneasy, like before their dating was just some imaginary thing that I didn't have to believe. But now she's kind of making it more real, even though they're split.

"Look at me, Derrick," she says. When I do I see that she's turned that stare away from the stop sign and directed it at the fool sitting shotgun. "Nick's smart and fine and true," she says, and I can barely stand to hear it. "And Nick's also a total dick when things go wrong during basketball. I used to come home and cry after Marion East lost—

not because I care, but because Nick would be mean and angry and just ruin the night every single time. So finally my dad sat me down and told me I didn't deserve that. That if a man takes out his frustrations on other people then he's no man at all." She looks away again, down at the dashboard like she's really thinking about that conversation. "I told Nick that, and he kept on. And after you lost to Hamilton he got so angry he scared me. So that was that. No more. He can go be smart and fine and true with someone else and make her life hell after each game."

I see a light click on inside our house. I know I better bolt soon before my mom comes down here and embarrasses me to death. I wait until Jasmine looks back at me and then I hold that look, stare right into those perfect brown eyes. "I won't do that to you, Jasmine," I say.

She shakes her head. "You already did!"

"I won't ever do it again," I say. "I promise."

She looks back at me, then down at her hands. "Yeah," she says. "Sure."

"I mean it," I say. She doesn't respond then, just looks sad and reflective, as if she's waiting on something. Then I realize that—even after all that's gone down—we're here in her car at the end of a Saturday night. I think I know what she's waiting on, so I lean over real slow. I put my hand on her chin to lift her face to mine and start to kiss her.

She pulls back. She puts one hand on my chest to push me away, and the other hand to her temple like she's got a headache. "For real?" she says. "Really? You thought that was the time to try to kiss me?"

I start to mumble an apology, but every word I say just makes her angrier.

"Stop, stop, stop!" she says. "You don't listen to anything! Just get out." I sit for a second trying to think of what to say. "Get out, Derrick!" she yells.

So I do. I close the door to her car and she screams out of there like she's on fire, and all that's left to this long, awful night is the walk up to my house, where my mom's waiting by the door.

17.

We lose. And we lose. And we lose.

To Indianapolis Northwest by six. At Howe by nine. At Anderson by three. None of those are as embarrassing as the Ben Davis game. In truth, we played better at Anderson than we have in a month, but they're still Ls, like Fs on a report card. We trudge home with them each time, feel their full weight on us. Bolden's eased off, trying to encourage us more than usual, probably because there's still a month and a half left in the season and even he can't bear to be angry and miserable for that long, but he's not fooling us. We've taken all the early season potential and run it into the ditch. You are what your record says you are. And with a week to go in January we are a 5-8 team on a six-game skid.

Up north, meanwhile, Hamilton's unblemished: 14-0. This isn't lost on my Uncle Kid any more than it is on me. So when he's waiting outside the Marion East doors when I get out of practice today, I know what's up.

"How's practice?" he asks. I know he's just trying to sound nonchalant. Kid's got that itchy, twitchy look he gets when he's up to something. He's tapping his foot like he's keeping time to some song nobody else can hear. He can't make eye contact with me. He somehow looks skinnier than ever, his face even more ashy.

"Same old," I say.

Kid's eyes light up. He looks right at me for a second. "Word. I bet old Bolden's still running the same practice schedule he did when I was lacing 'em up."

"Probably," I say. It's not that I have any allegiance to Bolden—I mean, the man screwed our season up by keeping me pinned to the pine instead of letting me lead us straight out—but there's something about the way Kid says this that makes me defensive. So I don't say anything more and turn toward home.

"Hey, D!" Kid shouts, and hustles to catch up with me. "Hold up! I just want to catch you for a second."

"Well, go on then," I say, my tone sharper than I'd intended. I'm just not in the mood for foolishness, though, not with Muncie Central looming—not exactly the easiest team to break a losing streak against.

Kid raises his hands like I'm mugging him. "Easy, D," he says. "It's just your Uncle Kid, man. I'm not trying to mess you up." He backs up onto a lawn on 34th and the frozen ground crunches under his heels. "But be honest, D-Bow. You know this season isn't what you had in mind. You deserve better than this."

I can't argue with him there, so I just nod and stare back.

"You remember what we talked about that night before your first game?" he asks.

"Yeah, Kid. I remember." A car creeps by slowly and Kid stares at it, then gives a quick nod to the driver. I turn my head to see if it's that black Lexus that used to follow him around, but it's just some old friend of his.

Kid turns back to me then. "Just want you to know all that's still out there for you. Good life up there at the Academy, D. They'll take care of you. All I'm sayin'."

"Well, you said it then."

With that, I turn toward home again, but Uncle Kid falls right in step. We don't say much more, even when he tries to draw me out by talking about hoops, how the Pacers are making a move in the standings and how the Hoosiers are faring in the Big Ten. At this point, I just don't care—truth is, I'd trade the Pacers losing all 82 if we could just get a few wins ourselves.

When I get to my door, I expect Uncle Kid to go on, but he's standing right at my shoulder when I turn the key. I walk in, expecting to hear Jayson blaring beats from his room or arguing with Dad about finishing his homework before he turns on the TV or pestering Mom to order pizza instead of cooking limas and meatloaf. But there's none of that. Just eerie silence, as quiet as those old abandoned houses Wes and I used to explore when we were kids. When I call out *Hello?* though, I get two voices responding in unison: "We're in here."

That's when I see Mom and Dad at the kitchen table, waiting, a third chair pulled out for me.

When Mom sees Kid, something flashes across her face and her young smoothness is creased with anger. "What's he doing here?" she asks.

"Just let him sit, Kaylene," Dad says. "Like it or not he's got some things to say on this subject."

Uncle Kid's still a damn good player, but he's a poor salesman. Even I can tell he's too jumpy for his own good, pushing me so hard to leap to Hamilton Academy that he makes me want to stay at Marion East.

"It's all there for the taking," he shouts after my mom makes a cutting remark about how few black teachers Hamilton has. He pounds the table with his fist and then stands and paces the living room like a nervous man outside an emergency room. "You can't not transfer, Derrick. You have to."

Even I can see that Kid has more invested in this than just my basketball career and education, but before I can say anything Mom shoots him down: "Sidney Bowen, don't you dare stand in my living room and tell my son what he has to do! Only two people get to say that, and he's grown enough to make up his own mind on this."

"But, Kaylene," he pleads.

"But nothing," Mom says, taking his plea with the same patience she shows to students who forget their homework. "Whatever love you have for those pretty, white people is your business, but don't come dragging it into my living room."

"It's not about me loving white people!" Kid shouts back. Mom struck a nerve and now Kid's got his back up too. The room feels like a pot about to boil over.

Dad, ever calm, tries to ease the heat back just a bit. "Sit, Sidney," he says, then reaches over and puts his hand over my mom's—the only man alive that can do that when she's angry and expect to keep that hand. "The adults in this room yelling isn't going to help the one teenager make a decision." He takes his glasses off for a second and wipes his face with his hand, a weary gesture, but when he sets those glasses on the table and looks at me without them I can see the calm in his eyes. His face seems to relax, easing away the wrinkles that are starting to form around his mouth and temples and he looks—just for a second—like the man I've seen in the pictures from before I was born, the one my mom fell for: smooth skin the shade of almond butter and a patient smile that says he's got all day just for you. "Instead of shouting over each other, let's just write down a list of pros and cons."

My mom sighs, impatient with my dad's methodical take, but she knows he's right because she gets up and tears a fresh sheet from the message pad on the fridge. When she sits back down she says, "Fine, let's hear all the great reasons why my son should go to school in a different damn county."

Uncle Kid clears his throat, but my dad just shoots him a look—*Don't you dare, man*—and instead Dad starts off. "Academics," he says. My mom, who's been resisting the idea of a transfer at every turn, lets her pen hover over the paper. "Kaylene, you know it's true. You can't even pretend. Hamilton might be the best high school in the state. At Marion East, when a kid manages to make it to senior year without dropping out, you'd think it was cause for a parade."

Mom relents and writes it down. Then she looks at me, fire in her eyes. "But don't let anyone say it's because they're better than us. You give our kids all the benefits they get and we'd be sending people off to every college you can name."

"Safety," my dad says.

"Oh, come on, Thomas," she says. "Don't be one of these fools who thinks every black kid's toting a gun in his jacket."

"Safety," my dad says again. "Tell me the last time someone got shot while waiting for their parents to pick them up in Hamilton County."

My mom juts her jaw out, but she gives in again and scribbles

Safety down on that pad, pressing so hard she might be etching it in the table underneath. Just as quickly, though, she writes an entry under the Con side. "Discipline," she says. "Sometimes having things easy isn't best. You get through Marion East, you know you have discipline. Wasn't it just last year one of Hamilton's players got arrested with enough drugs to start a pharmacy?"

"Fair enough," Dad says.

"Now, wait!" Kid pipes in. "You think Bolden's 'discipline' is going to be good for Derrick?"

"I don't recall asking for your opinion," Mom says. "But, yes, I'd say that's about the best thing Bolden has going for him."

There's a long, silent standoff between them. The dead air in the room fills with the ghosts of Kid's old run-ins with Bolden, his senior-year suspension that started his long fall from grace. Not even my mom has the brass to bring that up though, so soon enough they're back to the list.

At first the fact that Hamilton Academy's better goes on the pro-transfer list, but my mom cancels it out by saying nobody ever got better by taking the easy way. Uncle Kid dares to pipe up again and says I should go where I'm wanted, but again Mom counters by saying Hamilton just looks at me the way some people look at a pair of shoes in the window: just something to use and wear out.

I have to wonder if they're ever going to ask me how I feel about all this. Here they are, making lists for the biggest decision in my life so far and not one of them has bothered to ask me where exactly I stand on the whole issue. But then I realize they're avoiding another big question: what about Dad's job? So I finally chip in. "They still gonna give you a job, Dad?" I ask, and the three of them stop cold.

My mom starts to say something, but finally just shifts her gaze to Dad. It's his show now. "That's what they say," he says at last.

Uncle Kid straightens up like this is news to him. "Well, that's it then. You can't pass up a job, man."

"No," Dad says. "That's not it. We make do as it is. I'm not sure I want to get ahead on my son's back."

I understand what he's saying. It's noble I guess, but the way I've been feeling about Bolden and my teammates at Marion East lately, this kind of cinches it. "But we could use the money, right Dad?"

He waits before he answers. He and Mom trade a long, meaningful look. He can't deny it. "Yes," he says, and looks away from me.

"There you go," Kid says.

"Stop it, Sidney," Mom says. She narrows her eyes at him. "I don't know what skin you got in it anyway," she adds, enough to make Kid fidget like a man waiting for test results from the doctor.

Then my mom turns to me and lays down the verdict: I'm supposed to visit Hamilton Academy on Saturday since we don't have a game that night. Check out the campus, meet the coaches, hang with some of the players. Then Jayson comes bouncing in, headphones pumping beats. My parents stand, making it clear the conversation is over.

"It's just to get a feel for the place," Dad tells me later when we're watching the Pacers. "If you don't like it, you don't owe them a thing."

He says this to put my mind at ease, I know—and to keep Uncle Kid's expectations down—but it makes me anxious instead. Before he said that, I just saw Hamilton Academy as a better place to ball than Marion. I never thought about owing them anything.

"You all getting drubbed. Just thumped like scrubs."

This is Wes, and we're checking the items in Ty's Tower. It's Friday and we've got our game with Muncie in a few hours, but when Wes finally texted me, I was jumping at it. It is a blustery January outside, the wind ripping down 38th so the store's windows shake, but it's toasty in Ty's Tower and Wes is trying his best to talk smack—he's kind of giving it to me a little harsh, but I guess I deserve it.

"We gonna bounce back against Muncie tonight," I say.

"On Muncie? Hell, D, those guys are ranked. If you can't beat Howe, you gonna get run against Muncie."

"Easy, Wes," I say. I grab an Air Max from the rack and act like I'm about to take it to his head.

Wes laughs it off and then we just browse in silence for a while. Neither one of us has a dollar in his wallet, but that never stopped us from scoping all the gear at Ty's. We run our hands down the sleeves of Jumpman and Therma-fit hoodies, check the price tag on the Pacquiao M65 and try not to react, eye the jerseys and argue whether it's cooler to rock the James or the throwback Magic, but we're just killing time. Eventually we swing back over to the shoes and Wes just stares at those Timberland Earthkeepers again, looking like some lovesick schoolboy staring at his crush.

"I thought your Pops was hooking you up with those," I say.

Wes just hangs his head. "Nah," he says. He walks off and I worry that I've insulted him again. He's out the door before I can react, and I jog to catch up to him on the street, the air burning my lungs.

I catch him at the corner, but when I reach for his elbow he jerks his hand away. A car speeding on 38th sees us and honks its horn, taunting. I look at Wes and I can see the pain written across his face, making him look suddenly older. "Wes," I say, "man, I am sorry about the night after the Hamilton game. If I could undo it, I would. I know you were all into Iesha and I ruined it for you."

"Nah, D," he says. "I was mad at you, but it's not about the girl." He looks off down 38th for a second, some old man stare like he's a weary soul. "My dad never made it for Christmas," he says at last. "Called the night before and just said he couldn't make it. No excuse, no nothing. No kicks, either."

Thing is, even though he's telling me this to let me off the hook, it just makes me feel worse. My man Wes got stood up—at Christmas—by his dad, and I wasn't there for him. It makes me feel sick. "I'm sorry, Wes," I say. It's the only thing I can think of.

Wes breaks off that dead stare and turns back my way, like he realizes for the first time that I've been standing here, which seems fair enough. "It's cool, Derrick. I was pissed at you, but I shouldn't have held this other stuff against you. Not your fault my dad's too cheap to buy me a Christmas present." Then he smiles. It's that grin that just barely shows his teeth, and he looks like a ten-year-old full of mischief again, his amber eyes lit up with it. "Besides, Iesha's folks got some money, I think. Maybe I'll make her my sugar mama." He laughs at his own joke, a big, goofy sound—back to the old Wes.

I'm so happy to see him smiling and laughing, it takes me a second to pick up on what he's saying. Then it hits me. "For real, Wes?"

He nods, sly as hell. "It's not, like, official, but I'm pretty sure she's into me," he says.

"You daaaawg!" I grab him by his shoulders and shake him, but he just laughs the whole time. And who can blame him? A pint-size kid like Wes hooked up with a fine girl like Iesha Steadman? Uncle Kid has a saying for something like that: *That guy's making shots from outside his range.* I decide not to lay that one on Wes and just let him enjoy the moment. We walk down College and he tells me about her, talking Iesha up like she's the finest girl that ever walked Marion East's halls. I just keep telling him what a player he is, feeding his ego and keeping him happy. In fact, his happiness is so infectious that I feel lightened by it, as carefree as if this were mid-summer and not a thing in the world I have to do, instead of the toughest, meanest winter I can remember.

We kid around all the way back home, laughing like old times, and then when we hit my house Wes grabs my hand and pulls me to him, gives me a thump on my back. "It's all good, D," he says. "Now go beat Muncie and quit being in such a funk all the time."

We laugh one more time at that and then go to our houses. I cruise on by my folks with a quick *Hey* and settle into my room for the unbelievable boredom of the hour before I head to the gym. I even try to fill it up with some Friday schoolwork. I hear Jayson trying to rap along with Big Boi through the wall before I realize it. I might not miss crazy Coach Bolden or the dead weight of Tyler Stanford if I skip out to Hamilton, but there's one person I sure as hell will miss: Wes. I mean, not being able to hang with him made these last few weeks even worse, but if I'm spending five days a week, plus practices and games up in Hamilton County next year, Wes might as well be a ghost. And that just doesn't rate for me.

18.

A funny thing happens midway through the second quarter against Muncie: We start balling out. It starts simply enough. We're down five when Stanford gets tangled up in the lane, panicked and off-balance, but when the ball gets poked away it bounces straight to Devin who's alone in the corner to bury a three. Just one of those fluke bounces that go your way once in a while. But when Muncie tries to in-bound long up the court, they overthrow their point guard and I intercept the pass. It's such an overthrow that I'm almost caught off-guard, but when I gather it in, I look up—and there's Devin standing alone in the corner again. I fire a laser to him and he just takes his time, sets, and buries another trey. The whole series of events takes maybe five ticks off the clock, but just like that we're up one and the crowd is jumping after the back-to-back threes.

The Muncie players try to shrug it off, acting like it's just a little speed bump on their way to a sure win, but that's all it takes for us. We've been in-fighting and stumbling to loss after loss, but we're all hungry for a win. Next, Moose gets himself free for a deuce down low, and then

Nick shakes his man and drops in a teardrop. I get in on the act with a rebound bucket, then swat away a weak jumper on the other end to start a break that ends in one more three from Devin. Next thing you know we're heading for the locker room up 8 and feeling better than we have in a month. That's the great thing about hoops—a game can turn on a dime. I've seen it happen a million times, from the NBA to the playground. A team's just cruising along with a comfortable lead, trading buckets, feeling like they're almost destined to win. Then they lose focus, just for a second and *bam!* the other team pounces. Maybe it's a dunk or a blocked shot or even a hard foul that makes tempers flare. Doesn't matter. Once that adrenaline kicks in and the momentum swings to the other side, everything that happened before gets erased in a heartbeat. Give even a weak team a little spark, and they can burn like champions in a hurry.

Bolden doesn't change a thing at halftime. He doesn't even acknowledge that we're playing well, like to say so will jinx us. Instead he hits up the chalkboard. "When they go zone, they're extending way out," he says. "Look for quick flashes to the high post, right at the free throw line. Easy shots there. Or if they jump at you, our bigs can seal down low."

"I feel that," Moose bellows. "Their center's a stiff, fellas."

That draws a few remarks from the room, everyone puffing their chest out and swearing they can't be checked either, but Bolden puts a stop to that. He slams his hand flat against the chalkboard. "Listen! Stay focused. Trash talk isn't going to score buckets. Look for those gaps against the zone. If they come out of it to go man, then just spread and let Nick and Derrick drive on these guys."

There's silence for a second, and I see it flash across Bolden's face. He wants our heads in the game but he's worried he just killed our enthusiasm.

So he slams the chalkboard one more time, so hard the erasers pop off and fall to the floor. Everyone looks at him, wide-eyed. "Focus on our gameplan," he says evenly. Then he raises his voice, lets it boom out like he's ordering a freshman to run laps at practice: "Now let's go get a win!"

"Damn straight!" Murphy yells from the back of the room, and we rise as one to charge back out for the second half.

The next hour was a thing of beauty. Muncie made a run to cut it to two mid-third, but Nick spun in a reverse lay-up to push it back to four, then I jumped a pass and got loose like I was the first one to the gym. I was tempted to go for a reverse, but I kept it simple—just thundered one down two-handed as hard as I could. Right back to a six-point lead, the crowd on its feet, and that was all she wrote.

In the locker room after the game, it felt like instead of knocking off Muncie by thirteen we'd just got finished running Kentucky off the Rupp Arena hardwood. It's such a release to win that even Bolden gets in the spirit. When he walks in and hears that Moose has the music cranked up on that old boombox, he crosses the room real business-like to snap off the sound, only to crank it up the last little bit. The sound gets all fuzzed and crackly on that piece of junk, but we don't care, because the very sight of Coach Bolden turning up Kanye sends everylast one of us into a fit of laughter. Even Bolden laughs, and the locker room is transformed from all those losses, like someone just walked into a funeral home to inform the folks gathered that it's a false alarm—everyone's still alive and feeling fine.

The mood carries over into the night. Most of the team ends up at a house party held by some senior named Warrick Richards, a big sneering football player who stands at the door looking like the only person in the room who's in a foul mood. The only time he moves is to threaten somebody away from his parents' room, or to scare someone with a cigarette into going outside. Everyone else is having a big Friday night though. The living room is a mob scene, a swirl of colors as people dance to music and shout at each other over the noise. It seems like most of Marion East is there, from spindly freshman to jaded seniors. There's a massive pile of winter coats thrown in the corner. Everyone who comes in sheds their layers as soon as they feel the heat from all those bodies crammed into the room. Moose, loosened up by the win and most likely a few beverages being passed around in red cups, is dancing with no less than three fine girls, and when "Ima Boss" comes on the stereo, my man can't contain himself—he hauls his huge frame up onto a table, those three girls bouncing around him like they're in orbit, and the whole room erupts. The table sags like a diving board beneath his weight, but even Warrick Richards cracks a smile at Moose cutting loose—either that, or even he doesn't feel big enough to squash Moose's good time.

"You the boss!" hollers Wes, who's got Iesha practically hanging on him. He smiles at me, clearly loving the scene.

Moose hears him and hops right down off the table, getting up in Wes' face, rhyming along with the Rick Ross verse, and then the two of them shout the chorus back and forth at each other—Moose twice the size of Wes, but both of them giving everything they've got. By the last chorus the floor feels like the room's shaking as much as that table was under Moose. People are feeling so good that when I take a look around I see that even Tyler Stanford has a breezy up on him—he didn't do much more than add a couple garbage buckets, but you can see from across the room that he's talking game with confidence, smiling at her and giving her little playful touches on her arm. Amazing what a win will do.

Once things calm back down, I hang with Wes, talking my boy up to Iesha.

"You're laying it on a little heavy, aren't you?" Iesha says. She's a petite girl, perfect for Wes, with blue eye shadow popping against her mocha face.

"About my boy Wes? Nah. Every word I say is true."

She laughs and buries her head into his shoulder, and he mouths *Thank you* to me.

After that, I figure it's time to bounce. My curfew's approaching fast and I have that trip to Hamilton tomorrow. But when I tell Warrick thanks for the party—he just nods solemnly and thumps my chest with his massive fist—I see that behind him, in the kitchen, Nick is slinking out the back door holding hands with some girl who isn't Jasmine. And then I see Jasmine leaning against the kitchen counter, eyeing him. I figure the way things rolled against Muncie tonight this is as good a time as any to try my luck. After all, if even Tyler Stanford is getting some love, then why not me?

I linger for a second by the kitchen entrance, not wanting to look too eager. I nod to a few guys I recognize from school. They all come over and tell me *Good game*, hyping me like I took down Muncie all on my own, but it's just the kind of entrance I need. I look past them and see Jasmine checking me. I give her a little smile, and she smiles back, then looks down quickly into her cup, swirling it once in her hand as she does.

She says hey when I walk over and, remembering how she teased me for saying *'Sup* at the bookstore, I give an exaggerated tilt of my head, like I think I'm some gangsta, and drawl out a long *'Suuuuup, girl.*

Jasmine laughs, this sweet sound that erases all the tension from her face. "You look like you're feeling pretty good about yourself," she says. Then she smiles again, as if to herself, as she looks down at her cup again. I wonder for a second if she's drinking alcohol, but I know that's just not her style.

"What you knocking back there?" I ask, half-teasing and half-asking to know for sure.

She frowns at me then, tilts the cup my way like she's about to douse me with it. "It's Sprite, Derrick," she says. Then she looks around the party, sees Moose back up dancing on the table again. "Bet some of your boys can't say that."

"Hey, don't be spreading that news around," I say. "Moose isn't doing anybody any harm, but Bolden will sit him in a heartbeat if he finds out."

She jabs her elbow playfully into my ribs. "Oh, you're too easy Derrick," she says, laughing. "I'm just playing. Nobody wants to get Moose in trouble."

I laugh it off, feeling a little foolish that she suckered me so easily. She looks at me then, wide-eyed like she expects me to say something important, and I come up empty. Truth is, something about Jasmine still intimidates me. She lets me struggle for a few seconds before she picks up the conversation for me. "So, I hear you guys won tonight," she says.

"You got that straight," I say. "Muncie's no joke either."

"Well," she says, sloshing her drink around again, "that's great, Derrick."

I can see she's already bored with the subject, but I don't know what else to talk about. Sure, I got plenty on my mind, namely whether or not to head north for next season. But I can't talk to her about that. So I'm standing there trying to think of something to say that doesn't sound stupid—something that isn't about the party or the music or the basketball game, something that would actually interest Jasmine. So instead I say something stupider than all those things combined: "You want to get out of here with me?"

She looks at me like I insulted her mother. "Uh uh, Derrick. You didn't just say that." I start to explain I didn't mean it the way it sounded, but she's not having it. "You think because you won a basketball game I'm just gonna just sneak off with you?" I can feel people turn to stare at us. Her lips are pinched tight like she's debating whether or not to really tear into me. She doesn't say anything else, though, just turns so fast that all I see is those amber ringlets in her hair bobbing away as she makes a straight line through the door, cutting right through the heart of the party like there's nobody else there.

I can still feel people staring at me. They don't want to gawk, but I see their eyes cut my way. Finally, Wes emerges from a crowd of people near the kitchen and gives me a consolation fist-bump. "It's okay," he says. "She'll come around."

"No she won't," I say.

When I creep in the door my mom's waiting. She's sitting on the couch, back straight and eyes wide open while Jayson snoozes away with his feet draped over her lap.

"What time is it, Derrick?" She keeps her voice low enough so as not to wake my little brother, but I can tell she's spitting mad. I can just make out her silhouette from the streetlight bleeding in.

"Eleven-forty-five," I say.

She leans forward as far as she can without disturbing Jayson, then seethes at me. "Which is sure as hell not eleven." She points her index finger straight up, "I swear to God," then she lowers it toward me, "if you start missing curfew after games I'll put the brakes on this season so fast you'll think Coach Bolden's a soft-hearted little schoolgirl."

"I'm sorry, M—"

"Save your sorry, Derrick," she says. "Get home on time or I'll show you sorry. Now march," she says, pointing to my room. She raises her voice just a tad on that last word and Jayson stirs and wriggles on the couch. It reminds me of how he used to sleep fitfully on Mom's lap in the backseat of the car whenever we'd be driving home from trips to my aunt's in Louisville. "Don't you dare sleep in tomorrow, either," she whisper-shouts, then glances over at Jayson to make sure he's still asleep because she doesn't want him to hear what's next. "You be on time up at Hamilton. Being late is rude"

I obey. I go to my room. I look at my nightstand where that book I got to impress Jasmine sits barely opened. I set my gym bag on the floor so quietly you'd think it was a feather. I slip my winter coat to the floor. I pry my shoes from my feet without untying them. I peel off my jeans and drop them in a crumple on top of my coat. Then, sweatshirt and all, I climb into bed, the sheets cold against my legs, and wonder how I could have made such a mess out of a night that started with a win.

19.

It's no secret where we're going, so my dad doesn't have to slide up side streets like Uncle Kid did. Instead, he gets us onto I-69 early Saturday morning and punches it straight up to Fishers. When we hit the exit, it doesn't even seem like the right place because after we get past the gas stations and a sprawling hospital, we're out in the middle of a field that's barren and choked with snow and ice. Not what you'd expect when you're just a couple miles from a huge school like Hamilton Academy. It's just a reminder that the landscape is still catching up to the shift of people north. When I was younger, there was nothing up here.

Like he's sensing my thoughts, Dad says, "By the time you're in college, I bet this place looks as developed as downtown."

We cruise past a park, empty in winter except for a couple people bundled in coats while walking their dogs across soccer fields that stretch to a distant row of trees. It all seems so foreign, all this open space. I find myself looking around for signs of city clamor. Not until we get a few more blocks and see Hamilton Academy rising above a neighborhood do we see life again. Then it's a snag of traffic backed up by a Starbucks and a series of neat, new stores: a bakery, a printing shop, a flower boutique.

"Nice places up here," my dad says while he merges onto the main road and shifts into the left lane. The way he says it, though, reminds me just a little bit of Uncle Kid. Not that my dad's anything like him in mannerisms, but here we are up in Hamilton County and he's stressing how nice everything is, just like Kid kept saying how everyone up here takes care of each other.

"So you think I should transfer up here, Dad?" I ask.

"Ah, Derrick," he says. He shakes his head as if pained by the whole process. "That's up to you, son. This is your basketball career and nobody else's." He looks at me, blinks a few times behind those glasses, this patient gesture to see if I understand.

Thing is, though, for as much as I get frustrated with adults telling me what to do, I sit here and all of a sudden I'd kill for some basic instructions. *Do this, Derrick. Transfer to Hamilton.* Or, *Forget these guys and stay put at Marion East.* And my dad's the guy that could do that. I mean, they're offering him a job, after all, and if he'd just tell me what to do I'd jump and be okay with it. But my dad has never been one of those fathers. He wants you to think for yourself, work things out on your own, which I guess is great when it comes to math homework, but doesn't help me a single bit right now when I'm more conflicted than I have ever been in my life.

While I tease all this out—my dad's potential job, my mom's allegiance to Marion East, my frustration with Coach Bolden, my friendship with Wes—the car keeps rolling. Down 116th and then up to 126th—that same grand entrance that Uncle Kid took me in. The trees are bare now. January has made the grounds as beige and dreary as any other in Indiana. But even on a day like this, the high school seems to rise up like a cathedral compared to squat old Marion East. Standing by the top step is the Hamilton coach, Henry Treat. He's tan in winter, with almost a bronze tint to his face. He's wearing the same practiced smile he always does, whether his team's playing poorly or balling out. I see it widen just a little, pushing his glasses up just a tiny bit on his face. He runs a hand through his thick black hair, almost a nervous tic, like he's always got to make sure it's just right. As my dad and I climb the stairs to meet him, he extends that hand first to Dad, and then to me. He squeezes hard, gives my hand three solid pumps like he's trying to prove through his handshake that he's a perfect, God-fearing man.

"Good to meet you, Derrick," he almost shouts. Then his smile opens up to reveal his perfect bright whites. "Let me show you around our little school here." There's something about him I immediately dislike. I don't know what—maybe it's the way he walks with his back straightened in perfect posture or the way he drops his voice into some fake humility when he says *our little school* or maybe it's just instinct when I see someone wearing a navy blue Hamilton Academy sweatshirt. It's not that he does anything wrong. In fact, he's a perfectly nice guy. But I can feel myself bristling as we head inside the school.

The hallways gleam. It's like walking into some kind of museum, everything polished and spotless. You get the feeling if you so much as scuff your shoe on the floor you'll get kicked out. There are no dented lockers, no chipped floor tiles, no torn posters, no places where graffiti has been painted over with a shade that doesn't quite match the rest of the wall. There's no doubt that this place is a totally different world from Marion East.

"I want to show you our pride and joy," Coach Treat says, smiling at us again.

I figure we're heading to the gym, but Coach Treat must know that my parents care about more than hoops, because next thing I know he pushes open double doors that reveal a massive, shining science lab. It looks like something you'd see on a crime show on TV: there are beakers and bell jars of all shapes and sizes; there are cylinders and flasks and funnels; burners and torches and microscopes; computer-looking monitors I don't know the name for hooked up at every desk. Now, science is not my thing, but I can hear my dad almost gasp. It's not like he thinks I'm going to all of a sudden turn into some physicist if I come up here, but I'm smart enough to know this lab is a symbol for something else. When you come from a school that has a science lab with a couple tarnished beakers and a tattered periodic table hanging on the wall, and then you see this? Well, you'd have to be pretty dim not to see which is the better school.

"Now, me?" Coach Treat says. "I couldn't tell you the first thing about how to use this equipment. But our teachers here do a great job. We even have a retired professor from Indiana come up and guest lecture a couple times a year. The kids, they actually seem to enjoy this."

It's just more salesmanship, I guess—trying to make himself sound like a regular guy even as he shows off the advantages of his school—but it is impressive.

"Let me show you some other classrooms," he says. He takes us down wing after wing of the school, answering my dad's questions as we walk. I learn that Hamilton Academy has "college days" each semester when recruiters from almost every school in Indiana visit to talk to students about their campuses; that they rank third in the state in students who graduate with advanced placement credits; that students have a chance to take summer trips to Spain or Italy or France. And, he adds, the bulk of costs for those who can't afford it are covered by donations and scholarships. We've just finished strolling down sophomore wing and seeing where I'd have homeroom next year—a computer lab that has brand new Macs at each desk—when Treat finally turns to me again. "You're awfully quiet, Derrick. You have any questions?"

"Nah," I say, then catch a glare from Dad, and add. "No, sir."

Treat smiles. "Well, maybe this will wake you up a little." With that, he makes a quick turn and we walk down a little hallway lined with trophy cases. They're surprisingly full for a school that was just 2A not too long ago. I see the plaques for each time they've won our Regional and their State title trophy from last year, but these are flanked by trophies for every sport you can imagine: women's volleyball, men's golf, softball, racquetball, lacrosse, tennis, everything. Then we hit the end of the hallway and Coach Treat offers me a quick smile before he pushes on the thick double doors, which open with an automatic whoosh.

He's got all the lights up in the gym, as if it were a game night, even though we're the only people there. The effect is amazing, like we're walking into some sacred ground. Their gym is huge, bigger than some college arenas, and I know that when Hamilton Academy takes the hardwood every single one of those 7,000 blue seats will be filled with faithful fans, not to mention a handful of college scouts scoping for talent. The court is polished so high I can see my shoe's reflection with each step. The windows above the bleachers on the east end let in some winter sunlight. They've got the scoreboard lit up so it reads HAMILTON 63 VISITORS 63, with the time at 0:05. Treat points to it and says, "Looks like we've got just enough time for one last shot." Then he walks over to the scorer's table and picks up a Hamilton East jersey. He looks down at it and smiles, then shows me the back, where I see my last name and my number 25 stitched in white. He tosses it my way and it flutters right into my hand. "See how that fits," he says, so I peel off my sweatshirt and hand it to my dad, then throw the jersey over my t-shirt. When I look up, Treat has a ball in his hands and he's standing at the top of the key.

Like some schoolboy, he starts to call the play-by-play as he dribbles: "Five ticks left and Hamilton's ball on the inbounds. It comes to the top of the key, and they're looking for Derrick Bowen here." It's silly, but infectious—no player can resist it, no matter how old they are, so I play right along.

"They look for Bowen on the baseline." I flare along the baseline, arms extended for the pass.

"But it's a fake!" I drop my hands and dart back toward the bucket.

"Alley-oop for the win!" He lobs the rock toward the rim, and even in my jeans and street shoes I rise easily to catch it and flush it down. Treat cups his hands around his mouth and imitates the noise of a crowd going wild for the win. That coaxes a little laugh even from my dad, who until that moment seemed far more interested in the classrooms than what might go down in this palace.

Coach Treat, smiling so big it's like we just won a real game, strides down the lane with his arms outstretched. When he gets to the baseline where I'm standing he offers his right hand in another handshake and then pulls me into him and gives me a few slaps on the back. "Let me tell you something, Derrick. Things like that can happen if you come up here. And it's a whole lot better when you've got a gym full of rabid fans cheering you on."

The tour's not done though. Dad and I follow Treat off the court and down the tunnel to the locker room. When he opens the door, I see at last the depth of differences between Marion and Hamilton. Sure, the classrooms are nicer, but learning still comes down to what you put in. And, man, that gym is crazy slick, but it's still all about what you throw down between the lines. But the locker room? This is what I'd imagine Big Ten locker rooms look like. There's plush blue carpet wall-to-wall with the Hamilton Academy Giant staring up like a menace in the middle of the floor. Lining two walls, there are spacious wooden lockers polished to a shine just as high as the court, with a clean, crisp jersey hung in each one, and two or three pairs of fresh kicks tucked in the slot below. There's a whiteboard stretching across an entire wall, clean and impressive compared to the dusty old chalkboard Bolden still uses. Beneath that, there's a rack of new leather balls, not a worn one in the lot. There are blue folding chairs with cushioned backs stacked by the door. There's a cooler propped open with Gatorade and cokes on ice. Even the showers look nice—clean and new, instead of the old stained things we have down at Marion, where you stand on an old cement floor that smells of mold.

But that's not all. The crowning touch, on the wall opposite the white board, is a flat-screen TV bigger than any I've ever seen in my life, and it's currently playing Hamilton Academy highlights on a loop.

The screen's so big that when I see Lorbner dunk on some chump or see Deon Charles leave someone with a crossover, it feels like they're actually there in front of me, flesh and blood. I notice too that the TV is hooked up to a fine-looking stereo, with speakers about a half-foot taller than my boy Wes. On cue, Treat picks up a tablet that's resting on a chair by one of the lockers, scrolls down it for a second or two, then taps it, and just like that an old Tupac track comes trucking out of those speakers. He's playing a censored version, but I don't care. The sound is incredible and makes that old junk in our locker room sound even worse by comparison.

Treat smiles at me, clearly proud. I bet he couldn't tell you Tupac from Jay-Z if he saw pictures of them, but he knows what impresses players. He raises his eyebrows, as if to ask *What do you think?*

"As my friend Wes would say, that," I offer, "is butter."

He laughs, though I can tell there's a moment of confusion. He can't tell if what I said is good or not, but he seems pleased, satisfied like a man who has everything going according to plan.

I steal a look at my dad. He's just staring down at his shoes, his mind totally somewhere else.

Lorbner's too big for his car. He rolls in a red Audi A7, a brand new model. It looks pretty sweet on the road and it's the baddest ride I've ever been in, but I can't help think that Lorbner looks like he's driving a bumper car. Part of that is because Deon Charles sat behind Vasco, rather than behind me, and made his big man push his seat up to give some leg room in the back. We cruise up Southeastern Parkway, and then Vasco zips onto I-69 and lets the car roar a little bit. We get to the next exit in the blink of an eye. I have to hold myself back from audibly oohing at the car's get up and go.

Charles leans up from the back seat, says, "That's how we roll up North."

The idea here isn't to impress me with Vasco's wheels, though that doesn't hurt. I know the goal is to have the two best Hamilton players recruit me. Coach Treat shook my dad's hand about twenty minutes ago. They left me to hang with Lorbner and Charles—no particular instructions, other than to meet back up in a couple hours so my dad could get me.

"We'll meet some of the other players for lunch," Vasco says. He's got no trace of an accent, but he speaks in this formal, rigid kind of way, like everything he says is part of some memorized speech. Off the court, he doesn't look quite so imposing. You can see in his face that he's still just another teenager, with a few pimples and little thin whiskers where he missed shaving. If you were just looking at his face, you sure wouldn't think he was the top big man in his entire class.

"Hey, hit up some music, V," Charles says, slapping his big man on the shoulder.

Vasco does as he's told, but what comes out of those speakers is stuff I've never heard before, some kind of rhythmic, synthed-up thumping without any lyrics.

"Awww, V, what is this shit?" Charles asks.

"My car, my music," Vasco says calmly.

Charles looks at me, shaking his head and rolling his eyes. "Man, I've been working for two years to get this kid to listen to real music. Maybe you'll have better luck with him."

The two of us laugh then, sharing some fun at Vasco's expense.

Immediately I feel more at ease with Deon Charles than I ever have in almost a full season running in the same backcourt as Nick. Vasco doesn't find us funny though. "My car, my music," he repeats.

That just makes Deon laugh harder, like Vasco's performing some kind of stand up. "Don't worry, Bowen," he says. "V's actually got a cool side to him. It just takes a long time to see it."

We zip down 116th Street, past stretches of new condos and houses, all of them gray and almost featureless, like some conveyer belt just rolled model after model right out onto the lots. Soon, though, the lawns start to get bigger and I can only see the houses tucked way back up the winding drives because all of the trees are bare. We hang a right and cut through a neighborhood that looks like it must be home to millionaires only. I see clear blue water behind some of the houses, and boats anchored to little docks.

"Hoo, check that," Deon says, tapping on his window. When I look I see a black Lamborghini parked in front of a mansion. "And Vasco thinks he's a bad-ass in his Audi," Deon adds, shaking Vasco's shoulders as he teases.

I widen my eyes and nod to Deon, trying to find the right response to seeing such riches, but inside I'm twisted in a knot. It's nice, all of it. More than nice: the kind of thing I can't dream of unless it's attached to a larger dream of an NBA contract. But I can't shake the feeling that things up here are too perfect, like somehow I don't belong in a place like this. I mean, what would these people think if I were riding in Uncle Kid's bucket instead?

On our left I see a country club. Even in the dead of winter the fairways look so crisp that if it weren't blustery and cold you'd expect men to be out there, chipping away a Saturday. We curve on around, Vasco taking it at a steady cruise now that we're in residential areas, and then finally hang a right on another main road. Every now and then I see water to our left again, and it looks like a massive lake, one I didn't even know existed up here. I see a sign saying FALL CREEK ROAD AHEAD and though I recognize the name, I know this is a far cry from where I walk along Fall Creek Parkway.

Vasco makes a quick turn and we screech into a parking lot, a two-story restaurant rising in front of us. The three of us walk through the cold, Vasco in front. He opens the front door for me and Deon. When I finally get in and my eyes adjust to the darkness, I realize that it's basically just a sports bar. But like everything else up here, it's a cut above anything I've seen. Flat screens everywhere. Here they're situated above fireplaces with leather couches facing them; a shiny bar stocked with bottles that just look expensive; big, leather booths with a small flat screen next to each one; even a stage in the corner, where a lonely mic stands next to a couple amps and some stools. The place is packed on a Saturday afternoon, the bar boisterous with guys watching early college games. I feel a little overwhelmed until Deon points back to a corner. "There we are," he says. Then I see a cluster of guys decked out in Hamilton Academy blue, like a splash of sky there in the dim restaurant, all of them waving to us to come over. Vasco tells us to go on, but then he drifts off, like he doesn't really care about joining his teammates.

The starters I know, but as Deon makes a round of introductions, my head starts to swim and the names get all jumbled. They all have their different looks, different faces, but each one wears the same sure smile that seems to be uniform up here, like Coach Treat has trained each one of them. They're perfectly friendly, but I don't feel a connection with any of them. It's not just that they're white—in fact, only about half of them are—but they just make me feel as if I'm some kind of alien. Only Deon keeps things light: any time someone asks me about the school he tells them nobody wants to talk school on a Saturday; when one of them chuckles when I look puzzled by some items on the menu, Deon snaps that there are some things down in the city that might confuse some spoiled kid from Fishers. Every time he does something like that, the other players laugh. I feel conflicted—it seems like they're only laughing with Deon because they have to. But they're nice. Every single one. No matter how uncomfortable I feel there's not a thing I can point to for an explanation why.

"Don't worry, Bowen," Deon whispers at one point. "They're more nervous than you are. They know if they don't impress you, you're gonna drop 30 a game on them for three more years."

At last the food comes—massive burgers with fries piled high beside them. Then everyone starts chowing, and things become easier. After all, we're just a bunch of guys getting their grub on and watching a Big Ten game on the big-screen. I'm about halfway through when I feel a hand on my shoulder. It's Vasco. Until that moment I'd forgotten that he ditched us at the door. "When you're done, I want to talk to you," he says, again very formal, so much so that it's kind of ominous. I find myself worrying that I made some mistake I'm not aware of, like the Rich People Police are going to tell me, *Sorry, kid, but we have to ask you to go back to Marion County now.*

Vasco has no such thing in mind; he just wants to get me off to the side to talk privately. We stand at the edge of the bar section. It feels kind of strange, like Vasco has taken me as close as possible to a world we're not allowed to enter as high schoolers, but I get the feeling that if he wanted to he could step up to that bar—forget his acne and wispy facial hair—and order whatever he wanted without anyone saying a word.

"Never mind those guys," Vasco says, nodding toward his teammates. "You and me? We are different." He looks at me like he expects me to jump in, but frankly I don't know what he means. "There are some good players over there," he explains. "Every single one of them has a chance to play in college. But they are not like us. Derrick, you and me, we can stop the game. Do you know what I mean?"

I nod. Now I do understand. There are those times when I get zoned in when it feels like everyone else is in slow motion, or like I've got everyone on a string: fake one way and watch everyone jump, then dart the other way. Or there are times when I see my teammates look at me, some small hint of need in their eyes that they'll never admit, but a look that says: *You take over now, D.* "I feel you," I tell Vasco. Then again, I watched Deon torch us pretty good, and I bet he feels like he can stop the game sometimes too.

Like he's reading my mind, Vasco says, "Even Deon. He's a good player. A very good shooter. He'll be a nice off-guard at a good school for four years. But he needs me to get those looks. There are only two people in this entire place who have a shot at the NBA, and they are both standing right here." He looks down at me from his 6'9" height and lets that sink in, his face forming that same serious expression that Coach Bolden gets when he's trying to drive a point home. Then he looks around and kind of frowns and shakes his head. "That's why you and I don't feel at home in places like this. I mean, there is nothing wrong with that, but we belong somewhere else. We know this is all just temporary, just four years we have to go through until we can really make our mark. These other guys? It matters because it is going to be the best time of their entire career."

Vasco grabs my shoulder then, turns me back toward the table. He's a powerful guy, because he moves me about as effortlessly as my dad marching Jayson back to his room for misbehaving. As we walk, though, he drives home his point. "I don't care about Hamilton Academy, Derrick," he says. "I'll win championships here with or without you. And then I'm never looking back. But don't hurt yourself by staying down at Marion East because of some sense of duty." He says that word *duty* like it's a punch line. "You are going the same places I am. You just need to decide which school can best help you get there."

As he says that we arrive back at the team tables. Vasco sits down and starts cracking jokes with his teammates, joining in their banter while they watch the game as if he's just one of the guys, like everything he said never happened. Then he catches me looking at him and gives a nod, only it's so quick I can't even be sure. He could be conveying some secret just between us—*it's just about you Derrick, not the schools or the coaches or anyone else*—or it could have just been a meaningless twitch.

Either way, I have to hand it to Vasco. No way did I expect him to lay that trip on me. I'm pretty sure Coach Treat's thick, sculpted hair would have turned gray on the spot if he'd been listening in. And I have to admit it: For some reason it makes me like Vasco more than anyone else I've met in Hamilton County.

We head back to Hamilton Academy. Deon uses the last few miles to hammer home some selling points. He explains that Coach Treat is a lot more relaxed than he seems on the surface. He insists that the school isn't some hyper-strict place where nobody has any fun. And he stresses, over and over, that if I'm on board, they'll have enough talent to go on an unprecedented run, taking state title after state title. Vasco basically nods along, like a student half-asleep during a history lecture.

When he pulls into the parking lot, I see my dad sitting in his car, engine running so he can stay warm, a sad little cloud of exhaust rising while he waits. As soon as I see him, I feel this surprising little lift, like I've been away from home for a month in some foreign land. I try not to let that excitement show to Deon and Vasco though. I give them some fist-bumps as we part. I thank them for showing me around. When they tell me that they'd love to team up with me next year, I tell them I'll think about it. And I mean it. Forget school pride, forget coaches, forget arena capacities: Lacing 'em up with those two would be a thrill every time out.

Just as I'm about to cross the parking lot to my dad, another car pulls up. It takes me a second, but then I remember where I've seen it—it's that black Lexus with the tint job that was following Uncle Kid around for a while. It pulls in right next to Vasco's Audi. As soon as the engine stops, out pops a slender white guy—a little gray at his temples but still a young, athletic face—in a Hamilton Academy jacket. I don't know this guy's name, but I recognize him as an assistant who spends every Hamilton game perched right next to Coach Treat. He gives a quick nod to Vasco and Deon, but he's here to see me. He extends his hand, thrusting it at me like a threat. "Hey there, Derrick," he says, his breath visible in the cold, "I'm Doug Campbell, Coach Treat's top assistant." He says all this in an overly friendly way, like I'm supposed to all of a sudden like him because he sits next to Coach Treat. There's something too slick and hurried about him, and I don't like the way he keeps shaking my hand while he talks. When I look over his shoulder toward my dad, he leans in, pressing the issue. "Hey, now, Derrick. I know these guys have been showing you around, and I know the success we've had up here speaks for itself. That gym? That school? I know that's enough for most guys." Then he lets go of my hand, only to take a card from his pocket and press it back into my palm. "Some guys need a little more encouragement though. You got anything special you need, you just call me," he says.

Then, before I can say anything in response, he lets go of me and turns toward where my dad's parked. "All yours now, Mr. Bowen," he shouts, waving to my dad like they're old buddies.

We're almost back to Fall Creek Parkway before either of us says anything. It's as awkward as watching a movie with your parents when some sex scene comes on. You just want to pretend like it's not happening. Finally, my dad asks, tentatively, "Well, what did you think?"

"I don't know," I say. I want to elaborate, to explain how I like the idea of playing with Deon and Vasco, how it would be great to get out from under Coach Bolden's control, but that it's mixed with some kind of uneasiness—a distrust, I guess—of some of the people up there, especially the very last one to talk to me. I can't seem to get my head around all that, much less explain it to my dad, so I just repeat, "I don't know."

"It's okay, son," he says. "I don't know either." And then we cruise the rest of the way in silence.

20.

After my visit to Hamilton on Saturday and a slow Sunday grind of church and homework and, finally, another brief attempt to read that book I picked up to impress Jasmine, I'm ready to hit the gym on Monday evening. It's February now. We've only got five games left until Sectionals start. Maybe I'll be on the North side next winter. But if I'm going to make anything of my freshman season, we've got to build on that nice game we had against Muncie. So I hit up practice with a little bounce in my step, only to see that nobody's out on the court when I arrive. All the balls are put up, the baskets are still raised, and the lights aren't even on yet. For a second I think maybe I'm just way early, but when I open the locker room doors, I see my teammates, each of them seated at their locker and still in their street clothes.

Coach Murphy stands along one wall with his arms crossed. He doesn't even look at me when I come in, but says, "No practice tonight. Team meeting."

I head to my locker, full of dread. Nobody's making eye contact. Team meetings in the middle of the season never mean anything good.

I find myself expecting the worst—Moose got busted for drinking on Friday night or somebody's quit because of playing time or—and this one hits me with a cold chill—word's out about me visiting Hamilton and Bolden's going to call me out in front of everyone. When I reach my locker I see a single sheet of paper and a pencil sitting on the seat.

"That's for the meeting," Coach Murphy says. "Just go ahead and sit." When Coach Murphy's barking out orders, I figure things are about to get real.

One by one, the players file in—Nick, Royce, Stanford—and one by one their casual expressions change to stone cold seriousness as they sit there in silence at Murphy's orders. Moose tries once to crack a joke—"Who died?" he shouts—but nobody laughs.

Eventually, after we've all been stewing for a good fifteen minutes, Coach Bolden walks through the door, an epic frown etched on his face. He takes his sweet time, turning his stare on each of us one by one. I'm more sure than ever that something is about to go deeply wrong.

"Friday night, something important happened," Bolden begins, not breaking that frown even as he speaks. I figure that's it—someone got busted drinking at the party. I wonder if it's Moose. I immediately start writing this season off as lost and begin looking ahead to next winter up in Hamilton County.

But Coach Bolden pulls out a folding chair, sits down on it and leans forward. When he does, he looks up at us with his face emptied of that anger. "What happened was," he says, "we played good basketball for the first time in a month."

You can feel a sigh of relief coming from every locker, like the comedown in a car that's narrowly missed a crash. We're all too smart to relax though. We know Joe Bolden never called a team meeting to give everyone a high five and hand out donuts. Sure enough, he looks down at his hands, which are clasped in front of him as if he's about to say a prayer before Thanksgiving dinner. He gives a deep sigh before looking back up at us with that hard stare of his. "The problem is it's not going to happen again—" he holds up his hand to fend off any protests that we've turned a corner, that we're rolling now. "No. It won't happen again because that happened by chance. All it proved is that we can be a good team if we'd just get out of our own way."

He nods a signal to Murphy, who strides into the center of the room. He stands there for a second, straight as an oak, and slowly swivels his head back and forth until he makes eye contact with every last player. His stare isn't as imposing as Bolden's, but when it lands on me I can't help but look away, still nervous that somehow everyone can see my betrayal as plainly as if it were stitched on my shirt. "You each had a pencil and paper on your chair when you came in," Murphy begins. As he talks he paces around the locker room, enjoying his moment in the limelight. "What Coach and I want you to do is simple. Imagine we're playing Lawrence North in the Sectional Finals. We're down one, with the ball, only five seconds left. We've got one last shot to win it. Got it?" He looks around and everyone nods, like we're in the classroom and eager to prove to the teacher we're following the lesson.

"Now imagine," he begins again, "just imagine to yourself, who you think should score the next bucket. Don't say it out loud, and don't tell the person next to you. Just think about it and keep the answer to yourself." He pauses again, then glances at Bolden, who just nods right back as if to say, *Go ahead.* "Now write that answer down on your piece of paper, fold it up, and hand it to Coach."

A few guys write down their answer immediately, get up and hand it to Coach, who accepts each ballot without even looking at the player, like he's just a ticket taker trying to get people through the aisles. I know what my answer is: It's me, since I'm the best player on the team at creating my own shot. But something about the way this is playing out makes me pause. It feels like a trap of some kind. I look around the room for some cues, but everyone is keeping things to themselves. Even Moose looks away as quickly as he can, jots down a name on his paper and hurries it up to Coach Bolden. At last, I figure there's no downside in writing my own name. After all, if I get the most votes that will at last be a signal to everyone in the room who the best player on the squad is.

The only person to wait longer than me to take their vote up is Nick. He gives me a long look as he walks back to his locker, then gives a quick shake of his head like he's disgusted.

Once we're all seated again, Bolden starts to unfold the ballots, reading them like they're the names of the dead at some memorial service.

"Moose," he says, then crumples the paper and lets it drop. "Derrick," he says, again crumpling and dropping the paper once he's read it. Then it's Devin, then Royce, then Stanford—and at that a few guys stifle laughs since the only person on the planet that thinks Stanford should take a big shot is that thin sophomore himself. He opens the next piece of paper and pauses. "Me," he says. "Somebody wrote 'Me.'" He stares at the paper again in disbelief, then holds it up for us to examine, like evidence at a trial.

"Sorry, Coach," Moose says. "That one was mine."

"Good Lord, son," Bolden says. "Sometimes I wonder about you." Everyone laughs at that, even Moose, but soon enough Bolden is back to the ballots, reading name after name as the crumpled papers form a little mound at his feet. When he's done, he looks up at us. Then he stands and walks to the chalkboard and asks: "So who had the right answer?"

By my count, I got four votes to two each for Moose and Nick, but even I'm not stupid enough to shout it out. Instead it's Nick who raises his hand. Bolden points at him with a piece of chalk, and Nick says, "Derrick got the most votes, Coach." Hearing him say that is about as shocking as hearing Pastor Baxter tell the congregation there's no Heaven. But there it is: Nick Snarks owning up to the fact that I'm the one the team wants taking the shots that matter most.

"Yes," Coach says, "but that's not the right answer. Not at all." Just like that, the pride I felt a moment ago deflates, and—against my own will—I start thinking back to Hamilton Academy and how nobody there was so intent on breaking people down. I don't have time to sulk though, because now Coach shouts at us, nearly jumping off the floor with the force of his volume: "What's the right answer?"

Nobody says a word.

"I'll tell you the wrong answer," he continues. "The dead wrong answer is *Me*. Now, only Moose actually wrote down that word, but be honest for a second. If you wrote your own name, you were really writing *Me*. How many of you did that?" Moose raises his hand straight off, since he can't hide it. After a beat Stanford raises his hand too. "Be honest!" Coach shouts. Finally, Royce and Devin lift their hands too. I put mine up, my palm so hot with anger at this whole ordeal that I feel like people can see it glowing like an ember in the air. When I look at

Nick, I see that he's not man enough to admit it. He just has his hands folded in his lap like some choir boy.

"Wrong answer, all of you," Bolden shouts. "Who knows the right answer?!" Again, there's silence. One by one, the heads in the locker room drop, each of us shamed by our own ignorance, by the anger it brings out of Coach Bolden. "Coach Murphy," he says, his tone calm again. "If we're down by one with five seconds left in the Sectional Finals, who do you want to make the last bucket?"

Murphy, who'd retreated back to the door as Bolden read off the names, steps forward again. "Coach, that's an easy one. I want Marion East to make the last bucket."

"Right answer!" Coach shouts. And then he scrawls it on the chalkboard, pressing so hard that you can see flakes of the chalk fall off as he writes. "Marion East! It doesn't matter what person makes it, as long as they have Marion East written on their jersey! And, damnit boys, until you get that we'll just be fighting ourselves, playing basketball way below our potential."

I feel sick. Angry, too, at having to be yelled at even after a win, but sick because I know—somewhere deep inside, no matter how much I want to deny it—that Bolden has a point.

After a few more minutes, Bolden chases the reserves out, leaving just me, Nick, Moose, Royce, Devin and Stanford. Bolden brings us into a semi-circle by the chalkboard.

"I want to tell you guys something," Bolden says. He's calm now, talking to us like we're just chatting over a lunch table. "We still have time to be good. We might just be six and eight, but I swear on all that's holy we can make some noise down the stretch. But everyone in this room needs to give something up."

He takes up his chalk again, and writes on the board:

5 –

4 –

3 –

2 –

1 –

"We've got five starting spots and six players in this room," he says. "Follow me here."

The first name he puts up is Moose's at the 5, which is no shocker. But he turns to Moose as soon as he's done and says, "Moose, you've got to give something up for us. Can you do that?"

"Sure, Coach," he says. Everyone knows there's no other answer acceptable.

"You've got to give up your body. We're going to beat teams by running right past them, going up-tempo every chance we get. And that's gonna hurt like hell on you. Every time we do conditioning, you find a way to opt out or Coach Murphy gives you a breather, but every game from here on out you've got to run until you're ready to drop. Then I'll give you a breather and put you back out there to run again. Will you give that to us?"

"Can do, Coach," he says, but all of us are silently wondering just how long Moose can last in an up-tempo game.

Then Bolden chalks in Varney and Bedford at the two and three spots. Immediately, I realize that means it's coming down to me and

Nick at the point, but I don't so much as breathe. "You two are keeping your starting spots," Bolden says, "but you need to give us something. You're going to give up touches. You'll still get yours, but our first option to score is somewhere else. If you can't give that to us, then I'll find somebody else to put in your spots, even if they can't shoot a lick."

They nod obediently.

Then Coach turns to Stanford. He puts a hand gently on that slender shoulder. "Stanford, you need to give us your starting spot. Son, someday you'll be a load down low. You're agile and skilled, but you need to spend a year lifting weights and eating steak and eggs. You'll still get minutes, but they're gonna be to spell big man there—" he points to Moose—"when his legs get wobbly."

Stanford nods, accepting his fate.

"Good kid," Bolden says. "You keep working and your day will come."

I realize, of course, that that leaves me and Nick with only the point guard spot and a post position. Everyone in the room knows something doesn't add up, but Bolden starts in again before anyone can even react.

"That leaves you two," he says. "Here's what you have to give up." He pauses, gives us a real long look like he might just kill us and bury us in a shallow grave if we don't man up. "You need to give up your stupid grudge against each other. I thought you'd be smart enough to figure out that the two best players on a team need to work together, but it's been months now and you two are still fighting like dogs over a chicken bone. Just let it go, you two."

"It's done, Coach," Nick says. He doesn't look at me though.

With that, Coach writes Nick's name in at the 1, and I feel a stab of anger in my heart.

"That leaves you, Derrick," Bolden says. He stares at me, and everyone else stares with him. I'm the only one left he has to address, so it feels like everything suddenly hinges on me, the kind of pressure I'd love if it were those Sectional Finals and we were down one, but not with this kind of treatment. "There's only one spot left, and it's at the four. Now when I told Moose he needed to give us everything he had physically, I didn't tell him that he's only got the second worst job. The toughest one is for you, Derrick." He lets that challenge hang in the air for a second while he gauges my reaction. I try to show no reaction at all. "The goal is to get our five best on the floor, but to do that it means every night out you're gonna check the other team's four. And every night out, he'll be bigger and stronger, and he's gonna try and take you down on those blocks like he's about to mug you. And I'll tell you, Derrick, sometimes he will. You have to give to us the embarrassment of having some big take it to you now and then."

"I can do that, Coach," I say. There's nothing else to say, I suppose. I mean, every day—every single day—I've stayed after practice to work, and this is how I get rewarded. But I can't exactly say that. So I repeat, "I can do that," and nod my head. Bolden looks as if, of all the players he's addressed, I'm the only one he doesn't believe. I see this little flicker go across his eyes, like he senses something off. He lets it pass. I guess he's put a lot of effort into planning out this night, so he's not going to let it go sour now.

"If you do that, Derrick, then we all have to give you help every time your man catches it in the paint." He looks at everyone else, making sure they understand. Once he's satisfied they do, he scrawls my name next to the 4, completing the lineup. A few guys fidget, and Moose steals a glance at his watch. We've been in this locker room a long time. Coach, even though he has his back turned, somehow senses it. "We're not done yet," he shouts, his voice reverberating off those walls.

He turns to us and smiles. "I haven't told you what you get back," he says. "If you'll all give those things, what you get back is a chance to do something special. If we work our tails off on the defensive end, when we get defensive stops, we're going to do something." He shoots his gaze back at Murphy, who we'd all but forgotten. "What are we going to do, Coach Murphy?"

"Run the other team the hell off the floor," he shouts emphatically.

"That's right," Bolden says. "We get that ball and we're gone. First pass is to Nick, and you're pushing it right up the floor. And, Nick, you better bury whatever grudge you have with Derrick because he's your first look for a bucket." He turns to me again. "You think there's a four man in the state that can keep up with you in transition?"

"Not unless he plays for the Pacers," I say, trying hard not to grin at the prospect of getting out on the break with open space.

"We'll run teams until they quit," Bolden says. "Or at least until they have to go small like us. And then let's just see if there's a team out there with four perimeter guys as good as ours." He looks around one more time, making sure we're with him. "What is it you guys say? 'You feel me?' Well. Do you?"

"I feel you, Coach," Nick says, setting off a chorus from everyone else. I'm a little late to chime in, and I get that look from Bolden again—that little flicker across his face like he just remembered an insult he hasn't quite forgiven.

"Be back here tomorrow night, usual time," he says. "And be ready to get after it."

At home, I manage my way through a normal dinner without having anyone bring up anything about basketball. For once, I'm glad my parents force us to talk about school, happy to hear them gently argue about some political issue I could care less about. Later, Jayson pops into my room.

"How was practice tonight, D?" he asks. I know he's just trying to put off doing his homework, but I also know there's no easy way to get rid of him. For his age, he's got a hyper-developed sense for when somebody's trying to brush him off. I've seen him wear down even my mother when she tries to give evasive answers about what he's getting for his birthday. So I figure I better answer him straight.

In fact, I tell him every last detail. And as I do, I feel myself getting slightly angry again at having been pushed to the 4-spot. I lean back on my bed and look around my walls. I bet nobody ever asked Derrick Rose or Chris Paul to play a forward spot. Good coaches are supposed to let players do what they do best, not experiment with them like they're in some chemistry lab. I know Coach Treat isn't asking me to come up to Hamilton so I can bang it out down low with some bigs. Hell, no. I'll be running the show from the point. Jayson must sense my dissatisfaction, because he doesn't respond. He just sits there under my LeBron poster, biting his lower lip. I realize that I haven't even been looking at him as I talk, just unloading on him like he's some shrink.

"Anyway," I say, "that's the plan. Doesn't matter to me. Whatever."

Now Jayson looks annoyed, his eyebrows pinching down in the same pained look my mom gives when you disobey her in public. "What do you mean 'Whatever'? Don't you care?"

"Yeah, but—" and I stop myself right there before I spill all the transfer plans to Jayson.

"But what?"

"Nothing, Jay."

"Nah. What's up?"

He's starting to get that pestering tone like he does with my parents so I give him something to latch onto. "I just mean this year's about in the books anyway. We'll do what we can, but the problems this team has won't get fixed until next year." In a way, concealing my plans to transfer makes that transfer more real than ever before. After all, if it weren't something I wanted to do, I wouldn't have to lie about it.

"That's some mess, D," Jayson says. He stands up, so angry he seems on the verge of tears. "That's not the Derrick I know, man. I mean, I'm sorry but Coach Bolden is right."

He looks at me real quick and then looks away, afraid that he's said too much and I'm going to flip on him. "What do you mean?" I ask. I realize he's scared, so I sit up, put my hands on my knees, and repeat my question: "Seriously, man, what do you mean?"

He pauses now, bites his lip. He looks toward the door like he'd rather make a run for it than say what he wants to say. Finally, he starts in. "He's right that you guys don't play together. It's like you and Moose work it out, and then there's a second team with Nick and Devin and Royce. Two teams. And half the time it ain't even that put together— just a bunch of guys fighting each other."

"Don't say ain't!" I snap, channeling my mom's anger at any improper grammar under her roof. I motion toward the door. "Just go on, Jayson. You don't understand."

He slinks out and I immediately feel bad for snapping at him. But I've had enough. Here's all I want: a squad that can compete, a steady spot at the point. Give me that, I can roll from there. And it seems like everyone down here just wants to put things in the way. It makes me so frustrated I feel like ripping down all those posters from my wall, one by one. It's like I can see all those big-time ballers staring down at me, laughing because I can't even run point for a high school team that's below .500.

I try to read for a while, but I just can't focus. The words all blur and bleed on the page, everything blotted out by my own frustrations. I put on some headphones and try to drown everything out, but even that doesn't work. I turn out my light and stare up at the ceiling in my dark room. *Hell with it*, I think. I don't need this. As much as I want to say that, I keep coming back to two things. The first is Nick, who gave me that stare after he handed Coach his ballot, and then didn't raise his hand when Coach asked who voted for themselves. It's been bugging me all night. At first it bothered me because I figured Nick was lying. But now it bugs me because he may have been telling the truth. I mean, maybe that stare was because he voted for me.

That possibility changes my view of Nick just a little bit, even if I don't want to admit it.

And then there's the other thing, which is this: Jayson didn't tell me what I wanted to hear, but he's never been wrong about a basketball team in his entire life.

21.

The ice is gone. During the winter, Fall Creek gathers bits of ice at its edges, little thin plates forming around sticks and discarded beer cans and plastic bags from the gas station. We're just in the first week of February, but the weather has given Indianapolis a little tease, a crisp day edging up toward the 50s, and with that the ice is all chased away and the creek seems to flow a little more freely. Anyone who's been through an Indiana February knows this day is fool's gold. Things will snap back below freezing. The wind will come knifing down the streets. Snow and sleet will come back to sting your face, maybe as soon as tomorrow night while we battle with Bishop Chatard. But right now, with just a little light remaining in the day, the warmth lingering in the air feels like summer reaching out from the future, reminding everyone just to hang in there and soon enough life will be nothing but long, leisurely days of pickup at those courts just down the bridge from where I'm standing now, days of AAU ball in muggy gyms, of cooling off with 64-ounce drinks in the blasting AC of a convenience store, of the smell of barbeque billowing out of King Ribs on Keystone.

I wonder now what summers will be like if I'm up at Hamilton Academy. I'll still live down here, of course, but there will be summer games up there, semi-organized workouts, more structure than just AAU ball. That will be better for my game, I know, but it will mean more time away from my neighborhood, away from Wes and Jayson, and a lot less time just basking in my summer. I lean over the rail, look down at the water again. The ice is gone, but all that garbage remains. The light on 30th turns green and traffic flows west behind me. I think about heading home, but I want to just take a few more minutes for myself to come down from practice.

The past week has been a mixed bag at practice. Playing the four-spot takes some getting used to, especially when we get bogged down in half court. Now, rather than looking for seams to drive, I'm setting cross-screens for our shooters, flashing to the high post. In a way, I get Bolden's thinking: I can score down low, and my mid-range J is still better than my stroke from three, but I just feel handcuffed. In the thick of things like that, I get one dribble, maybe two, to free myself, and for as good as I was spotting cutters from the perimeter, looking to kick it back out from the paint takes some getting used to. Then there's guarding the opposing four. It's no fun. Just body-to-body the entire time, fighting not to get sealed, trying hard to figure out when to front and when to play behind. Even Stanford—*Stanford*—has made me look silly on a few drop steps, and I have to rely on Nick and Royce and Devin digging down to help me out. That part I hate almost as much as anything else—I can stick a man out in space, no help needed, but having to get bailed out time after time is kind of an embarrassment. None of this tires me out so much I don't stay to work on my shot, but sometimes I imagine that I'm honing my J so I can use it against Bolden next year.

Granted, when we get a stop, we score before half the twos are even across mid-court. But that's why they're the twos. We'll see how it flies against Bishop Chatard.

"If it isn't the legend!"

I turn to see Brownlee, strolling up the sidewalk to where I'm standing, his shout brings me back to the here and now at Fall Creek. He looks shifty. He licks his lips once and then bites at the part of his goatee that's just below his lower lip. He looks around like somebody might be following him, but then when he gets up close to me he smiles and extends his hand like we're old pals.

I give him a firm handshake and look him in the eye, practicing the manners my parents taught me even though the last person on earth I want barging in on my solitude is this fool.

"You boys gonna keep up what you had rolling against Muncie?" he asks.

"I hope so," I say.

He offers a nervous laugh, licks his lips again. He's got a Purdue sweatshirt on that looks like he's been wearing it since Gene Keady was coaching. "Of all the times to have a full week off. Man, you get to playing like you did against Muncie and you just want to line the next team up. Just keep on playing."

"I guess so," I say. I'm trying to be polite, but I wish the guy could take a hint. Instead, he gives this stare across Fall Creek like he's looking out from a mountain peak, and gives a long, slow sigh.

"I suppose next year this time you won't be hanging out on this corner," he says.

"What's that supposed to mean?" I know what it means, but there's something about Brownlee that gets under my skin.

"I'm no idiot," he says. He looks back toward me and gives me that full-of-himself look, his eyebrows raising in mock surprise and wrinkles creasing in his forehead, like when he started lecturing me at the park last summer. "Hell, Derrick, soon as your uncle told me about what he had working at Hamilton, I was angling on it too."

"What?" I ask.

Like a sky blotted by a cloud, his face darkens in an instant. His skin seems a shade deeper and the eyebrows return to their resting position. All of a sudden he looks like a middle-aged man who's not trying to fool anyone. "I figured you knew, Derrick. Your dad isn't the only person Hamilton's offering a job to. Your uncle's trying to get a coaching spot out of this, just some little made-up position like Associate Coach for Player Development, but, man, it's a job."

It all clicks into place. That Lexus. Coach Campbell, its driver, offering me whatever I wanted. Kid splitting from the park and high-tailing it from church when that car came near, and then him, more than anyone else, pushing me up North—*This is where people look after each other, D.*

"I'm not proud of it," Brownlee says. "They saw right through me anyway, but I made my play. Told 'em I was a friend of your family's from way back and that I had a little sway. Thought maybe they'd throw me some green, some kind of something, if they thought I could help convince you to transfer. But I guess they have ways of knowing when that's true, because my phone never rang when I asked them to call me back."

We stand there in silence for a little bit, the last of the day's sunlight fading. There's a sour taste like old milk in my mouth. It's all I can do not to spit into Fall Creek. Part of me wants to walk from

Hamilton just to pull the rug out from under Uncle Kid, but deep down I know that helping him is just another reason to transfer. The problem is, now it feels like I have to.

"Your uncle's a good guy, Derrick," Brownlee says. He's not looking at me now, like he's reading from a script printed on the blacktop on the courts. "Best kind of guy to hang with. Fun as hell. But he's not much of a man sometimes. And I'm allowed to say that because I'm not one either, sometimes. But then I saw you play the other night against Muncie, and all of a sudden you looked so young to me. I know you feel all grown, but you're still a young pup. So what kind of person would I be if I made a buck on a kid? Well, I know—the same kind of person that kept making promises to your uncle when he was your age. Made promises and then just screwed him as fast as they could." He pauses, pacing out the ending of a speech that must have been rattling around in his head for a while. "I don't know why it's so hard for grown folk to just let kids stay kids for a while."

PART III

22.

As soon as our five hits midcourt for the tip, little murmurs ripple through the crowd, the way the high school hallway buzzes with the news of a student getting booted for behavior. Everyone knows something's off. Even Bishop Chatard's players can't hide their surprise when we come out small, and their four man—a senior named Drew Chapman who has the arms of a wrestler—scowls around in search of his matchup.

I steal a glance up in the crowd toward my family and see confusion there too. Uncle Kid and my mom are half-shouting at each other and motioning toward the court, my dad in between them with a pained look on his face. *Focus*, I tell myself. Worry about all that later.

Chatard controls the tip and they ease into the frontcourt, waiting to see where the mismatch is. They don't search for long. Chapman bulls his way into the lane, puts his body on mine and then opens up, his shoulders a white wall of muscle sealing me on the blocks. "Ball! Ball! Ball!" he shouts, and when he gets it he drop-steps and powers it in, bullying me back onto the baseline like I'm no more than a gnat. I try not to look discouraged, but as I inbound the ball to Nick I can hear those murmurs in the crowd turn to grumbles. Any fool can see that putting a freshman guard at the four is a disaster in the making.

I shake it off, make up my mind that I'm going to get the points back on the other end, but other than a flash to the high post when Nick just offers me a feeble pass-fake, I spend the whole possession bumping off of Chapman like a pinball as I set screens for Royce and Devin. After a few reversals, Royce tries to force one into Moose only to have it poked away, and we sprint back down to the defensive end, a chorus of exasperated sighs serenading us as we go.

This time I dig in and put up more of a fight. When Chapman tries to seal me, I dance around to front him. When he spins to the other side, I beat him to the spot. He fights for position, but I edge him out a little bit with my knee, bumping him just enough to uproot him. Still, after all that, they run a little cross-screen for him and he gets an entry pass just off the right block, only about a foot from where he caught it before.

"Double!" Nick shouts from up top, hoping to chase the rock back out of Chapman's hand. Chapman gives it up all right, but all three perimeter players have come crashing down to help, so the Chatard guards have their choice of looks at a three. Nick makes a mad run at their shooter, but it's too late. Nothing but net, and a quick 5-0 hole for us.

I inbound to Nick again, and look ahead to see Royce and Devin sniping at each other, probably arguing about who was supposed to help with Chapman in the paint. Our crowd has gone from odd murmur to rising disappointment to utter silence, so much so that I can hear Devin shout as he turns away from Royce, "This is bullshit."

So much for Coach Bolden's little experiment to get us to play together.

Just then though, Nick dribbles over to me while he's still in the backcourt. "D, this time down, just keep screening for Moose until Chapman has to switch onto him."

My impulse is to tell Nick to mind his own damn business, but there's an earnest look on his face. For once, he's not masking anything behind a cocky grin or a disgusted sneer. So I give it a shot. I down-screen for Moose, then turn right around and back-screen for him. Nothing doing. Then I slide down to the opposite side and cross-screen for him when the ball reverses. This time, he rubs shoulder to shoulder on me, shedding his man, and—just like Nick said—Chapman has to switch onto him.

I turn to watch Moose go to work, but am shocked to see Nick ignore him completely. Instead, he waves Devin down from the top of the key and then dribbles over to my side. He waves Royce down to the opposite baseline, though it takes a second for Bedford to obey. Finally, with everyone flattened out, he motions for me to come to the perimeter. At last, I see what he's doing. He gives me the rock on the right wing, and then shouts at everyone: "Iso. Just give him space."

And all of a sudden I'm singled up with a 6'8" center who moves like his feet are in cement. He does the smart thing, sinks his heels back into the paint and uses his length to try and scare off a J, but he still has no chance. I bounce left once, twice, then lower my shoulder for one power dribble to get him to move. He lunges with all the grace of a bulldozer, and—zip—I cross between my legs and rip past him to the rim, even baiting him for one last lunge to draw the whistle as I kiss in a deuce.

"There it is, D!" Nick shouts.

Our crowd follows suit, realizing at last the upside to Bolden's gamble: we get their bigs in space and they've got no prayer.

I concentrate on my new form, even though it still feels a little stiff. I rattle in the free throw thanks to a friendly roll. My bucket's given us a little bounce. We all know now that if we can just get a stop or two we can make things real nasty for them on the other end.

Bishop Chatard didn't get to 13-4 by being dumb though. They stay patient, reversing and reversing while they look for an entry to Chapman. After about twenty seconds, he beats me to the right block and I'm sealed again. This time Devin—and only Devin—sprints down to double. Chapman gets a little full of himself and tries to force one up between us, but it's a skimmer off the front rim, glass, and then safely into Moose's sure hands.

We know what to do. Moose pivots and rifles the outlet to Nick at the hash. Bedford, Devin and I sprint like our lives depend on it. Nick pushes, while Devin and Bedford fill the outside lanes, setting up at the arc. Chatard's perimeter players sink on Nick's drive, then fan out to defend the three. And all the while I keep running. Chapman? That kid's a memory. He's probably still got his heels on the mid-court stripe when I slice down the lane, take a little scoop pass from Nick and rip one down one-handed.

Our crowd rises to its feet at once, and lets loose a sound that shakes the hardwood under my feet. I take a moment—just a split second, since any more than that will bring Bolden down on me—to pose post-dunk at the baseline. Knees still bent, arms spread and fingers wide like I'm a landing plane. I spin, then haul ass back to the other end so they can't lob one deep to a cherry-picking Chapman. When I get down there, Chapman's huffing in disgust by the elbow, waiting for his teammates.

"Enjoy it while you can," he sneers.

"We can play that game all night," I answer.

Then we both shut up and the war for position starts again.

It's punch and counterpunch into the fourth quarter. We'll get a couple stops and sprint down the floor for easy buckets. I get free runs to the rim. If their wings help, then Devin and Bedford get nice, long looks at threes. Even Moose gets in on the act a few times, catching Bishop Chatard relaxing when they do stop our break, just long enough for him to fill late and muscle one in right at the rim. But they pound us on the other end, working and working until they find Chapman or throwing bodies at the boards, taking advantage of their size for second, third, fourth chances until they get one to drop. Despite all this, neither coach is willing to budge. No matter how many times I run past Chapman for an easy look, they refuse to go small. And no matter how many put-backs Chatard pours in, Bolden won't do anything but give Moose minute-breathers with Stanford and Chris Jones, with the rest of us getting a total of maybe five minutes rest.

By the time we're midway through the fourth, everyone's gassed. Chapman looks like he's about to pass out, and I can feel welts already rising all over my body. Even Nick, who has crossed the line first on every single sprint of the season, looks a little rubber-legged from our relentless pace. Moose looks like he needs an ambulance.

With three minutes to go, Moose gives up a cheap one—his fourth—on their big man, to stop him from an easy deuce. The crowd settles into a lull. Everyone in the gym cranes their neck to check the scoreboard. We're clinging to a three-point lead. It's like the crowd senses the need for one last push. They have seemed almost as tired as the players from the constant back and forth on the floor, but now they rise up, give us the kind of support they haven't since the Hamilton game. I glance up at my people and see all of them—Mom, Dad, Jayson, Kid, even old Brownlee—standing with their hands cupped to their mouths, urging us on. And I swear through the blaring noise of the crowd I hear one voice knife through: Wes shouting, "Keep fighting, D! Keep fighting."

Nick huddles us up quickly before Chatard's center takes his spot. "Ain't no quit now!" he shouts. Then he leans in. "Listen! You remember early when D screened and screened for Moose until they got crossed up?" We all nod. "Just the opposite this time down. Moose you screen your ass off for D. I'll take care of the rest." Everyone's too tired to argue, so we just go take our spots on the lane.

I don't even budge while their big goes through his ritual except to bring my jersey up to my mouth. I put my head down and suck some salt from the jersey, then close my eyes trying to gather some energy. I can smell Chapman next to me, his sweat smelling more like old apples as the game wears on. He leans against me on the first free throw, mostly to annoy me since it's a two-shot foul.

The first one rattles off, and the crowd gets louder while the ref chases it down. On the second one, we all crash into the lane, Chapman lodging a forearm between my shoulder blades, but it manages to find bottom, so Moose scoops it up to inbound while the rest of us slog down the court, nursing a one-bucket lead.

Devin and Royce set themselves at the arc. Once Moose makes it down, he starts screening for me like Nick instructed. Mustering up whatever juice I have left, I come flying off a downscreen with my hands ready. No look. I spin and rub off Moose's back-screen, but Chapman slips through. We work and work, but Chapman hangs on, grabbing and bumping just enough to avoid a whistle. My calves are burning from all the cuts, but finally Moose lands a solid screen on Chapman and I go flying free toward the free throw line. Nick gives a pump my way and then slides a left-handed bullet behind me. I turn to see that both of Chatard's big men chased me, leaving Moose all by his lonesome at the rim, where he gathers in Nick's dime, and—too tired to throw one down—lays in a gimme just as a Chatard guard swipes at him. The hack doesn't even register on a guy Moose's size, but it draws a whistle, and all of a sudden we're up four with a plus-one coming. The crowd responds, hitting their highest volume of the night. As the bleachers rock, I steal a glance at Chapman, who slowly but surely hangs his head, the sign of a beaten man on a beaten team.

From there it's all sugar. They force a three and start fouling, and by the time it's done we walk off with a 74-64 win that looks a lot easier than it was.

As we head to the locker room, I see Wes hanging over by the bleachers, extending his hand to give me a quick five. In the locker room, everyone's feeling good, but it's really only the reserves dancing around and acting the fool. The five that went the distance are so beat we don't have the energy to join in. Instead, I just trade smiles with Nick and Devin and Royce and Moose as we lean back in our lockers, exhausted. Those looks say it all, though: It's like we made it through a war together. No matter what happens in the future, we'll know what it means to really get after it. Moose has just enough juice left to ham it up though. He slides down out of his locker and lays down flat on the locker room floor. "I need a nurse!" he shouts. "I demand that all you sophomores go out and find me some honeys to come tend to my wounds. Just tell them 'Moose needs some love' and they'll come running."

That draws the laughs he wants, but even he doesn't have anything else left in the tank. He literally crawls back to his locker and sits against its base, draping a towel over his head.

At last Coach Bolden comes in and motions for everyone to simmer down.

"You got mixed up on who was supposed to help in the post at least a dozen times. You gave away cheap fouls. When guys came off the bench they let the energy level drop, so the starters had to go wire-to-wire. We took rushed shots in the half court."

I can't believe it. After that Bolden's going to walk in here and bust on us. If I weren't so exhausted I'd just walk out of this locker room and keep putting one foot in front of the other until I got to Hamilton Academy.

"I don't know what else to say," Bolden adds. "You got anything, Coach Murphy?" He stares at Murphy, but I can see a wry old smile creeping into Bolden's scowl. The old man was putting us on.

Murphy pipes up on cue. "I'd say we better warn the rest of the state. Because tonight we found a basketball team at Marion East!"

Murphy extends his right hand in front of him and we rise as one, put our hands in. Bolden reaches his leathery hand into the middle of it, resting it on top. "Way to work tonight, boys," he says. Then he slaps the stack of hands. "Team!" we shout in unison, then hit the showers.

It's just one win. One tooth-and-nail victory over a pretty good team. It doesn't change anything, not in the long run. I figure next year this time I'll still be up north, just hammering people with Vasco and Deon, but as I lean back from my tray of food I revel in the post-victory glow. The satisfaction of it seems to sink in now that I've eaten, and I can feel my muscles relaxing and readying for sleep. I watch Wes and Iesha across from me at the table. They've barely eaten, picking at their food once in a while when they can take their eyes of each other. They're squeezed up so tight they don't even take up half their booth. Behind them, the restaurant is brimming with people from school chowing down and workers picking up forgotten trays and mopping up spills.

Wes finally breaks his gaze with Iesha, asks me what my folks said after the win.

"My mom was juiced," I say, "but my dad never says too much about hoops. He just said 'Good, clean game.'" I roll my eyes just a bit at the injustice of it—any other kid with my talent would be getting mountains of praise from their father but Dad acts like it's a crime to care too much about sports.

"Well, at least your dad's there," Wes says, and I immediately feel bad for complaining. I see, though, that Wes is mostly making a play for Iesha's sympathies, which he gets. Damn if I wouldn't give back that win to have Jasmine rub up on me the way Iesha's on Wes.

Right then, Jasmine herself walks in the door. Problem is, there's a guy right behind her. He looks a few years older, is dark brown with a thin beard along his jaw line, pricey studs flashing in his ears.

I look out the window, like there's something far more interesting in the middle of 38th than up at the front of the restaurant. Last thing I want is to have Jasmine see me checking her when she's on a date with some new kid. Iesha undermines me, though. "Hey, girl!" she shouts. "Jasmine! Come on over here."

Jasmine turns and waves, then walks toward us, her boy in tow. When she arrives, she chats it up with Jasmine and I just try to pretend like it doesn't matter to me one bit. Every time I look up, Jasmine checks me out of the corner of her eye, probably trying to gauge how jealous I am. Then she does it again—that quick wink she gave me months ago in the parking lot after practice. It stuns me. Is she really flirting on a date with another guy? And as for him, he just stands there with his hands shoved in his pockets, not saying a word.

Once Jasmine has my attention, she turns back to him. "Where are my manners?" She grabs hold of his arm and motions toward our table. "This is my friend Iesha and her boyfriend Wes. This is my friend Derrick." I could swear she stresses friend. "This is James, everyone, my cousin visiting from Anderson."

"Oh," I say. All of a sudden I remember my manners too, and I stand and shake his hand. "What are you doing all the way down here on a Friday night?"

He finally speaks, his voice a whispery little song you wouldn't expect out of a guy who looks like he does. "Our parents were all getting together so I told Jasmine I wanted to come see some basketball."

"What'd you think?" I ask.

"I think y'all balled out," he says. "Especially you, man."

I smile, but try to rein it in. "Thanks, man," I say. "We got a long way to go to be good." I sit back down and there's a lull in the conversation so I can't help myself. "What'd you think, Jasmine?"

She pauses, smiles. "I think you played real hard, Derrick," she says.

Then they're off to order their food. Just like that my heart is racing faster than it did in thirty-two minutes of ball. I should know better, but that smile of hers makes me want to tell Hamilton Academy to get gone. I remind myself they have plenty of fly girls up there too.

"Poor Jasmine," Iesha says. She looks at her friend with an expression of pity.

"Why?" Wes asks.

"That girl has Derrick Bowen fever bad," Iesha says. Then she laughs and looks at me.

"Nah," I say.

Iesha leans back in her booth, tilting her chin down and looking at me like I'm crazy. "Then you aren't watching the same girl. You see the way she looked at you and made a point to tell you that's her cousin? She's sending you all the signals, D. You two are the only ones who don't know it."

23.

A Saturday night at Cathedral isn't exactly like taking on the Bulls at
the United Center, but the place gets pretty hostile. Cathedral isn't too
far away from Marion East, just up on 56th on the East side, but it's
a private school, and they just love to think they're superior, like this
mini-Notre Dame. Problem is, they have been superior on the court
lately. We always play them tough, but I can't remember the last time
we beat them. They're good again, maybe the best team we've played
since Hamilton, and they're sitting at 16-2. Their best player, Colvin
Lovelace, is a junior who's already signed to play for Ohio State in a
couple years, and he's no joke.

Their gym's packed to the rafters, everyone decked out in their
green and gold. Meanwhile, there's a little splotch of red in the corner
representing the Marion East faithful, all of them sitting silently while
the band rips through the Cathedral fight song and their cheerleaders
bounce around the floor.

I'm making my way through the lay-up line, trying to get myself
loose, when Moose comes my way. He shouts my name over the noise

and motions for me to come up near center court. He points up behind their basket where a half dozen green-and-gold banners hang, each celebrating championships at various levels. They're satiny and shining, and look brand new compared to those old beat-up banners in our gym. "They got a nice gym, don't they," Moose says.

"Yeah? So?"

"Well, last year when they came down and beat us, that son of a bitch Lovelace kept making fun of ours. Said the city should close it down."

It's the first time I've ever heard someone talking trash about a gym. It's not like they play in some palace, but I can imagine my mom's tirade if she heard that—nothing makes her angrier than for people to think they're better than us.

"Hey look, D," Moose continues. "I know you and Nick ain't never gonna be tight. You've gone after each other's throats too long."

"I hear you," I say.

"But he's never gotten a win over Cathedral. And, man, I don't have that either. So when we hit the court tonight, gather up all that anger you've had toward Nick all year and take it out on these guys instead, okay?"

"I got your back, Moose," I say.

As if he heard our whole conversation, Lovelace strolls over. He stands a few feet away from us, almost toeing the center court stripe, and flashes a cocky smile while he dribbles lazily back and forth between his legs. "At least once we whip your ass, you guys won't have a long bus ride back to that shack you call a gym."

Usually, Moose just laughs that kind of stuff off, but now his back stiffens and his face draws tight. "You best shut the hell up," he says.

"You're awfully touchy tonight, man," Lovelace says. "I thought fat boys were supposed to be happy."

Moose takes one big step toward Lovelace so he's just inches away. "Say that again," he says. "Say that again and I will kick your ass up and down this floor."

I jump in between them, trying to calm Moose down. Within seconds the referees are there, not wanting to deal with a fight even before the first whistle. Murphy's also there, pulling Moose back toward our bench. The Cathedral crowd goes suddenly quiet, like they're all holding their breath to see what will happen, but there's a chorus of shouts from the Marion East corner. I sneak a peek long enough to see Jayson and my mom leading the way, my dad tugging at their sleeves trying to get them to sit back down.

When we get to the huddle, Bolden is scowling. "What the hell is wrong with you?" he screams at Moose.

"That asshole called me fat," he says.

This stuns Bolden for a second, and even he can't help but let a smile replace that scowl. "Moose, you know I love you like a son. But I have to say, it's not like the guy was lying." Everyone laughs now, Moose included, because it is a rare thing indeed for Coach Bolden to crack a joke.

Once the laughter dies, that tightness pulls back into Moose's face. "Yeah, but you're allowed to say that," he says. "Not Lovelace." And I realize that whatever happened between Moose and Lovelace in previous years sticks with Moose pretty deep. Maybe because Lovelace is that blonde, All-American type boy, everyone's darling, and he'll get a lot of hype as the next big Buckeye recruit, while Moose is just Moose.

Nothing special to anyone outside of Marion East. When I see that look on Moose's face, his anger infects me. Oh, it's gonna be a ruckus on that floor tonight.

When the ball goes in the air, it gets physical straight off. Every time someone snatches a board, they come down with their elbows out, just daring someone to step in. It only takes a couple minutes before Moose and Lovelace get tied up going after a board. The crowd goes into a frenzy calling for a foul, for a technical, for blood, and while the refs blow their whistles like mad, they're a little timid stepping in. That's two man-size players going at it, and nobody wants to be on the wrong end of one of those elbows.

They finally get them settled. After that it's a whistle about every 15 seconds as the refs try to gain control. It helps me out, because the guy I'm guarding—a 6'6" standout named Victor Range—starts easing off in how aggressive he tries to fight me on the blocks after he gets a quick foul for backing me down. The stop-and-start rhythm from the whistles only gets everyone more aggravated: first the fans, then the coaches, then the players. After Varney gets whistled for his second on a ticky-tack reach 30 feet from the bucket, Nick has to go talk him down before he gets T'd up.

The call forces Coach's hand too. He's got to send Stanford in at the four, and slide me back to the perimeter to protect Devin from his third foul. You can see the apprehension etched into Stanford's face, like *I don't know if I want a piece of what's happening out there.* So Murphy, always the cheerleader, jumps up as Stanford heads to the scorer's table. "Get in there and knock these guys around," he shouts.

"Damnit, Murphy," Bolden says. "We don't need these kids more worked up than they already are." He calls me and Nick over. "Don't worry about trying to 'knock people around.' Just get guys calmed down!"

"Yes, Coach," I say. And I most definitely mean it, but I swear that court has an energy of its own, like one wrong move might spark an explosion. It's like those days at school when a few guys get in each other's space and everyone just kind of stops and backs away—nobody wants to say the wrong thing to make it escalate.

Next time down on D, Lovelace sets a back-screen on me and throws his shoulder into my head. No whistle. On the other end, Nick spins into the lane with his elbow leading the way. Every time through the lane there's a bump, a push, a hold, and the refs give up calling everything and turn to pleading with us, trying to talk the players down at every loose ball. The result is ugly, with Cathedral up 10-8 with under a minute left in the first, half their points on free throws. On our next trip I get a look on the baseline, but as I rise I hear Murphy's voice in the back of my head trying to correct my form, and the shot comes off flat. Pops off the front iron. Stanford keeps it alive, and when the rock swings back to me I attack the rim. I get a smack across the bridge of my nose, but I finish with a little finger roll, knotting it at 10. My vision blurs and I squint to keep my eyes from tearing up so I'm not sure what happens next. I just hear Nick shouting at me—"Ball! Ball! Ball!"—and I see the rock rolling free again. I might still be reeling, but I know enough to scoop it and attack again. Only this time I'm dishing out the punishment.

I give the slightest glance toward Nick who's widened to the wing, and then take one last dribble and bring it strong. Only when I'm in mid-air do I realize it's Lovelace who's back, and only when it's too late does he realize he should have just conceded the bucket. I bring it one-handed right on top of him. And that whole gym just shuts up. There's just the sound of the rim giving way, then a delayed eruption from the distant corner where the Marion East crowd hollers, and then the horn to end the first.

Bolden was right about me running into guys too good for me to just dunk on. But as I swagger to the sideline, I glare back over my shoulder at Lovelace, just to let him know he's not one of those guys.

As we gather at the huddle my teammates are all worked up now. Chest bumps and trash talk all around except for Nick, who just makes his way straight to the bench. When we all simmer he leans over to me and says, "Good finish, but you're lucky you didn't get whistled, D."

He points to the floor where Lovelace is standing at mid-court with the Cathedral coach. Lovelace's got one hand over his nose, a small stream of blood running out, and both of them are pleading with the refs. It's only then that I feel the throb in my elbow where I must have caught him good, fending him off as we went up. "Don't worry," Nick says, "mashing his face is the best thing you've done all year." He gives me a quick little smile, letting me know we might have a lot of noise between us, but for tonight we're on the same mission.

Then Coach Bolden kneels down in front of us. He reminds us of all the things he said pre-game, about helping in on Lovelace, about being patient with our sets. Then he stops. He furrows his brow like he's mad, but then he gets this wicked smile, the kind where you can't tell if he's happy or angrier than ever. "You know what?" he says. "Remember the game plan. But thanks to Moose and Bowen here, you guys aren't in a basketball game. It's a damn dog fight, and you've got three more quarters of it. Lace 'em up, boys, because this ain't for the faint of heart."

Moose has a time of it while they tend to Lovelace's nose. His backup is thin as a rail, and every time down we just feed Moose on the blocks. Bucket, bucket, bucket. On the defensive end, since we don't have to dig down on Lovelace, we get out into their perimeter guys and fluster them a little. Finally, Nick gets a rip and sails it out in front for me to go chase. Another chance to throw one down, this time two-handed with a little swing on the rim for emphasis, just enough to make them burn a little. Just like that, we're up 7 and Cathedral wastes a timeout.

On the way back to the bench, Moose takes a wide arc toward Cathedral's sideline, pausing just long enough to jaw at Lovelace. "You pretty boys. A little nosebleed and you're cryin' for your mama." Nick grabs Moose by the elbow and leads him toward our huddle before any of the Cathedral guys can snap back. "Those fools are about to quit!" Moose shouts to us.

Problem is, just as he says that I glance over to see Lovelace checking back in. Boy means business now. You can see it on his face. His nose is swollen and his eyes are still red, but he's got that same look—like an animal on the hunt—that Moose had before tip.

Just like that, it's on again. Holds, elbows, staredowns, whistles. And very few buckets. If one of us goes on a 5-0 spurt it feels like an onslaught, but neither team can get separation.

At halftime, even Bolden doesn't have much to say. He mostly just lets us rest. We look around at each other, silently wondering if we bit off more than we could chew, if maybe those Cathedral guys are tougher than we bargained for. Royce walks back and forth in the locker room, trying to keep a twisted ankle loose, and Stanford keeps stretching out his neck, trying to work out the kink from where he got a Lovelace forearm. Moose just stares at the floor a few feet in front of his shoes. Once in a while he mutters some little curse under his breath, but he never looks at anyone else. Finally, with just a couple minutes left before the second half, Murphy pipes up. "Come on now. We can't be sitting around worried about our bumps and bruises. You know they're over there feeling pain too. Let's make 'em hurt more in the second half."

Bolden, who usually cuts Murphy off any time he starts going down that road, nods his head. "Coach Murphy's right about that much. Let's go now." We gather in our circle, put our hands in, yell *Team* and break, filing out of that locker room like soldiers marching into battle.

When we get back on the floor, it's more of the same. Sometimes—between the missed jumpers and the thumps of bodies hitting the floor for loose balls—you can even hear the crowd groan, like just watching this game is painful. Cathedral can never quite get the lead back from us, but for most of the second half they chip and chip, getting down to two, to one, but each time Moose wills his way to the rim or muscles in a put-back to stretch the lead back out. Varney's battled fouls the whole time, so it's been me, Moose, Nick, Royce and Stanford, with no easy run-out dunks coming my way like I had against Chatard, no easy chances to get some separation from these guys. Instead, they start sagging back in on Moose, since Royce is our only real threat from range—I get looks, but my legs are so tired I'm a little gunshy.

It feels like it goes on that way for hours until, all of a sudden, I look up at the clock and it's crunch time. *Winning time*, I tell myself. We've got the rock, clinging to a 40-38 lead with just over a minute, but as physical as this game's been, Coach wants us to keep running offense—pull back for a second and they'll rip it from us. *Winning time*, I tell myself again. With Nick out top looking to feed Moose again, I fake a baseline cut and then pop off of Stanford to the elbow. Nick feeds me right in rhythm at the foul line, and   bang   I bury a dagger with a whistle.

Too good to be true on the road, though. The refs call a moving screen on Stanford. A damn moving screen after a game played like a cage match. Bolden goes ballistic. Murphy has to grab him by the shoulder to calm him down. But the result is no bucket, and Cathedral gets the rock back down only two. Just like you could feel the nastiness on the floor earlier, you can feel the energy change on the floor now. Cathedral's crowd rises in unison. While we're still shaking our heads about that whistle, they rush the ball up. There's a crispness to their offense now that's been missing all game, and then it happens: with 20 ticks left Royce gets clipped by Lovelace and loses his man in the corner. Three.

The crowd explodes and for the first time since the first quarter, we're behind. Nick rushes it up to the frontcourt and calls time. The whistle sounds and we all start for the bench, until we hear the roar of the crowd behind us. There the ref stands—same one who tagged Stanford last possession—rolling one arm over the other to signal a travel on Nick. He does it with some emphasis too, like he's proud of putting the screws to us. It's an absolute phantom call, a complete joke, but as soon as Nick starts to plead his case the ref just holds up his hand like a traffic cop. Nick has to drop it before he gets a T, but the whole scene sends the Cathedral folks into a frenzy, and I can hear—mingled in the jeers and cheers—a mocking laughter that makes my face burn. I hear my mom's voice raging in my head: *These private school sons-of-bitches,* it says. *They think they're so high and mighty.*

Fouling is all we can do. Moose gives a lunge at a driver and sends him sprawling on the floor. It's a little Hollywood act, but it's a miracle we don't get a flagrant out of it. The hard foul is all it takes for Cathedral's players to jump in, chests puffed and mouths running. One of them even cocks his fist to take a swing, but Lovelace grabs him. "No sense in that," he says. "Don't stoop to that thug's level."

A blind man could see that word—*thug*—hit Moose like a slap. We all jump in to calm him down before everything gets out of hand.

Nick huddles us up before the free throws.

"I oughta kill that fucker," Moose says.

Nick shakes his head. "No, big man. Let's just keep our cool and make these last fifteen seconds count."

We break for the free throw, but Nick grabs me by the elbow, pulling me toward mid-court for just a second. "You got one in you?" he asks.

"Sure," I say.

"No, I mean, you got a three in you?" He looks at me and widens his eyes. "They're chasing Royce everywhere—but you can get a look if you want one."

"You get me the rock and I'll put it in the hole," I say.

"You damn well better," Nick says, but I don't hear that old threat in his voice. Instead, this is his form of encouragement.

I hurry down to the lane before the ref hands the ball to the shooter, then watch as he calmly sinks both. Cathedral hurries back on defense, except for their point guard, who gives some mock pressure on Nick to try and eat some clock. Nick rips past him and waves me toward the right wing. He zips into the front-court with about ten ticks left, then drifts toward the left wing like he's looking for Royce. I keep bouncing on my feet, staying ready to cut to the open spot when I get a chance. *Head straight*, I tell myself, *Get open with your feet but stay straight on the shot.* The whole Cathedral defense drifts over to the other side. Then Nick darts back my way with a lightning cross-over and zips me the rock. He leads me a little toward the baseline to make my man's recovery just a little harder, but that means I have to pick 'em up and put 'em down to reel in the pass. I catch it just the slightest bit off-balance. *You got time to gather*, I think, so I get my feet under me, bend my knees, rock the orange back toward my shoulder and rise.

Head straight, head straight, head straight.

I let fly.

It immediately feels short, my tired legs doing me in, so I give it a little body English to urge it home. I feel the crowd hold its collective breath while it hangs in the air, this whole brutal game hanging with it.

Front rim. Back rim. Up. And *through*.

Tie game. I check the clock for a split-second before racing back to stop a desperation shot: three seconds left. I sprint down, trying to locate my man, my heart pounding like a bass drum. Then I hear a gasp from the crowd cut through the distant cheers of the Marion fans. I turn back just in time to see that Nick's jumped the in-bounds. I see the Cathedral guard still standing there with his hands outstretched to where the pass should have arrived, while Nick puts a spin dribble on

Lovelace and whips toward the rim like a cyclone. It's all done in a flash. He floats a bunny up on the glass just before the buzzer, and it banks safely home, quick as an eight ball ricocheted to the pocket. Ball game!

The next thing is a sprawling tangle of bodies dressed in red and green unis taking over the Cathedral court. We dog-pile Nick in celebration, everyone yelling—not even words, just joyous shouts of a team receiving a miracle win. Moose lifts Nick from the pile for a second and holds him up, the way linemen lift up QBs after touchdowns, but that's just a reason to pile on again, and the celebration continues until Bolden and Murphy—who showed off a pretty good vertical of his own when the game-winner fell—remind us that we're supposed to be dignified and shake hands with our opponents.

By that time, half the Cathedral players have hit the showers. In fact, I see more Marion fans than Cathedral players, our crowd streaming down to the court. Jayson runs over to me, so excited his eyes are about to pop from his skull. "That's what I'm talking about," he shouts, and gives me a quick high five before running off across the court, spurred by adrenaline. I see Uncle Kid and Brownlee laughing with each other, their faces suddenly young with happiness, as if they were the ones who just hit the big shots. And I see my parents—only I can hardly believe it's my dad. My mom I expect to see pumped up, but it's my dad—calm, quiet Thomas Bolden—who's high fiving her and shouting at the rafters like he just won the lottery. He catches me looking at him, and he gathers himself really fast. He smoothes out his shirt and says, "Good game, son."

"Good game?" my mom shouts. She grabs my dad by his shirt and shakes him like she's angry. "That's only the best basketball game ever!"

My dad gives in to the sheer joy of it all. He laughs an easy, open laugh I don't see from him as often as I used to. "Okay, okay." He gives me a quick bear hug and then steps back. "That was a really good game."

I stand there, the whole post-game circus swirling around us. I have this feeling that there's something terribly important I need to tell Mom and Dad, but I can't figure out what it is. I don't get time to figure it out either, because I get blindsided by one of my teammates who's hugging me and pushing me toward the locker room all in one motion. I can hear whoever it is laughing as they push me, and I give in too, still giddy with the win. Then we stop, and I look down to see who it is. None other than Nick Starks, hugging on me like we're long lost brothers. Truth is, I don't care one bit. Not after that game.

"That was a big-time shot, D-Bow," he says.

"Yours was even bigger, Nick," I say.

Then there's Murphy, hovering by the locker room door, and he leans over to us. "Remember fellas—to win, we needed 'em both."

24.

That game. It's like there was life before it and life after it, and there's no going back. It feels the way some people talk about having a near-death experience. Nothing's ever going to be the same.

At practice we're as crisp as we've ever been. Bolden still has me at the four, but it's like a red light's turned green. Guys sink down to help me in the post and then jump back to the perimeter seamlessly. When we get a stop we're off to the races—the twos never have a chance to get their feet set.

All of it, to be honest, is enough to make me re-think heading to Hamilton. How could I line up against Moose next year? Square off against the guys I've gone to war with? It just doesn't seem right. But then I remember the job they're holding out to my dad, and even the angle Uncle Kid has working. I can't take that away from them.

In a couple nights we've got Baptist Academy, and the twos keep imitating their flex offense, cutting and reversing and cutting and reversing but getting nowhere. And it's not just because they're the twos—the starting five seems to move like one animal now, waiting to pounce. This time it's Bedford, who darts past a screen and tips a pass. Nick scoops it up and we're off. I leave Stanford standing in sand and I don't even have to call for the ball—it's like it just appears, magically, one step in front of me, so I can catch it in rhythm and push it ahead against the one guy back, an undersized and overmatched sophomore who tries to square up for a charge, but just gives me a nice, open lane to slide past him, gather and rip one down.

"There it is!" shouts Devin. He was trailing and gives me an enthusiastic chest bump like he'd have never dared even a week ago.

Bolden blows the whistle. "Good one to end on," he says. "Let's just not get to thinking we're gonna run past Baptist that easy." His voice is full of fire, but not quite at the level it usually is. Even he knows it—Baptist is gonna get rolled.

Friday, I get home from school with a couple hours to kill before I hit the gym so I poke my head in Jayson's room. He's kicked back on his bed, thumbing through an issue of *SLAM*, but he pops his head up. "You ready for tonight, right?" he says.

"That's the truth," I say. "You gonna be there making noise?"

"Most definitely, D." He gets off his bed and crosses the room to give me a fist bump. "You guys keep it rolling."

I see the excitement in Jayson's eyes, and I know that what I see there is happening with all our fans. All of a sudden, people believe. Then his face goes serious and he says, "Hey, Dad." I turn and see that dad's at the door. He's got this blank look on his face, like he's sleepwalking, and I can see my mom staring at him from the hallway. Something's up again.

Dad, still staring blankly past me, pulls his keys out and jangles them for a second. "I'll give you a ride tonight," he says.

I hesitate, then look back over my shoulder, like maybe Jayson can give me some insight, but he's back on his bed and buried in his magazine. I start to say that I can walk, that it's not that cold a night, but my mom clears her throat. "Go with your dad, Derrick," she says. When I check her face and see that stern stare, I know there's no debating.

I pack up my gear and climb in with Dad, who demands we leave an hour early. In the car, Dad doesn't say a word, just pulls out of our drive and starts toward school, his fingers rapping out a nervous rhythm on the wheel.

We head out, but instead of going on to Central, he immediately heads north on College.

"Dad," I say.

"Just trust me, Derrick," he says.

I pretend like I'm going to be late for the game, but my dad knows better, and takes his time along 38th before hitting Fall Creek to Keystone. It's like Uncle Kid's game with me before the season started all over again, as I see the scenery change as we push north. I almost feel a sense of panic, like I'm suffocating in the car. I have the impulse to unbuckle and tear out of there at each red light. It's one thing to get this kind of treatment from Kid, but I expect different from my dad. I mean, if he wanted me to transfer to Hamilton he could have just flat-out told me a hundred different times. Besides, I already know what's at stake for him, and I know that's why I should transfer even if the Marion East locker room suddenly feels a lot more like home than it ever did before.

We keep on, but unlike my trip with Uncle Kid, this time we stay on Keystone, all the way past the interstate and over 86th, then on into the mall—the rich people's mall. It's called Keystone at the Crossing, but more than once I've heard my mom call it Caucasians at the Crossing when she thinks I'm not listening. I don't say anything, but it seems about the strangest time in the world to be heading to the mall.

My dad parks, but he doesn't turn off the car. Instead, he just watches the pretty people go in wrapped in their expensive coats or come out of the mall loaded down with merchandise, as if February 11 were Christmas Eve.

He must feel me fidget, because he sighs and looks at me. "Derrick, I've been sitting back just letting you handle this decision all by yourself. And no matter what I'm about to say, it's still your decision. But I got to thinking, and it seemed wrong that a father wouldn't give any advice. So here goes." He takes a deep breath and holds it for a second, like he's about to dive into deep water, then he exhales and squints his eyes in concentration. "Son, your mother is the best woman I know. If it weren't for her, I'd be nowhere. Whatever drive you have in you, it came from her. But there's one thing that she's wrong about— not that I'd ever say this in front of her. She thinks it all still boils down to black and white: there's these white people up here living the good life, and black folks down on Patton getting cheated."

"You don't think that's true?" I ask. I don't say so, but it seems to me that the view out of our windows is pretty good evidence that Mom's right.

"It's not that it's not true. It's just so much more complicated than that. If we'd have driven the other way on Keystone, we'd have seen some white people that don't look this—" and here he points out the window like he's accusing people. "If you try to make sense of everything by black and white you'll drive yourself crazy, and you'll end up hating the idea of success. If you just get angry at people with more money and bigger houses and college degrees, then where does that leave you? I mean, that's what we should want. And if you're too busy resenting it, then you forget to try for it. I know this. When I lost the grant money for college, I was mad at everyone else—at least at everyone who never had to worry about money for college. But I had to get past that and get to work. Pretty soon there was your mom. Then you and Jayson. No time to get bitter about things."

"I hear you, Dad," I say. I figure this is his way of saying the same thing Kid is saying: Transfer to Hamilton. It's best for me.

He keeps on, and I realize he's not made his point yet. "The thing is, I went to college for a couple years, and I learned some things. And one is this—there are better ways to be successful than letting someone buy you. I mean, that's what Hamilton's trying to do, right? Buy us? I could use that job, but we're paying the bills. We'll be okay. And then there's one more thing that your mom taught me. These people aren't the enemy in everything, but maybe basketball's sacred ground. I'm not going to sit here and pretend that I've cared about sports my whole life. But, damnit, Derrick, if there's any justice in the world we should at least be able to beat their asses in basketball."

That line is about as foul as my dad gets, so I know he's not playing around. Still, I take a sideways look at him just to be sure. He turns and stares right at me. "You saying what I think you're saying?" I ask.

"Still your decision, son. You like Hamilton Academy, then go there. But if you do it because you think I need that job I'll never forgive myself."

I sink back into my seat and take a few seconds to watch the people float by. There's something that makes me feel almost powerful as I gaze at them, like they're just following their little paths, not even thinking, while I sit here with my dad mulling my decision. It's almost like the feeling I get on the court when I see the opponent lulled into their offensive set, just going through their pattern, and I just sit back and wait to jump a pass, like they've forgotten about me, but I'm onto them.

"Dad?" I say.

"Yes?"

"I gotta get to the gym."

25.

We kill it. I mean, we kill it from the tip and we keep on killing it. At each timeout, Bolden keeps reminding us that we've got to play four, that we can't blink on these guys, but we know. We see it written on the faces of the Baptist Academy players: they're done. We jump out to a double digit lead early and there's no fight left in them. Bolden keeps on urging us, but he doesn't have to. After that Cathedral game we're like a pack of wolves with a taste for blood. Devin and Royce bury J after J, I get runouts with Nick, Moose muscles his way to the glass time and again, and every once in a while Nick just takes a clear out for himself, schooling his man with spins and crossovers and step-backs until that kid just hangs his head because he knows he's beat.

Even when Bolden starts to rotate the bench in—first Stanford, and then Jones, and then the young perimeter guys who never get minutes—the domination continues, and by the time the final seconds are ticking away, the starters are all kicked back at the end of the bench, enjoying the end of a 74-38 laugher.

Bolden rises, getting ready to go offer the opposing coach a handshake, but he pivots on his heel and comes back to us first. "First, be gracious," he says, as if he can sense that we're pretty full of ourselves. "Remember what it was like when you got blown out, so you know how these kids feel. And second, remember where we're going." He points at the court. "This game's over. You got to be thinking next game already. That's what good teams do—they want next! So decide right now if you're that kind of team."

The buzzer sounds to end the game and Bolden's gone again.

"Shiiiiit," Moose says. "That man just can't ever be happy."

Nick laughs, but it's more a kind of sharp burst than the sound of someone amused. "True enough, Moose," he says. "But he's got a point. Let's start thinking Broad Ripple right now."

And with that we rise, follow our coach down the sideline and methodically shake hands with the kids we just ran out.

It's late, but I figure it's not too late to call.

I chilled with Wes and Iesha for a while, and then came home to kick back with Jayson, my parents, and Uncle Kid. We demolished a couple pizzas and watched Durant get to work on the West Coast, and nobody so much as whispered about Hamilton Academy.

Everyone started dropping off at halftime of the Thunder game, so I pulled out the book I saw Jasmine reading. I don't know why I do it. I sure don't want Kid or Jayson to see me reading some book by a woman author or I'll never hear the end of it. But it's become a way to take my mind off of all the other noise in my life, and now that I'm getting close to the end I feel compelled to go ahead and see what happens.

Tonight, though, I can't focus at all. I put the book down and listen to the sounds of the house at night—the click and hum of the heater, the shudder of the front door when a gust of wind rips past—and I feel a nervous energy in me still. Some of it, I know, is leftover game buzz, no different from any other win or loss that seems to stick in my veins hours after the gym lights have gone dark. This is more, though. I know that after my visit to Hamilton, after our turnaround in this season, and after my dad taking me up North earlier today, that the time has come to make a decision. Transfer or stick it out? Even with my dad telling me not to factor in his job, I can't pretend that Hamilton Academy isn't offering quite a bit—and to me too. The chance to play with other All-Stars, the chance to go to an elite school, the chance to play in the State Finals every single year. There's that pitted against everything I know—these blocks, my teammates, hanging with Wes.

And just like that, I know what I want.

I put down the book and look at my clock. 11:45. Late, but I figure a young guy like Coach Campbell is still up.

I dial, and on the third ring he picks up, sounding as alert as if it were noon.

"Campbell here," he says.

"Coach, this is Derrick Bowen from down at Marion East."

He chuckles a little. "I know where you're from, Derrick. Question is what are you doing calling my number at this hour."

"Well, Coach, I just realized that there is something you could do for me."

"Name it," he says.

So I do.

26.

It's still not the Roy Hibbert treatment, but now when I hit the halls of
Marion East, heads turn. They know who I am. So the whole trip down
freshman wing with Wes is a string of *'sups* and fist bumps. Even Mr.
Jenks, who still shakes his head at every wrong answer like it's the one that
will finally doom America's future for good, acknowledged my game on
the way out of Algebra II. "You study for this exam," he said. "We need
you out there come playoffs." When we rounded the corner Wes turned
to me and said, "Man, you guys must be ballin' out if Jenks notices."

So it's all good, and now when I see Nick and the crew kicking
our way from senior wing there's no iciness, no staredown like we had
back before the season started. Now it's cool all around. Nick even gives
Wes the time of day, asking him how things are rolling with Iesha.

The only thing I wish were the same is the presence of Jasmine.
I still remember her giving me that long look at the beginning of the
year, but now she's all but disappeared. Sometimes I'll see her down the
length of the hallway, but she's too far away for me to call out without
looking desperate. Or I'll see her in the courtyard, bundled against the

cold as she heads home while I've got to stay behind for practice. Or maybe I'll see her at lunch, but she always seems to be finishing up just as I'm about to sit down. She's always just out of reach.

"D?" Wes says, and I realize I've been spacing. The whole team has gone on their way, and Wes must have just asked me a question.

"Sorry, man," I say.

"I was just asking if you wanted to get together later and cram for that Algebra test."

"Sure thing," I say. "Besides, there's something I want to talk to you about."

This perks Wes up, but there's an uneasiness in his face, the way Jayson looks when Mom and Dad call him into the living room to talk.

"It's cool," I say. "Don't sweat it." I tell him I'll check him later and we head our different ways down the hall.

Practice. Man, come mid-February even the most dedicated player starts to feel about *practice* the way Iverson did back in the day. That drudgery of hauling your bones out to the court to go through the same drills. It feels like an eternity until Friday, when we get to stomp on Broad Ripple, and it's a full two weeks after that when Sectionals start. *Practice.* In my head, it can start to sound just like Iverson said it.

But not this year. It might be February, but we're still finding ourselves. And if I feel a little weary for yet another drill, all it takes is a few minutes on the court with my crew and I'm alive again. Today it's Devin who brings the energy. He gets himself rolling in the half court drills and starts dropping them from 20, then 25, until Bolden shouts at him to take game shots. Devin raises his eyebrows at coach as if to say *If they fall, then they're game shots*, but he's smart enough not to actually say that.

Still, it feels like every day we find a new way to attack people, and I can see Bolden's eyes grow excited at all his weapons. He's like a kid with a bunch of new toys, just wanting Christmas Day to last forever. So today, with Devin hot, he tells the 1s to run an offense just called "Screen for Devin," which is exactly what it sounds like. Except what we find—and what Bolden tells us he expects—is that the defenders get so busy chasing Devin that the rest of us get the easy looks. I get a back-door cut for a jam. Moose seals his man after the screen for an easy deuce. Royce picks and pops for a fifteen-footer. And Nick just blows by fools whenever he wants to. I mean, this offense is humming. By the time Bolden orders us to stop with a shout of *Free throws*, it feels like we're about to burn the gym down we're so hot.

Murphy comes over to where Moose and I are practicing our free throws. He's almost bouncing he's so pumped. He toes the baseline at the bucket and feeds us, firing chest-passes so crisp they pop in our hands. "I tell you guys," he starts as he watches Moose find bottom, "Lawrence North thinks they're gonna stroll through Sectionals, but we got a wake-up call for them." He quiets while Moose eyes another one, watches it bounce a few times on the rim, then—not being able to contain the old player in him—leaps up for a quick tap-in when it rolls off. "I mean, Tagg's a player, sure," he starts again. He zips the ball to me. I square up at the stripe, going through my routine even as I hear Murphy's chatter. "But Tagg's just one guy. We'll come at them in waves. Just isn't gonna be the same team they beat earlier."

I get a friendly roll and receive Murphy's pass. I give a quick wink to Moose because we both know Murphy likes to talk us up like we'll never lose another game. Even if we feel that way ourselves, we always get a kick out of the most optimistic assistant coach in the long history of optimistic assistant coaches. "I'll tell you another thing," Murphy says, just as I'm about to go into my shooting motion, "we get to regionals we might just knock Hamilton Academy in their teeth too."

Just the mention of the school feels like a kick in the gut. It wrenches my form at the last minute so my free throw goes up like a knuckleball and bangs hard off the back rim.

"Come on now, D-Bow," Murphy says as he chases it down. "You can't get distracted by a little bit of chatter. What's up?"

"Nothing," I say, looking down at my shoes. "I just don't want to get too far ahead of things. We got Broad Ripple Friday night."

There's a reason we usually hang at my house instead of Wes'. It's not that his place is nasty or something, but sometimes there's a sad feeling to it, like his mom is just barely holding it together. There's always stuff scattered on the floor—envelopes, their dog's toys, dirty laundry— and sometimes it smells like there's something off in the kitchen. I mentioned it once to my mom and she just told me it took some brass to criticize a woman for how she keeps a house after her husband splits.

I can tell sometimes it gets Wes down. He'll meet me at the door and squeeze his way out before I can come in or holler from the other side to wait and he'll be right out. But his mom takes care of him, cooks a dinner for him every night and makes sure he's got clothes that fit, which is more than can be said for some kids on our street. And tonight

Wes seems easy, kicked back in a chair in their living room while his mom fixes dinner.

"So what's the word, D?" he asks.

"There's been some hassle going on in my world that I haven't told you about," I tell him. He leans forward like he's interested, but I see a little twinge in his face like he's hurt I've been hiding something from him. I figure the best thing is to just plunge ahead. "About halfway through the season I started getting recruited by Hamilton Academy to transfer up there next year."

Wes flops back in his chair and throws his hands up. "I knew it!" he shouts. "Every time we get someone with some skill in the city, someone wants him to sell out and transfer." Then I see it flash across his face—the knowledge that I might actually go. His eyes widen and his chin snaps up. "You're not gonna do it, are you, D?"

I was planning on stringing him out, play up all they were offering and how much better the school is, but when I don't answer right away, I see panic in his face. I realize that the prospect of me transferring would be devastating to him, that no matter how much he should be confident in himself—he's smart, he's funny, he's got a fine girl in Iesha—sometimes he thinks whatever popularity he has hinges on the fact that he's best friends with me. So I squash all the drama quick. "I'm not going anywhere, Wes," I say. "I'm a Marion East Hornet to my bones."

"Straight," he says. He stands up and walks over to give me five, as juiced as if I'd just hit a game-winner. When I told my parents an hour ago, they didn't exactly jump up for high-fives, but I could tell they both thought I was doing the right thing.

I crane my neck to look into the kitchen, like what I'm about to tell Wes is a huge secret I don't want his mom to hear. "It's not like they didn't have something to offer," I tell him. "And I kind of took them up on something."

Wes furrows his brow, worried that I might have done something stupid. I just hold up my hand for him to chill and then run back to the front door real quick. I open it and grab the box I left on the porch, then bring it to my boy Wes. He just stares at it like there's a bomb in his hands.

"Go on," I say.

He lifts the lid and, there, staring back at him are the freshest pair of Timberland Earthkeepers in the city, the very kind he'd hoped his pops was getting him for Christmas. He stares at me dumbfounded, searching for something to say. Finally he manages to ask me where in the world I got these.

"They got a real smooth assistant up there," I say. "Coach Campbell. He told me if there was anything I wanted, he'd get it for me. So I told him I wanted a pair of new kicks."

"But doesn't that mean you owe him now?"

"Wes, I figure if the man's stupid enough to think I wear size eights, then I don't owe him a thing."

Wes laughs at that, then settles into a broad smile, relaxing at last in the knowledge that the kicks in his hands are his. He lifts one from the box and eyes it the way a jeweler might inspect a new diamond. "You did that for me?" he asks.

"I didn't owe any coach from the North side, but I owed you," I say. "You're my boy and I let you down."

"Aw, man. I told you not to sweat that."

"I know, but that's because you're who you are. I just thought you'd dig these things."

He admires the Timberlands again. "Yeah," he says. "That's the truth." Then he rips his old sneakers off his feet and throws them in the corner. "We need to see how these things look out on the blocks," he says. Then he hollers at his mom that we'll be back in a while and the two of us head out into the city, Wes so obsessed with his shoes it's a wonder he doesn't bump into every streetlamp.

27.

The locker room is pretty tame. We went up to Broad Ripple and dismantled them, then came home tonight for our regular season finale: a 20-point beatdown of Meridian. So, sure, we're enjoying it—the music's playing, Moose is clowning, and everyone's feeling good—but it's not like we're overjoyed. That's the thing about reeling off six straight—you kind of come to expect the wins, so this last one over Meridian doesn't feel like anything special.

Coach Murphy comes in, clapping and shouting as he strides to the center of the locker room. "Come on, boys! Let's make a little more noise than this. Way to end the season."

As soon as Murphy stops with his chatter, Coach Bolden puts his hand on his shoulder. "That's all right, Murphy. Let them stay cool about it. I like that better."

Then Bolden raises his hand and we all know to listen. Nick clicks off the music, Moose sits down, and the most anyone does is peel off socks or jerseys while their eyes stay on Coach.

"I don't need to tell you we have something going in this locker room," he starts. "Not a lot of people know it. You spend a month losing to teams like we did, people forget about you. Well, they'll remember us soon enough."

That draws a few shouts from the squad, like we're choir members shouting Amens. Bolden smiles—a real, genuine smile—and I realize that the winning has made him a new man too, like he's all of a sudden some twentysomething coach just rising in the ranks, full of energy.

"Boys," he says, "it's been a long time—too damn long—since I've had a team on a tear like this. But we've got all week before Sectionals start for us on Friday. We're gonna use that week to get even better, but I want you all to remember what made us good to begin with. Sacrifice. Unselfishness. Dedication. Hard work." He eyes us, each and every one, making sure those words sink in. Now there's no hesitation or second-guessing—everyone nods earnestly. Man, we'd lace them up and practice now if it weren't against the rules. "And no foolishness. A lot of teams have messed up their playoff runs before they even get started because they lose focus off the court. So keep your heads on straight." I could swear his eyes linger on Moose for an extra second.

"Now bring it in," he says. We all rise and head toward the center of the locker room, a mass of bodies standing together, arms raised. Bolden grabs the top hand, but rather than hitting it he grabs on for a second. "Our season's just getting started," he says. Then he slaps that hand.

Team!

I exit the gym and pull my hoodie up against the night wind. Just as I do, I see a figure—long and lanky—approaching me quickly. I tense up. These blocks aren't as dangerous as some people think, but you never know after dark.

"D-Bow," the voice says. Then I recognize it. Uncle Kid. "Where you headed, little man?"

I bristle at that term. *Little man*—it doesn't sound any better coming from my uncle than it does from guys like Brownlee. But I also stiffen because I know Kid wants something, that he's still trying to make some kind of play. "Home," I say and head toward Patton.

"Well, hang up a sec," he says and breaks into a quick jog to catch up with me.

I so don't want to deal with this right now. There's part of me that feels like Uncle Kid cursed this season when he drove me up to Hamilton before our first game. Now that things are humming for us, I don't want him screwing my head up again. It wasn't just ten minutes ago Coach told us to keep our heads straight off the court. But you can't walk on family so I slow down for him.

"You all brought it again tonight," Kid says, sounding all enthused. I don't say anything, so he just keeps going, a nervous rhythm to his voice. "I mean, you guys are really mashing it now. Just in time for the stretch run, you know what I'm saying?"

"Yeah," I say. I'm almost to our block and I figure if I can just keep giving him a *yeah* or a *sure now*, he'll never get around to his point. Then he'll know better than to say much in front of my parents.

"You and Nick just stickin' daggers on those clowns," he says. Then he falls silent. I know he's leading up to it, trying to find just how he wants to say what he meant to bring up all the time. "I just want to make sure, you know, that as sweet a ride as you're taking right now that you haven't lost sight of the big picture."

I stop. I turn and face him. He's still a tick taller than me, but he's the one struggling to look me in the eye. Instead he looks left and right and then down at his feet. I feel bad all of a sudden. He's a grown man, and every last thing makes him ashamed. I'm tired of wasting time out in the cold though. "What's up, Kid?" I say, and I realize I'm the one with the tone of an older person soothing a child.

"Your dad told me you said no to Hamilton. That right?" he says. He still can't look at me. "I mean, they went all out for you. You shouldn't let them down."

"I think I'd be letting down some other people if I went," I say.

Kid steps back like I've offended him. "Now, D. You told me you were all but gone."

"When?" I shout, my breath making visible puffs in the night air. "When did I say that?"

Kid kicks at the sidewalk. "Now you know you let me think that. I mean, I had something going up there too."

"Why can't you get the same kind of job at Marion East?"

"With Bolden?" he shouts. "Are you kidding me?"

Kid looks desperate, his eyes casting about like he's searching for something in the night. I flood with anger at him for doing this to me—except that for as much anger as I feel, I feel every bit as much sympathy for him. The man looks like he's about to cry. I feel like I've let him down. "I'm sorry, Kid, I just—"

He shakes his head. "Sorry don't cut it, man. I mean, I've been there for you, D. All those summer days down at the court. All those hours. Was it your dad taking you down there? Your mom teaching you all those moves? Naw. Naw. Your Uncle Kid. And now here you are, about to bust out, and me?" He grabs at his coat, and then motions his hands at the night like he's trying to throw something off of him.

"What, Kid?" I yell. I see a light click on down the block, and I realize we're getting loud. A car pulls to the corner and flashes its brights at us. But who cares? The cops aren't going to beat it down here for people shouting. "What do you think I owe you? What?"

He looks at me square then, and nods his head. It's like he was waiting for just that question. "Just one conversation," he says.

"Well, this is it. What else do you have to say?"

"Not with me, D," he says, then motions to the car that brighted us. It comes rolling up slowly, and I take a step back. Only when it gets closer and cuts the lights can I see what it is—that same old Lexus with the tint job. Coach Campbell from Hamilton Academy.

He leans his head out the window and nods to Kid, who backs away so Campbell can look directly at me. He narrows his eyes at me, looking cold and tired and basically pissed off.

"Did you get those shoes I sent your way, Derrick?" he asks.

I play dumb. "Last pair of shoes I got were my AdiZeros, and my dad bought those for me."

Campbell doesn't seem in the mood to play. He turns off his ignition and steps out, not looking one bit bothered by being a Hamilton County white boy far from home. He points at me. "You might not think a pair of shoes is much, Derrick, but you told me what you wanted and I got them for you. That means something."

I glance at Uncle Kid but he just looks down at the sidewalk, not wanting to deal with the fact that he set me up like this. I turn back to Campbell. "Yeah, well, those shoes weren't for me. I don't know why you think I wear a size eight, but—"

"Stop it, Derrick," he shouts. "You and I both know how this works. You could have asked for anything. Didn't have to be shoes, but that was your call. And then earlier this week your dad tells Coach Treat 'Thanks but no thanks'? That's not right."

I look around us. The light in the one house is back off now, like those folks decided this wasn't any of their business. I take a deep breath, the cold air stinging my lungs. "I don't know what you want now. I can't get the shoes back for you."

"I don't want the shoes!" he shouts. "I want you to make good on your end." Then he softens his tone, like we're good pals again. "Derrick, Hamilton Academy is the best place for you anyway. Don't waste your talents down here because of some sort of pride. I think you have this idea about us that isn't who we really are. It's fun for players up there. You got to talk to Vasco and Deon. You had a good time with them, right?"

Another deep breath. "I made my decision, Coach Campbell," I say.

I tried to say it in the most respectful, sincere way I could, but something about my tone must have hit Campbell wrong, because he snaps again. "Unmake it Derrick. You accepted that gift. And all it takes is one phone call from me, and you'll be sitting out these playoffs with a nice suspension. That'll change the way people see you, even some college recruiters."

That sends a chill through me more icy than anything the weather can offer. Just like that I can see everything we've built—all this momentum for Sectionals—start to crumble because of me.

Uncle Kid steps up. "Wait a minute," he says to Campbell. "There's no cause to threaten him. I want him to go up to Hamilton too, but—"

Campbell pivots toward Kid now. He points at him. "Hey, you're the one that kept saying it was a sure thing. Don't back up on it now." Kid throws his hands up again and starts to protest, but Campbell just waves him off and turns back to me. "You know what you're throwing away, right? Not just for you, but for your dad? Your uncle?"

"Coach," I say. "I've made my decision."

"Fine," he says. He pulls a smartphone from his pocket and lets his index finger hover above it. "You're about to live with the consequences."

I figure he's bluffing, but Uncle Kid's not taking any chances. He walks over to him and snatches the phone from Campbell's hand quick as if he's thieving a lazy pass. Campbell startles, but has no idea what to say. "Now I told you not to threaten my nephew," Uncle Kid says. "What I had with you was business, but this"—he points at me—"this is family. And if you so much as look funny at my nephew again I'll make some calls so you can forget about driving south of 38th Street again as long as you live."

The two men stare at each other then, their breath visible in front of them.

"We clear?" Uncle Kid says.

"Clear," Campbell says. He holds out his palm and Uncle Kid drops the phone in like he's handing a child a piece of candy. Campbell starts back to his car. Uncle Kid walks over to me and gives me a quick squeeze on my shoulder to let me know we're cool. "I hope to hell we see you in Regionals," Campbell says. Then he starts his ignition and rolls up his window.

I bet he can hear me when I holler though. "Look for me there," I shout. "I'll be the one hanging from the motherfucking rim!"

28.

Sunday. I'm up and dressed for church obediently. It's like my close call from last night has me walking the narrow line, because halfway through the service when Jayson tries baiting me into laughing at a woman squeezed a little too tightly into her Sunday dress, I don't even blink. At one point I do crane my head around to see Uncle Kid slinking in, late as usual, but he just nods at me in a way that says, *No need for either of us to talk about last night. Ever.*

Pastor Baxter climbs into the pulpit. As he does, I see the light through the stained glass windows grow dim. There's supposed to be one last big winter storm coming, but I try not to think about that. Baxter sends his gaze across the congregation and I could swear he lets it rest on me for just a beat. Then he starts in. He talks generally about a fight to save funding for public schools and asks us to pray that our mayor finds courage and wisdom. He talks for a little bit about a streak of violence on the East Side and asks us to pray for the grieving families.

And then he pauses, smiles a little bit, and looks again at me and my family. "But I know where I'm preaching," he starts again, "and I know what time of year it is. Later this week, some of the young men in this very congregation will take the court for Sectionals. And I know that in Indiana, that event ranks up there with a Presidential election.

"I am not like some men, who will profess to believe that the Almighty takes an active part in the outcome of such events. I believe He is too concerned with any number of other things to worry about who wins in a high school gymnasium on a Friday night." Some congregation members laugh at that, but you know there will be more than a few prayers said for—or against, I suppose—Marion East come next weekend. "There is something religious though, to be learned from those young men who go out and fight the good fight."

Pastor Baxter opens that massive Bible that rests on his pulpit, and asks us to heed the day's text. It's one I've heard before, but like so much else that goes on in church, I've never given it too much thought. He tells us about the faith of the mustard seed, that faith—if it's real—can move mountains even if it's that small.

"We see this every year in basketball," he says. "A team overmatched, a team nobody gives a chance, a team that maybe has taken on losses all year. Yet in that locker room there is faith. In their hearts, faith. In their minds, faith." Some of the congregation nods along now, and I hear an Amen or two. "And that which is in your minds, which is in your hearts—that is what moves your hands. That team with faith, true faith, they take the court, and—oh, my! —you just watch the miracles they perform. They might be smaller, slower, younger, less celebrated than the squad they're facing, but they take them down. You see it happen every year. They begin in faith, and it is rewarded, and then—minute by minute you can see it happen—that faith grows and is rewarded more, until at last they are the ones playing like champions. Yes, in fact, they are the champions."

The sermon goes on from there. It turns out Baxter's message isn't about basketball after all. Instead, he wants people to know that if we could just have that kind of faith in our everyday lives we could, in fact, move mountains. But I don't hang on those words quite the same way. All I know is that for the first time in as long as I can remember, I'm inspired by church, and I can't wait to get to that locker room on Thursday night. My mom must sense it too, because she reaches out on the last full-congregation Amen and she squeezes my hand. I glance over at her, and her eyes are on fire, like she's ready to take the court herself.

We hit up breakfast at the Donut Shop, like always, and by the time we're leaving for the bookstore, even my dad can't hold back the flood of basketball talk. We all play out different scenarios—who we might play Friday night, which team is more dangerous, how we match up in the post and on the perimeter—but every time we keep coming back to the same prediction: after the byes, it's going to be us against Lawrence North for the title on Saturday night. Man, I can't wait to get another crack at Tagg and Patterson, only this time I'll keep my cool.

Later, as I wander through the aisles at the bookstore I find myself regretting that night at Free, when I started that noise with Tagg and Patterson. Not only was it stupid since it was two on one, but it cost me my one real shot with Jasmine. And then—*bam*—like thinking about her makes her appear, I see her in that same spot I did months ago, reading and drinking tea. It almost stops my heart she looks so good. I have the urge to jump behind a rack of books to collect myself before talking to her.

She sees me first though. "Hey, Derrick," she says. She smiles so big I think maybe Iesha was right, maybe Jasmine really does want me. "Been a long time since I've seen you around."

"Things have been crazy," I say.

"Basketball?" She sounds disappointed when she says it, like after all this time that's really the only thing I've been doing. I don't know, maybe she's right, but I wish she could understand just how much basketball means to me. It's not just a game—it's my whole future.

"I've had some other things going on too," I say.

She puts her book down and takes a sip. "Like what?" she asks. She picks up a pen and gives a quick little bite on the end of it.

I stammer around for a second, not knowing what to say. I look over to where Jayson had stood months ago, teasing me while I tried to chat up Jasmine, but he's not there this time. It's just me and her. One more chance. Then I realize that this is the chance—the chance to say what I've been waiting to say to her for a long time now. "I've been reading some too."

"Yeah?"

"Yeah. Enough to know that if a flood ever comes, I'll save you just like Tea Cake did for Janie," I say, dropping the knowledge that I made it through that book she was reading the last time I saw her here.

She stops cold. She puts down the pen. Looks at me. "You read that book?"

I just nod, cool as a man who's just knocked in the killer bucket.

"Well, Derrick Bowen," she says. "There might be hope for you yet."

"You don't know the half of it, Jasmine," I say.

She smirks at me. I know I've overplayed my hand. But I also know this look—she's about to tease me some. "Don't get too full of yourself just yet," she says. "You do know that Janie shoots Tea Cake later, right? It's not like some happy ending."

"Yeah, well, I might have skimmed some parts," I say, teasing right back. This one brings a real smile from Jasmine, then a laugh. And that laugh, it's golden, so pure I can't believe the whole bookstore hasn't stopped to appreciate it.

Our moment can't last though. Jayson comes running up to tell me it's time to split because the weather's taken a turn for the worse. Even in his hurry, he's got time to embarrass me. "You're Jasmine, right?" he asks.

"Yes," she says, smiling.

"When you gonna finally come around and get with my boy here?" he says. "I mean, the man's about to lead Marion East to State and you can't give him the time of day?"

"You have got to be kidding me," she says to me, but then she laughs and buries her head in her book, overcome by the fact that the younger Bowen talks even more trash than his older brother.

It starts as rain but turns to ice in the afternoon. It sounds against the windows—*tick tick tick*—like someone's teeth chattering. At first, it's just an excuse to huddle inside and watch TV, alternating between a Sunday game and the weather updates, the meteorologist getting more breathless each time they turn to him, like he's waited all his life for a winter storm like this one. A couple times, I hear the eerie sound of a long honk out on 36th followed by the crunch and crack of cars colliding, doomed to it by the ice on the roads. The sleet keeps up into the night. I know as I drift off that the odds of school on Monday are pretty slim.

I wake up to more than just a cancelled school day. The whole city is covered in a sheet of ice. This time when we click on the television the meteorologist looks more frazzled than breathless, that look of a man who's been on for too long. By morning, a big patch of Indiana is in a deep freeze and, the weatherman says, there's no relief in sight since the temperature isn't likely to push past freezing until mid-week.

"Hells, yeah," Jayson says, which earns the threat of a smack from Mom. But with the city shut down even she doesn't want to get our day off to a bad start, since we're all stuck inside together.

There's not much to do but watch movies and wait it out. I text Wes and he comes down—wearing his old kicks instead of the new Timberlands since he doesn't want to get them messed up with the weather. He tells me that we're lucky, that big chunks of the city are without power.

"And forget driving," he says. "I about fell three times just walking here."

"Yeah, well, it's not like you're some fine-tuned athlete," I say. "You could trip just trying to walk and chew gum."

He laughs it off and we settle in to watch some old gangster movie while my mom's back in her room reading a book, but as we do we hear the sleet kick up again. This time it comes down so hard it sounds like someone's tapping in nails on our walls. We get up during a commercial and poke our heads out just to see. Our street looks glazed. The new batch of sleet is laying a new coat on top. Now and then bursts of hail mix in and it pops off the street like popcorn. In all my life, I've never seen a storm like this, the sleet and hail coming down so thick you can barely see across the street.

"This keeps up we'll never go back to school," Wes says.

"Cool with me," I say. Then it dawns on me. "But if we don't have school they'll push back Sectionals too."

By Wednesday there's no change, except that some power is coming back on. At least the sleet has stopped. I keep checking the weather hoping that the cold will break and every time it's the same story— maybe tomorrow. The only traffic on the streets seems to be the salt trucks. But the ice must be an inch thick, which means they're not having much success.

Coach Bolden calls all the players, tells them just to hold tight and try to stay focused. We have to be ready to go when the weather finally breaks, no matter how long we have to wait.

The weatherman has also caught on to the fact that this storm might interrupt the basketball playoffs. Now when he gives his bleak forecast, he also adds a little basketball calendar below it. The first games are tomorrow. At this point it seems fifty-fifty that they'll go.

I text Wes and we kick it to watch more movies, but even we're getting antsy. Jayson's about to jump out of his own skin after being cooped up for three days. My mom keeps inventing reasons she's got to go visit a neighbor—just so she doesn't have to deal with three boys who are bored to death.

I text Jasmine to see if she wants to hang, but she's on lockdown until the roads improve. When I tell her I'm so bored I don't know what to do, she suggests I try reading another book. *There's more than one, you know,* she texts. I pause, wondering where this tone's coming from, but then I remember who I'm dealing with.

You just messing with me, right? I say.

You're finally catching on.

In that way the day passes, achingly slow, until by dinnertime I'm basically rooting for night to come so this day can be done with.

In bed, I toss and turn, idle so long that I've got all this pent up energy. Every few minutes I imagine I hear the sleet kicking in again. I think about Sectionals getting pushed back a week, killing our momentum, but when I get up to check the window each time, it's just a dry, windy night. It's all I can do not to text Jasmine, but I know nothing looks more desperate than some guy texting late-night.

Somehow, sleep finally comes.

Then it's Thursday morning. When I wake up I see the sun peeking through my window.

Mom peeks her head in my door. "Snap to it," she says. "School's back on, boy."

"Yes!" I say, more excited to hear that news than any freshman ever.

We got a first-round bye, so we don't lace 'em up for another night, but it's game on at last.

29.

Roncalli comes out of the Thursday night game, but they're nothing to sweat. Everyone knows that this is just a formality to get out of the way before the rematch with Lawrence North Saturday night.

Only problem is, nobody told Roncalli.

They come out crisp after playing last night, but it's like we're still in the deep freeze from the week. Roncalli is like so many teams full of white boys in the state. You can handle them, but if you're not ready to go they'll execute you to death. Oh, and they can shoot. Their first five trips are a pick-and-pop three, a backdoor layup, a spot-up three in the corner, two free throws, and one more drained three when Moose gets switched onto a guard. I don't think any of their shots even scrape iron. We're in a 13-3 hole before we're even loose. We're playing at Lawrence North's gym, and it's like we've turned these guys into Lawrence North.

Bolden calls time. In the huddle the looks on everyone's faces are as glazed as the streets in the middle of that ice storm. "Let's go!" Bolden shouts, but guys just shake their heads. It's like we've been punched in the nose and have no answer. "We're playing like it's

December again. Snap out of it!" This draws some *Yeahs* and *Come ons* from the huddle, but even as I join in I can tell it all feels hollow. It's hard to say why, but we've just got no bounce to us.

We break the huddle. Our next possession you'd think we'd never even practiced together. Royce and Devin bump into each other on cuts through the lane. Then Nick throws a lob to the rim for me—except I'm busy setting a back-screen for Moose.

As we backpedal on defense, Nick shoots me an angry look like it's all my fault, and I gesture back to let him know it's not on me. There's no time to really go there though, because Roncalli's hustling the ball up. Unless we want our season to end right here we better dig in.

That's when it happens. Just as the Roncalli guard crosses mid-court, the gym goes black. A gasp passes through the gym. Instinctively we all rush back to our bench, thinking something might be really wrong. The safety lights pop on, giving enough light to see that everyone's still just sitting there, trying to get their bearings. It takes another couple seconds, but—almost as one—people realize it's just another power outage, like some aftershock from a week of outages. A spontaneous mock cheer rises from the crowd, followed by laughter. As it happens I feel all the tension melt out of our huddle. We start laughing too, and Bolden doesn't dare stop us. Moose stands and goes up and down the bench, giving everyone five, saying, "We're okay. We good. Let's just get back out there and run."

An official walks stiffly down to our bench and tells us that it's a fixable issue, and that each team will get a two-minute warm-up period before play starts again. That sounds good to us. Royce and Devin turn back to our crowd and motion for them to make some noise. "Game's still on!" they shout, and the crowd responds.

Nick comes over to me and bumps fists. "My bad on that last pass," he says. "I threw it before I really looked."

"It's all good," I say. "I've been sleepwalking out there."

"We'll get it going now," he says. Then he calls the rest of the starters in and we just lay it all out, admitting ways we screwed up and how we can get this thing turned around.

Bolden stands over us while we talk and then says, "This team's got to be the strangest one I've ever coached. It figures you needed the lights to go out to wake the hell up."

He doesn't even know the half of it. Because once those lights come up and we get loose, Roncalli's just another road bump. It starts on that first possession, when we slip through all their screens without a hitch and then Moose erases their big's weak shot in the lane. We rip it and run. Moose outlets to Nick, who races it up the right sideline. I fill middle and get it from Nick at the top of the key and, when Roncalli races back to stop the break, I pull up at the stripe and find Devin filling left wing—he sets his feet, fires, buries it.

Our crowd goes nuts, releasing all their pent up energy. Just like that you can see the shoulders on the Roncalli players slump a bit. They know we're here for real now.

Roncalli doesn't go down without a fight. After all, their season is on the line too. But by mid-second quarter we edge ahead, and there's no looking back. They make a nice run in the second half to slice it to four, but Nick races it right up on them, and then lobs it to me for a quick throw-down. There's plenty of game to go, but that lets them know that there will be no easy comeback tonight.

Finally, with about a minute and a half to go, the Roncalli coach pulls their seniors. We've opened it up to 12, and it's all over, so he wants to give them one last round of applause. Bolden takes his cue to pull our starters too, and we get a standing O as we walk off. Our crowd, feeling a little full of themselves—and I think it's Jayson's voice that leads them—starts chanting *We want North! We want North!*, and everyone in the gym knows who that means: Lawrence North and Marcus Tagg, who's been sitting over in one corner with his teammates all game, sizing us up. He stands as our crowd is chanting and motions to his teammates, who file out like they don't care one bit and sure aren't going to lose a second of sleep over facing Marion East tomorrow night.

"Let 'em walk," Moose says. "We'll run their asses out of here in twenty-four hours."

The gym is juiced. On our side, it's like everyone just camped overnight and woke up in their same seats, ready for blood. And on the Lawrence North side it's packed so tight people are standing in the aisles.

I know I didn't sleep. Not from nerves, but from excitement. Last time Tagg waltzed into our gym, we weren't half the team we are now. Nothing better than a shot at payback on his court. I take a few glances down at their end, but Tagg's all business, warming up with a purpose and getting himself into a lather. Patterson sees me though, and mouths something my way. I pause on my way to the back of the lay-up line, just for a second. I raise my eyebrows, like *What?* He just motions toward our goal, as if to tell me to keep on my end. I stare for another second, but I don't have interest in starting any nonsense—just want to let him know I'm not intimidated.

As the clock runs down to zero, we all make sure to bottom our last shots. As we head to the bench the crowd—every last person in the gym—rises and starts to clap, like they're urging the game to start. The place is as amped as I've ever seen a gym, but Bolden just runs us through our game plan and sends us out for the tip, simple as if it's a scrimmage. We get out there and Tagg still doesn't look at me. He just stares down at the floor like he's meditating. But Patterson can't pass up a chance to run smack pre-tip, so when he shakes my hand he grabs on for a second and leans in. "You ain't getting no miracle tonight. We get up on you not even the power going out is gonna save you."

I just give his hand an extra shake and ignore what he says. Just in case, Nick gets in my ear. "Best revenge is winning," he says.

"I feel you," I say, and then we dig in for the tip.

Lawrence North controls. They rip it at us—a quick back-screen to get Tagg free on the baseline, where he gives Royce a pump fake and zips past. Only this time the rest of us jump to cut him off. He pulls up, almost surprised at how prepared we are. When he skips it weak side and we recover so quick it's like we're all sharing the same mind, Lawrence North has to back it up and reset. Patterson's smirk is gone just like that. He knows it's a whole different ballgame than the one they cruised through a couple months ago.

They eventually work it into the post, but Moose gets a piece of the shot and after a couple tips, Devin crashes down and corrals the board. We have no chance to run, so Nick walks it up and puts us in our set. I slide into the lane and North's strategy with me becomes apparent quickly—they want to beat the hell out of me. I get a shoulder to the chest and an elbow in the small of my back before they finally get whistled for a hold. "Clean it up, guys," one of the refs says, but as soon as it's back in play I get more of the same. Devin gets loose on the baseline and gets a friendly roll to put us up early. Patterson races it the other way, but we get back, and again they settle in.

The rhythm of the game settles too. Other than the body checks on me, it's cleanly played, but both teams stay patient and work, work, work. The possessions stretch out for 30 seconds, 40 seconds sometimes. When a shot comes off, it's a war for every rebound. There are no easy looks. With the battle under the boards we never pick one clean to get our break going. As the first quarter winds down, we're clinging to a 9-8 lead, and Royce has done the unthinkable—he's shut out Tagg. He's had a ton of help from the rest of us, but the only time Tagg got a decent look he missed from range.

Patterson circles it back around to the top, holding for the last look of the quarter. They've got our side overloaded, getting a double screen set up for their two guard, with Tagg all alone on the other wing. Patterson's looking our way the whole time, and Moose and I keep talking to Devin, telling him to be ready for the cut. When his man finally does come off that screen, we give Devin some space to shoot through, but that's when I glimpse over at Tagg. He takes a step toward the perimeter, then plants his foot—I've seen this before, and I leave the play side and drop into the lane just as Patterson lets go of the lob. Royce is beat bad, and Tagg has a free run to the rim. I rise to meet him, but with his momentum he's got a little more lift than I do. I reach, and I just get a finger on the orange, enough to make Tagg mishandle it.

The ball drops harmlessly to the baseline as the first quarter horn sounds. I want to get up in Tagg's face—or better yet Patterson's—and let them know we're not gonna just lay down like last time. But I know better. It's just one play and just one quarter. I pump my fist once and head to the bench to get ready for more.

The second quarter is more of the same, except that Tagg—too good to contain forever—gets loose a few times to give them a slim lead. On our end, there's nothing easy. I get a put-back and a mid-range J to fall, but we don't get a single fast break point, which starts to wear on us after a while. Every dead ball, Bolden keeps shouting at us to stay patient, to keep fighting. And, really, what other choice do we have?

With about a minute left, Lawrence North gets the ball, up two, after Royce gets called on a travel. As good of a job as Bedford's done on Tagg, it's like he's left all his focus on the other end—he's missed three or four easy looks and turned it over a handful of times. He shakes his head in frustration, but then claps his hands once and digs back in on Tagg.

"You'll get it going," I shout at him.

"Just stay after it," Nick says.

But then Lawrence North runs it up and the time for chatter's done. They work, patient as ever. I can feel the burn in my calves and thighs on every cut, and the brutal pace of the game has lulled that raucous crowd into near silence, so you can hear the squeak of the kicks on the hardwood or the grunts of someone getting hit with a screen all the way across the court.

Tagg catches it baseline and tries to single up Royce, but Bedford stands his ground—he cuts off the drive, then keeps his feet on the ball fake. Tagg has to fire it back out top to Patterson. He backs it up to the circle and signals to his teammates. They've run it down to under 20 seconds, so I figure they're holding for one, but then Patterson—who's not really a shooter—gets a wild hair and tries a step-back three over Nick. It rattles out, Moose corrals it, and outlets it to me. I push, but Lawrence North races back again. I pull up at the wing with about 10 seconds left in the half.

I give it off to Nick and then go down to the block. For the first time in weeks, I get that itch to break out of this offense—just go demand the ball from Nick and have everyone else flatten out so I can work. But we've come too far to give in to that kind of impatience, so I back-screen for Devin, then turn right around and cross screen for Royce running baseline. This time, I lean a little to get a piece of Tagg, but I get away with it and Royce springs wide open on the baseline with a couple ticks left. Nick finds him in rhythm, he sets, he fires. And he misses short by a solid foot.

Halftime, and we're down 20-18. Royce shuffles toward the locker room with his head down. Nick and I rush over to keep giving him encouragement, but even as we do Nick shoots me a look that lets me know we can't be counting on Royce to knock anything down tonight.

In the locker room, Coach lets us gather ourselves and get some rest, but when we're silent for a few minutes, he looks around. "Hey!" he shouts. "Don't mope now. We're right where we want to be. Hell, last time around with these guys the game was over by now, and I was wasting time jumping Derrick's ass."

The players look my way, and I sit back, wondering why Coach is jumping me for something that happened months ago. Then Bolden laughs, followed by a few laughs around the locker room, and I relax.

"What I'm saying," he continues, "is we've come a long way." He lets that sink in. Murphy starts to clear his throat like he's about to chime in. Bolden holds his hand up, though. "But I'm saying this too—we've got a little further to go before we're done with this thing. Boys, we can beat these sons-of-bitches."

We jump out on them in the third, inspired by Bolden's encouragement. And even though Royce misses another J and a wide-open gimme at the rim, Devin picks up the slack with a couple threes. Then Moose gets back-to-back buckets down low, and—finally—we get a clean rip and Nick leads me perfectly for a throwdown. I don't mess around—no reverse, no tomahawk, just a straight on two-handed dunk, swift and sure. But when Lawrence North calls time, I at least pump my fist to our crowd, who's on their feet again for our 30-26 lead.

I spot my family immediately. They're about to fall out, even my dad. I swear Jayson looks ready to charge right down out of the stands. My mom and Uncle Kid are even giving each other a high five in celebration. I check beneath our bucket too, and make eye contact with Wes, who's in the middle of blasting out our fight song. And then my eyes drift across our fans, and I see Jasmine Winters herself—wouldn't admit to caring about hoops if her life depended on it—jumping up and down with everyone else, her eyes wide with excitement. I guess a Sectional championship can get just about anyone on their feet.

"Stay focused!" Bolden shouts, even before we're seated on the bench. "Those guys haven't won Sectionals three years running because they quit when they're down four!"

When we hit the hardwood again, I see Patterson and Tagg

arguing with each other, with Tagg poking him in the chest. No, they're not going to quit, but they're definitely feeling the heat.

Of course, they make their run. We nurse that lead long into the fourth, but Tagg finally shakes Royce and buries a three from the corner. Down to one. Their crowd rises and you can feel the surge in the gym. Nick brings it up, and takes a deep breath before setting us into our offense, a little gesture like he's trying to tell us to stay calm. There's still more than a minute left, so when we glance to the bench Bolden just makes a rolling motion with his hand: *Keep running the offense.*

We're in no hurry though. Even when I get a decent look on the wing, I back it out to Nick again. When I do, the whole crowd gets just a few decibels louder, Lawrence North fans pulling for a stop and our crowd urging us for a bucket. I've never heard a gym this loud. I ball screen for Nick and he drives right wing, then spins a bounce pass to Moose on the blocks. I spot at the top of the key and let the big man work, but when he turns he sees Royce back-cutting to the rim, free as the first man out for warm-ups. He catches it clean and rises just as my man dives down to challenge, but it's a pretty good look at the rim. It goes glass, front rim, and spins out, right into Tagg's hands.

Royce looks at the ref for just a second, and that's all it takes for Tagg to leave him. He pushes, and they've got a quick three-on-two with me and Nick back. I holler *Ball*, and step up to challenge Tagg. He rides me down into the paint, but I make him kick it out, and Nick races to challenge the shot. He makes their two guard skip it to Patterson, who's wide open on the other wing. It's a shot we can live with, but as soon as it leaves his hands you can hear the pause in the crowd noise while they wait. It bangs home on a line drive, and the Lawrence North fans go insane.

I peek at the clock—40 ticks left, plenty of time—but when Bolden calls time, Patterson makes sure to cross my path to the bench. "Ballgame," he says. "Have a nice trip home." There's about a million things racing through my mind to say, but I know to hold back.

In the huddle, Royce is banging his fists onto his forehead. "Shit, I'm killing us. It's on me, guys. This whole thing's on me."

Bolden just grabs his hands, makes him unclench and look up. "What the hell, Bedford?" he says. "We're down one with forty seconds to go in the Sectional Finals. Someone offered this to me a month ago I'd have taken it in a heartbeat."

He and Murphy draw up a play. The idea is to get it to me right baseline, with Moose posting up. If Moose doesn't get a solid post, he clears, and I solo up my man. Good enough.

When we break the huddle, Nick pulls me aside. "You get a look you bury it," he tells me. "But these guys aren't stupid. They jump to you remember you got four more on the floor."

"I know it," I say.

As we inbound, our crowd stands, but there's not as much noise now. Everyone's just locked in, waiting for the play to unfold. We're still in no hurry. When I catch it right wing and wait for Moose to post, I can feel the crowd getting antsy behind me. It's that slow building murmur of people who think we need to get a shot up right away. I ball fake to Moose, but he's pushed off the blocks, so he clears, and I get the chance I've been waiting for—just me and a ticking clock, one shot to win Sectionals. I give one bounce baseline, then cross back left, just setting my man up. I jab right and he bites, so I lower my shoulder and drive left, looking for a little pull up in the paint. I get a crease, but just like Nick said, the whole damn gym jumps into the paint.

My first thought is to force it on up. I can make it, even with Tagg racing at me. But I hear Bolden's voice in the back of my head—*There will be a guy who will knock that shot into the fourth row.* And Nick's voice—*You got four more on the floor.*

I pull up. It's too jammed up to drop it off to Moose, so I look to the perimeter. And there he is, all alone in the corner again—Royce, with his feet set and his hands out. I'll be damned if he doesn't want the three.

I put it on the money to him, and he pulls right in rhythm. And when it splashes down, the crowd sounds like a jet taking off, and I swear the floor shakes with the noise.

We bounce back to the huddle when Lawrence North calls time, and Bolden brings us back to earth. "There's fifteen seconds left," he says. "That's a damn lifetime."

When we break, Lawrence North has Tagg taking it out on the side, and I know what's up. I can't cheat off my man too soon, because he's right down on the block, but if they let anyone other than Tagg take the shot with the whole season riding on it, they're fools. I wait for Tagg to inbound to Patterson. But when Tagg fakes baseline and then cuts back middle, I jump it. I undercut his move and swipe Patterson's pass clean, then hold onto that orange like it's worth a million bucks.

They've got no choice but to foul. As I walk to the other end, our crowd is on its feet. They can smell it. Hell, they can taste it—a Sectional Championship.

But when I toe the line, they quiet down and they realize the thing's not done. Not with eight seconds left and me at the stripe.

That's when the Lawrence North crowd gets loud, trying to rattle me. I take the rock from the ref, line up my AdiZero on the stripe. Two dribbles, then I spin the ball once in my right hand. *Head still head still head still!* I let it go.

Bottom. And our crowd lets loose a wild yell. "One more," I hear Nick shout. And I hear that from all over. From the bench, from the crowd, from a voice in the band.

Two dribbles, spin, head still, release. Pure.

Lawrence North races it up, but it's all she wrote. They find Tagg in the corner, and Royce challenges without fouling, but Tagg's off-balance anyway. It rattles out. Moose corrals it, and we hear our crowd chanting *Three, two, one.*

Moose slings the ball up into the air in celebration, and I sink down onto the court. We did it. That's all I can think—*We did it.* Around me I see a stampede of feet. My teammates' kicks and the black sneakers of the refs, and the swarm of boots and kicks on our fans storming the court. In that sea of people I just feel an overwhelming sense of relief, like all those decisions, all those hours, they all mattered after all.

Nick finds me in the madness. "Last time Marion East did this," he said, "I was barely crawling."

"We did it," I say, that phrase still stuck in my head.

"We sure as hell did," he says.

"I didn't think it would end this way that first day of practice," I say.

"End? D-Bow, season ain't over yet."

That's when it hits me. We get to keep fighting. So, yeah, I get hugs from the family and high fives from Wes, and even a little flirty glance from Jasmine. And, sure, we cut down the nets and pose with the trophy right smack dab at center court on Lawrence North's floor. But there's a team doing this same thing up in Hamilton County, and next Saturday afternoon, we'll be lacing 'em up against those guys.

30.

Regionals are in Hinkle Fieldhouse at Butler, sacred ground for Indiana basketball. We have the first game, so there's plenty of sunlight coming through those high windows, making bright rectangles on the court during warmups. The crowd files in, filling up the lower level and then the rafters, and you can almost smell the hoops history in this place. It's ancient, and has a dusty feel to it, like no matter how many times they polish this floor and clean the aisles it's still going to have a little film on it. If it weren't for the huge scoreboard with the video screen above is, you'd think you'd walked right back into the 50s or something.

The place is full of school colors, the stands cut into quarters by school, but this kind of game—especially in Hinkle—brings out people who just want to take in some hoops, old Hoosiers bundled in their puffy coats and flannels, a program in one hand and a steaming cup of coffee in the other. There's a string of scouts too, trying not to draw attention to themselves by sitting at the top of the first level. But I see those tell-tale team jackets—Minnesota gold, Kentucky blue, Boiler black. Even on press row, there seems to be a buzz, with radio announcers chattering away and looking anxiously at the court. They know this is the game of the day, and even though the Pacers tip in an hour on the other side of the city, right now there's no doubt where ground zero is for Indiana hoops.

When Hamilton races out from their locker room, it's like they're under orders not to so much as look to our end of the court. I keep trying to catch Lorbner's attention just to see if he's got anything to say, but the whole team is locked in as if we don't even exist. When Coach Treat comes out, though, he can't help himself. He steals one look my way, and then turns his head like some guy who got busted checking out a girl in class, and makes a line for the bench. Campbell's right behind him, and he doesn't look up at all.

I go back to our lay-up line, getting loose and talking up my teammates to get them juiced for tip. I steal a glance to my people in the crowd. They're about ten rows directly behind our bench, packed in tight on the bleachers. They're with Uncle Kid like there was never any question at all about what uniform I should be in for the rest of my high school career. That static all long gone for me. The itch to jump to Hamilton died as soon as Uncle Kid sent Coach Campbell back to his car that night. Jayson sees me and gives a cocky head bob, the corners of his mouth pointed down like *These guys got nothing on you, D.* I take a bounce pass from Devin, dip my shoulder like I'm going to the rim again, then step back and let a J go— bottom. I turn back to Jayson and give him that look right back.

When I head to the back of the line, I see Campbell talking to one of the people at the scorer's table. I can't help myself. I take an extra wide arc toward mid-court, catching his attention just as he turns back toward their bench. He stops and stares.

"What?" he says.

I point to my shoes. "If I wanted kicks, I wouldn't be getting boots."

"Fine," he says. "I get it."

Then I point to our band behind our bucket. "You might find a fresh pair of Timberlands on one of our sax players though."

"Just go warm up," he says, clearly angry. I do just that. After all, I really don't want to waste time talking trash to an opposing coach. But when I glance up I see Wes laughing, knowing just what I was doing.

Bolden and Murphy don't have a lot to say to us. I mean, if you need a pep talk for this game, you're not much of a player. They just stress the same things as before—help on Lorbner, especially on his drives, and then rotate to close out on the shooters.

We take the court after the anthem. I feel it, that jumpy feeling in my stomach rising into my chest and head, like I'll pass out if I don't get this energy out. The Hamilton players all shake hands politely enough, but only Lorbner acknowledges me. "It will be fun beating you," he says, then strides into the center circle for the tip. I can't help but smile. You have to love that guy's cockiness.

But there's no time to think about that. Charles bodies up next to me, and everyone settles into their positions. The crowd noise rises in pitch. Flash bulbs go off on the sidelines, and my heart starts pounding like it's about to jump out of my chest. Then, at last, the orange goes up.

Lorbner controls, and they don't waste any time. They slip it down into the post to my man, just to see how we'll react, but he gives it up quick—they're not going to change their strategy just because we play small. They reverse a few times, then get it to Vasco on the shallow wing. Pump fake, jab step, then a quick fadeaway over Moose that banks home.

Charles picks Nick up full-court. It's not to try to turn him over, just some light pressure to stop us from running out. Nick brings it up and kicks it to Devin on the wing, who looks and looks before reversing it back to Nick, who sends it over to Royce on the other wing. Moose and I keep cross-screening inside, but it's like the perimeter guys are gunshy. They look at us. Maybe give a ball fake. But they don't do anything—no penetration, no post-feeds, nothing.

Nick finally drives and draws, then kicks to Devin in the corner, but instead of taking an open look, he drives into traffic and forces a tough runner, which comes off into Lorbner's hands.

This time down they work into Lorbner on the post. When we double it's clear they've got a plan—he kicks it out, but rather than looking for a three, they dump it right back to Vasco, who's re-posted deeper. I have no choice but to come help on his drop-step, but he just bounces a dime to my man, who lays it in.

Again, it's the same thing on our offensive end. I can't believe it. It's like after all these games of the O clicking, we've forgotten what to do. I fake a cross-screen for Moose and reverse pivot, sealing my man under the basket. "Ball!" I shout, but Royce is late in seeing it, and his soft pass gets tipped away and stolen. At least we get a stop on the other end, but next time down we're just as bad. This time it's Nick, of all people, late on a feed, but at least Moose corrals it. The problem is, he's so frustrated by not getting touches that he rushes things and travels along the baseline.

That's enough for Coach Bolden, who calls timeout. We're only down four, but if we don't get ourselves in gear it's going to be a lot more fast.

"Let's go," he shouts. "Don't tell me you're intimidated by the stage here. Nobody's given them the crown yet. Make them earn it for God's sake."

Maybe we left it all on the floor against Lawrence North. Maybe everyone remembers that beatdown we got from Hamilton last time. Or maybe we *are* intimidated by the stage. Whatever it is, something's off.

"Coach, can I make a suggestion?" It's Murphy, who almost never chimes in with strategy.

Bolden looks at him, his almond eyes intense and his wrinkles carving up his forehead. "If it's a good one, go ahead."

Murphy hesitates, but then dives in. He kneels down in the huddle right next to Coach and says, "We keep running our offense, expecting these guys to get lost on screens. They're too good for that. But I don't think they can check Nick and Derrick off the bounce. Why don't we get those guys isolated and let them take their men some?"

Bolden frowns. All year, he's put Murphy in his place, like Murphy should be happy just to be a water boy, but this time he relents. "Maybe you're right," he says. He slaps his clipboard down on the floor with a pop and quickly draws up a couple sets to let Nick and me penetrate from the top.

On their end, Hamilton splits a pair of free throws. We get it back down five. When Nick crosses mid-court, he motions to me. I'll get first crack at them. We just run a ball screen exchange, and everyone flattens out on the baseline with me at the top of the key. The guy guarding me backs up, and keeps looking over his shoulder to see if there's a ball screen coming. Then it hits him—it's just us up here, and he's got to check me all alone.

I jab at him a couple times, then take a hard dribble to my right, but cross it back between my legs like I'm looking for a jumper. He bites on the headfake and goes flying by while I duck in to the left elbow. Vasco takes a step my direction, but doesn't want to leave Moose alone on the blocks, so I get a nice, clean look at a fifteen-footer. I rattle it home, and I can see every player on our team exhale in relief. Then our crowd reacts and, at last, we've decided to get after it.

The pace is insane. Once we get it going, we keep it going. Nick knifes all the way to the rim for a deuce. I get another pull-up. Nick drives and dishes to Moose for a jam. I penetrate and kick out to Devin for a clean three.

But Hamilton has it cranked up just as much. Vasco has it rolling. If Moose gives him any window at all, he drains Js. If Moose tightens up, he's by him like a shot, finishing in the paint or finding shooters for looks. The buckets come so fast that even the crowd seems to get a bit worn out. By the end of the first half their cheers sound frazzled, and you can almost hear a sigh of relief when the horn sounds. Everyone needs a break. It's 40-39, Hamilton. As I walk off, I take a quick glance at some of those older guys who are just here to take in a game—they're smiling at each other and giving big-eyed stares, like, *Can you believe this is a high school game?*

I see games all the time where there's a breakneck pace in the first half, and the teams can't keep it up in the second. This isn't one of those games.

"Stay patient out there," Bolden tells us as we leave the huddle, but I inbound it to Nick and he darts straight for the rim, buries a little floater to put us up one with no more than three seconds gone in the third quarter. Nick flashes a quick grin over at Bolden, and even the old coach can't help but smile. When a game's flowing like this, not even Coach Bolden's warning can slow it down.

Vasco gets free for a 15-footer; I drive and dump to Moose for two; Charles loses Nick and drains a three; Nick finds me on a backdoor for a bucket; Vasco posts deep and gets to the line for an automatic two; I break down my man and find Royce for a deep three. The shooting is video game crazy. After a while you almost expect the nets to catch fire. There are misses, but they're so rare that instead of a groan, you hear a murmur of surprise from the crowd. The coaches—even the normally rigid Treat and Campbell—have almost relegated themselves to cheerleaders, pumping their fists after made buckets, pounding on the floor in hopes of a defensive stop. By the end of another quarter it's 62-60, Hamilton.

"Eight minutes," Murphy shouts. "Eight minutes between you guys and history!"

This time Bolden gives Murphy that old withering stare. "Can we not worry about our place in history right now? Let's just figure out a way to get some stops." He slaps his clipboard down on the floor and pauses, then rubs his hand across those deep wrinkles in his forehead. "Derrick, you take Lorbner," he says. Everyone in the huddle pulls back a little bit in surprise. Guarding four-men at schools like Broad Ripple is one thing; checking the best big in the state is another thing entirely. Coach senses our hesitation and explains. "Don't worry. He so much as thinks about posting we're doubling." He stares at Moose. "You see him start to slide in low, you come over even before they get him the ball. We just need Derrick to stick him out on the perimeter."

It's a plan. No crazier than going to four guards in the middle of the season. And just as we all leaned back at the first suggestion of it, we all lean in now. At this point, Coach could tell us to start shooting underhand and we'd give it a go for the old man.

They have the ball first, and run it right at us. As soon as Vasco sees me step out at him, he pauses for just a second and shakes his head. He's got this weird smirk on his face, but he doesn't say anything—not to me, at least. He backpedals to the wing so Charles can hear him, though. "Post this side. Post this side." He doesn't even shout it, doesn't sound urgent like a guy with an open look. He might as well be talking to Charles about where they're going to eat after the game. He calmly edges down toward the block. Moose starts cheating over right away, and puts a hard double on Lorbner just as Charles picks up his dribble—he's frozen out there, wanting to get it to his big man, but without a clean passing lane. The perimeter players float toward him, but Devin and Royce are in their chests. That leaves Moose's man, but he's slow to react, and when he finally does flash toward the high post, Charles is in a panic. He floats an off-balance pass that way and Devin jumps it.

Hamilton races back, but now I see a second benefit to our defensive alignment—they're confused over who guards who at the defensive end. Both their four and Lorbner follow Moose down to the blocks. I trail the play with a free run at the rim. Nick slips me a quick bounce pass and I finish strong at the rim. Tie game.

Next time down Hamilton takes its time. They reverse and

reverse, looking for a clean post for Vasco. I fight like crazy. Though he's got all kinds of size on me, I keep bumping him off his cuts just long enough so Moose can slide over too. I know we're getting him frustrated when he throws his hands up and looks toward the ref. Sure, I've been getting away with some grabs, but it's not like Vasco to let that bother him. After a possession so long the crowd gets lulled quiet—you can hear individual shouts for fouls, or people yelling *He's open* about Vasco even though Moose is hedging over—Vasco finally has had enough. He sprints out to the wing and claps twice for the ball.

Charles gives it up. When Vasco catches, I can hear the crowd murmur. Showdown time. But here, I don't need help. I get in tight on him, so no way he can rise up clean. He leans in on me, trying to get some space, but I stay up in him. He puts it on the floor, trying to back me down, but he's got to be careful not to just lower and muscle through me, so he settles for a 17-foot fade, a tough look even for Vasco. Front rim and off, and Royce crashes down to snag the board.

Two stops in a row in this game feels like a miracle, and our crowd reacts. They all rise to their feet as Nick brings it up. There are six minutes left, but you get the feeling that every tick counts now. Like Uncle Kid used to say, *This game got late awfully early.* We all feel it too, so there's no rush for a look now—hot as everyone's been, we know we need to get the best shot we can. Devin passes on a three from the wing. Nick drives into the lane but thinks twice about his runner. Even Moose kicks it back out when he can't get leverage on Vasco. Finally Nick dribbles to me for an exchange. When he gives it off he kind of makes a show of it, extending his hands on the pass and then holding them there. It's his way of saying that this is my game now. And why not? Nick's been working Charles pretty good all game, but he's running out of moves—that last time in the lane, Charles stayed on his hip pretty good.

I dribble out near the circle, just to gather. I hear a shout above the crowd roar, and I know it's Jayson: "You all day, D. You all day!"

I size my man up, but there's no messing around. I just push hard right and dip my shoulder, get it past him and get into the paint. Lean in to keep the ball away from him, and drop in a 12-footer.

Our lead, and Coach Treat's off the bench signaling timeout. Our crowd's jumping so hard old Hinkle might just crack in two. Our bench is up, and even Stanford is amped, pumping his fist in the air like he's the one who's been dropping buckets. The sweat stings my eyes and I taste blood in my mouth, maybe some damage from a stray elbow I was too juiced to feel at the time.

Coach Treat's no fool. They come back out and we see the problem right away. They go small, four guards to match ours, which means if Moose doesn't check Vasco he's got to check a perimeter guy. And it takes Hamilton about five seconds to put Moose all alone with his man. Moose gets broken down so fast we've all got to jump the driver. The ball gets kicked to Charles all alone on the wing. Three, and just like that Hamilton's back up one.

We run it right back. Now it's a bench player trying to check me. So they've still got problems too. He backs way off, daring me to shoot from range, but he can't back off far enough. I still take him to the rim, draw Lorbner, and drop it to Moose for two.

Back again, and it's the same story—Moose isolated, drive and dish for an open look. Buried again, but this time it's not a trey. Coach calls time now. After he and Murphy discuss it, they decide to stick with our defensive alignment. "It's pick your poison," Bolden says, "but I'll pick a back-up making plays against us instead of Lorbner."

Back and forth and back and forth. I get to the rim for a deuce, get to the line for two that rattle home, find Nick cutting back-door. And each time Hamilton answers with two of their own. With just under a minute, Vasco finally seals me in the post. Moose is too spent from chasing on the perimeter, so I get no help. It's a simple drop step and dunk for him to put Hamilton back up one. Vasco gives me a long stare as he backpedals. Like, *Answer that.*

I give Vasco a quick nod, let him know I plan to do just that. We cross mid-court and Nick pulls up instead of giving me the exchange. The crowd murmurs, thinking he's going to take it himself, but I know what he's doing. He's just running clock. We're down one, but it might as well be winning time right now. He crosses it back and forth, daring Charles to lunge, then pushes it toward the top of the key to back Charles off of the five-count. Each time, though, Nick just circles back toward mid-court.

Tick, tick, tick. Thirty seconds left. Our crowd starts clapping in rhythm and they sound like an army on the march.

Tick, tick, tick. Twenty to go, and everyone in Hinkle is on their feet. The benches, the fans, those old guys who think they've seen it all. I bet even those scouts up high are standing now, even though it doesn't matter to them who wins. This is it.

Tick, tick, tick, and at last Nick dribbles right to exchange with me. I make a sharp cut to come get it, trying to get separation in case

Hamilton wants to double, but Charles sticks with Nick, and I'm one-on-one out top again. I think about all those days on the Fall Creek Court, working with Uncle Kid after everyone else has gone on, the sun getting low and early evening air cooling our sweat—but we'd keep working. He'd check it to me out top. *Just you and me, D-Bow. Game on the line. Show me what you got.* And I think about how many times I've come home from that court to find my parents keeping dinner for me, how every time they give me warnings about investing too much in ball but how every time I can see how proud they are that I'm putting in the work. *You work at something, anything, it'll pay off,* my mom has told me a million times.

Now's the payoff. Has to be.

I explode left without warning. Get my man on his heels. He leans first, then crosses his feet—opening up the lane. I spin and get him pinned on my left side, see that I have an open pull-up at the stripe. But I also see rim, and instinct kicks in. I pass on the J and take one hard dribble to the rack. I set my feet and rise, ball cocked back in my right hand, when the body flashes at me. That huge, cat-quick Lorbner is about to meet me at the rim again.

He gets the angle on me, rises just an inch or two higher than me. Which is fine, because he just falls harmlessly back to the ground while Moose—left wide open—drops in the easy deuce.

The sound of our crowd is like an ocean, but each of us knows to sprint back before Hamilton gets an easy look. When we do, Coach Treat leans over the sideline and motions for time, then hangs his head like a man who's just found out his wife's been running around on him. That sends our crowd to even greater volume. I look up to see a mass of bodies in red and green, all of them jumping, hugging, high-fiving, almost overcome with the power of the game. I feel that way too. I realize I'm almost shaking with the adrenaline, my thoughts racing so fast they're just a jumble. Only when Nick grabs me on the way to the huddle— "Yeah, D! That's what I'm talking about!" he screams—do I come back to earth. Moose is already in the huddle, stomping on the floor and pointing down like he owns the court. "I told you! I told you all! Bucket to win and it's me, boy. It's me!" Then he sees me and stops. "Nice pass, D," he says, cool as if it was for some garbage bucket in a pick-up game.

Everyone laughs then, filling up with the notion that we've actually done it. Everyone, that is, except Coach Bolden.

"Hey!" he shouts. "Hey! We need one more stop. Get your heads back in the game!" He pulls out his clipboard one more time, draws up what he thinks Hamilton will run. Then he pauses, looking down. He looks back up at me and Moose and opens his mouth like he's going to say something. He doesn't, though. He just shakes his head, says, "Dig in, boys. One stop."

When we break, I make a line for Vasco. No matter what they run, I know it's ending up in his hands. I body up, and he looks down at me. "Thank you, Derrick," he says.

"What's that?"

"Thank you," he repeats. "You left me four seconds. I can do anything I want in four seconds."

I laugh it off as false confidence, but he just stands stock still, gathering himself for one last possession. The crowds are buzzing, but you can feel the nerves on both sides, everyone holding their breath for these last few ticks.

Vasco screens at mid-court to get Charles loose. He catches the in-bounds just in the back-court. I see that Nick's right on his hip, but I follow Vasco over to the right wing, looking out for screens. They don't even run anything for him though. He just stops with his back to the rim at about 25 feet, like he's posting up, and Charles sends a long pass his way.

I know there can't be more than two seconds left, so I stay anchored on Vasco's left hip so he can't turn to his strong hand for a turnaround. He catches and pivots the other way. I close, straight up on his right side now so he has no room to rise. He's got no other option but to lean way back for space. I jump with him, but I don't dare reach with so little time left.

By the time he releases, he's a good twenty-seven feet from the bucket. I hear the buzzer just a breath after Vasco fires. I don't hear anything else—no crowd, no shoes on the hardwood, nothing—while I turn and watch his shot arc toward the rim.

It seems to hang in the air forever, but when it falls, it finds bottom. And then there's more nothing.

31.

The car can't be Iesha's. No way she's rocking a red convertible Camaro, but that's what comes screeching in off Fall Creek, top down and Iesha smiling like she's the baddest thing in the city.

I walk over, wipe sweat from my face with the bottom of my shirt, and see that Wes is riding shotgun. And behind them, squeezed into that backseat so she looks a little uncomfortable, is Jasmine. She's sporting some shades so I can't see her eyes, but it sure seems like she's staring a hole in me.

Spring Break means trips to Florida for other high schoolers, crazy times on the beach and bad behavior in hotel rooms, but for us we're still city bound. And who cares? Sunny skies and temps in the 60s? A whole week without a thing to do? We don't need to go South to feel free.

"You want a ride?" Wes asks. "We got this from Iesha's uncle. Ours for the day. Gonna hit every damn block."

I don't answer right away. Instead, I just stare at Jasmine. I think about how it would feel to squeeze in next to her, how the wind would make us shiver but our bodies would be pressed up together.

"D-Bow!" I hear the shout from behind me and look back. It's Moose on the edge of the court, waving me over.

Three things happened after Vasco's shot beat us. Coach Bolden all but cried in front of us. He apologized, especially to the seniors. "It's on me, boys." He told us he was going to switch Moose back onto Vasco for the last seconds, since there wasn't enough time for Lorbner to drive, but that he decided not to at the last second. But we knew better. Without Coach Bolden, we'd have limped into Sectionals with a losing record and limped right out in the first round.

The second thing that happened was that the only person still in the Marion East bleachers when I came out after the longest shower of my life was my mom. I asked where Dad and Jayson and Uncle Kid were, and she just told me they'd be waiting at home. Then she hugged me. "You're too big to hold," she said. "But I know when my son needs his mama." I didn't admit how right she was, but she knew it. She drove me down to Circle Centre, and we grabbed some food and she told me it wouldn't hurt so much if I hadn't put everything into it. "You have bigger things in front of you," she said, "but I couldn't be prouder than I am right now." Then we talked for a while, like we hadn't in way too long, about things that weren't related to hoops at all.

The third thing was Hamilton won State. We knew they would. Moose and Wes came over and we watched it on TV. Moose just sat there all game with his arms crossed. When Vasco and Charles hugged it out at mid-court, Moose stood. He pointed at the TV. "That was supposed to be us," he said. And so we made a pact, right then, that nothing was stopping us next year. We were going to be at the court or in the gym every day, working. "AAU ball isn't enough," Moose said.

"Lorbner and Charles will get that too. We can't just keep up. We got to gain on them."

And so, on Spring Break, when everyone else is out having fun, we're at the court. That's fun too, but we're not just messing around.

"Well?" Jasmine asks. She lowers those sunglasses and looks right at me. She can still make my heart jump. I have a feeling like she always will. Wes bugs his eyes at me, like, *Come on, D, you want the girl to beg?*

"D-Bow!" Moose shouts again. I turn and his hands are on his hips. He's starting to look a little bit cut from working out, shedding that fat and looking pretty menacing.

"You want to come back in a little while?" I ask Iesha.

"It's Spring Break," she says. "Can't you take a break from ball for once?"

Wes starts to plead, too, but Jasmine cuts in. "Let him go," she says. "If I know Derrick, I know he's not gonna be any fun if he's still thinking about hoops."

"I'm fun," I protest.

Jasmine laughs, that high, easy laugh that she has when her teasing gets to me. "Oh, Derrick," she says. "Sometimes you're so easy."

Iesha puts the convertible into reverse, gives me one last look, then shakes her head at me and speeds away.

I turn to Moose, who's leaning against the nearest basket support now, taking a swig of water. He finishes, spits the last bit out, and tosses his water bottle on the ground. He points to the blacktop. "Let's go, D. We got next."